QUIET MONTH FOR A MURDER

QUIET MONTH FOR A MURDER

A Possum Walk Mystery

FRANCESCA PANE

Francesca Pane

This book is dedicated to my husband Fred who gave me three critical ideas for the plot when I had 'writer's block'. He has supported me throughout the countless hours of self imposed solitary confinement writing this novel. And to my daughters who cheered and pushed me on during the challenges. Special mention to Nadia Rose Design for the book cover design.

One

Day 1 – Early Evening

This was Mary Robbins' last day on earth. She didn't know it that morning as she welcomed her friend and neighbour Kate Trellow home after two weeks' holiday. She had no idea, as she tended her beloved orchids, that by the evening she would be dead.

Drugged.

Fried.

Her death would shatter Kate's world.

Possum Walk Over 50s Community would never be the same.

***

Mary Robbins felt blessed. Since John's hospitalisation for pneumonia, the kindness shown by residents of Possum Walk was overwhelming.

"I'll pick up some shopping for you, Mary."

"Would you like me to drive you to the hospital to visit John?"

Cooked meals appeared daily, too many to consume on her

own. People's generosity knew no bounds. It meant she had more precious time with her husband.

This afternoon's visit had not gone so well, however. Kate accompanied her and unfortunately witnessed John during one of his 'episodes'. Sometimes they could be unnerving. The women drove home from the hospital with little conversation. Mary wondered what was going through Kate's mind afterwards and decided to check in on her later.

The smell of the pea and ham soup Mary heated a few minutes earlier distracted her. It was too delicious to resist and she tucked into it with vigour. The flavours danced across her palate and she savoured every spoonful.

She sat back in her chair and glanced at the clock hanging on the wall. How peculiar. Feeling suddenly lightheaded, she barely made out the outline of the clock. It reminded her of a giant pendulum swinging back and forwards along the length of the wall. Her vision became blurry and she shook her head, blinking her eyes tightly to clear her sight. It made her dizzy and she lay her head on her folded arms resting on the table. Just for a minute, she reassured herself. Her blood pressure must be low. It happened from time to time.

It wasn't long before she realised something was seriously wrong. Her whole body ached. She barely had the strength to push herself away from the table and there was a funny buzzing in her ears too. The thump thump of a dull headache hurt behind her eyes. Perhaps she was coming down with the same virus that had gripped several residents in the past few weeks.

She frowned. Could the soup have disagreed with her? Who gave her the soup? A couple of residents had dropped by today.

Or was it yesterday? No, today. She must be getting sick, she thought. Her mind was usually razor sharp.

The thumping in her head was getting stronger too. In vain, she massaged her fingers at her temples. The tiredness was overpowering and she couldn't think straight. It didn't matter. She would remember later to thank whoever made the soup. After she rested.

Mary couldn't afford to get sick now. John needed her more than ever. She must stay well so she could continue to visit him. He always brightened up when she was there.

She stumbled as she moved away from the table. Her legs felt weak and unsteady. The front bedroom was only a few meters away. She just needed to lie down for a little bit. A wave of dizziness assailed her. The walls and floor moved all around her like a lurching carousel. How was she going to get to her bed. And started to panic?

"Let me help you, Mary." She heard the voice echoing from a distance. The blurred outline of a person stood before her, guiding her with gentle hands towards the bedroom.

"Oh, it's you," she said, relieved, grateful that there was a steady hand to help her. "I didn't hear you come in." The person didn't reply.

"I need to lie down," she mumbled before crumpling onto the bed and squeezed her eyes shut. The world wouldn't stop spinning.

She lay still, willing whatever gripped her to ease. Feeling drained, she was incapable of lifting her arms to pull the blanket over her.

"I think the soup didn't agree with me."

Had she said that out loud? She sounded so ungrateful she winced, which caused her head to throb that little bit more. The soup was delicious. She finished every drop. Soup was the penicillin of the Gods, her mother used to say. Funny how memories like that popped into her mind. Especially as she got older. How she'd missed her family.

"Undoubtedly. I put a little extra flavour in it for you." That voice again. She also heard a chuckle echoing around her.

She turned towards the sound of the voice and instead her eyes locked on the framed photo sitting on her bedside table. It was taken at John's retirement party. They were both smiling into each other's eyes. John had his arm around her. Even now, after forty-five years of marriage, he was so handsome.

"I miss you, my darling," she whispered. "I miss the old John."

He was disappearing piece by piece. Day by day. She felt helpless, unable to do anything but watch on, her heart breaking, as he struggled with his memory and everyday life. She dreaded the day coming when he didn't recognise her anymore.

"I'm so sorry for everything." Her sleepiness slurred her words. "I love you."

"Rest now, Mary." That voice again. This time it was kind, soothing. "It will all be over soon."

Mary let out a deep sigh. This winter had been challenging. The cold weather chilled her to the bone. Lying under the snug blanket which radiated a wonderful warmth made for a lovely change. Had she left the electric blanket on the bed after all? She frowned. Why couldn't she remember? She thought she'd removed it because she hated the artificial heat it generated.

Electric blankets were not the only choice. There were hot water bottles, she giggled.

However this sensation of heat was heavenly. She was the warmest she'd felt in years and wanted to close her eyes to give in to the blissful comfort. Frowning, she wondered for a moment if the heat was becoming a little too uncomfortable, then decided she didn't care. Totally relaxed and cozy, she curled herself further under the blankets. She recognized the pull of sleep edging closer. Maybe she would have more soup when she woke up.

As unconsciousness took over, her last thoughts were that life was wonderful after all. For the first time in a long time, she felt safe.

"Goodbye Mary."

Too late, Mary never heard the words laced with hatred.

Two

Day 1 - 10 Hours Earlier

Kate breathed in the cool winter air as she drove through the gates of Possum Walk. It was early morning. A mob of kangaroos grazed in the fenced off reserve opposite. The hint of sun peeping out from behind the clouds teased with a promise of a bright winter's day. It felt good to be home after two weeks away.

She made the right choice nearly three years ago after an early retirement. The move away from Melbourne city living to a semi-rural lifestyle was a gamble, one she never regretted. This place rejuvenated her. The pain of the past ten years finally eased. Losing Charlie, her husband of thirty-five years, to a hit-and-run driver left her heartbroken. And guilty.

"Welcome home, Kate." Mary Robbins stopped her gardening when Kate pulled up in the driveway.

"The orchids look amazing, Mary. I swear they've doubled in size since I've been away." She laughed and glanced at her own sorry excuse for a garden. "I wish I had your green thumb!"

Mary's orchids were her pride and joy, and she was the envy

of many resident garden lovers. She also happened to be the of the Northern Orchid Society and knew a thing or two about the exotic plants.

"Everything's ready for the Winter Orchid Show," Mary said. "My entries are safe inside ready for display," she added proudly.

"I'm looking forward to it." Kate attended every Orchid show, usually twice a year, since she met Mary. She loved the variety and beauty of the exotic plants. But alas, she'd managed to kill off one or two Mary gave her over the past couple of years.

"How are Hannah and the girls?" Mary was petite and barely reached Kate's shoulders. It didn't, however, prevent her from giving Kate the biggest bear hug.

"They are all doing well." Kate hugged her back. "It was wonderful to see the twins. They are growing fast and becoming a handful. Three years old yet so gorgeous. Hannah is a wonderful mother."

"Your daughter has been through a difficult time, but she's like her mum. Strong. Tough. She will get through this."

"It's difficult being so far away in another state. Sometimes I think of moving closer to support her."

"Hannah wouldn't want it any other way. You know that. She loves her life in Queensland and both Sam and she wanted to raise their girls there. She's going to be alright."

"Yeah." She knew what Mary said was true. Her daughter lost her husband to cancer a few months ago. After agonising about what to do, Hannah decided to stay in Queensland rather than come back to Victoria where she grew up.

"Is John still in the hospital?" Kate turned towards Mary's

garage. The door was closed and there were no loud noises which usually emanated from within.

"It's too quiet, isn't it?" Mary seemed to read her thoughts. "Do you know what I miss the most? The rattling of the pans and dishes in the kitchen. Waking up to the sound of John preparing breakfast for us both, the smell of sizzling bacon."

"I miss seeing him pottering around in your garage restoring the latest old car, doing whatever retired mechanics do." Kate shook her head in bemusement. "It's fascinating watching those rust buckets come to life under his hand."

"And trying in vain to muffle his swearing when things go wrong!"

They both laughed.

"Miss him so much," Mary continued. "On a positive note, the doctors say he's responding well to treatment. The pneumonia is just about gone. Should be home in a few days."

"That's wonderful news."

"Unfortunately, his memory lapses are escalating." Kate heard the worry in the other woman's voice.

She wasn't surprised when Mary confided a few weeks ago that doctors diagnosed John with early stage dementia. His forgetfulness and bouts of confusion were becoming evident. Others noticed too. People were understanding, yet Kate sensed Mary hated the pitying glances from well-meaning residents.

"How is the novel coming along? I suppose you had little chance to write whilst you were away."

"No, I didn't, but I jotted down some notes and can't wait to get back into it." Kate gave her friend a mischievous look. "I'm going to kill off Rhonda Kavich."

Mary glanced down the street at Rhonda's house and smiled, shaking her head. "Sometimes she may well deserve it that one. With all her carry ons and meddling. If you add me to your list of murder victims, please make the deed quick." She chuckled. "And messy!" she added with a twinkle in her eye.

"You know I don't write gory or bloodthirsty crime scenes, Mary. My murders are sedate and - charming."

"Charming, eh? Now there's a word I would certainly not relate to murder."

Kate laughed. "I couldn't help thinking about the plot on the flight home. It consumes me these days and I can't wait to finish the draft. The pleasure of writing has taken me by surprise to be honest. And what a rich tapestry of personalities and behaviours to tap into right here at Possum Walk."

"I suspect quite a few residents might want to get their hands on your novel after finding out what it's about." Mary chuckled. "They will desperately search the pages to discover if they're in the story or try to recognise others. You might be up for a lynching if you're not careful, my dear!"

Kate shrugged with a grin. "Discretion is the key. Readers might find a group of elderly amateur sleuths solving murder cases to be quite fascinating. At least I hope so. It took me until retirement to realise how much I love creating stories. I should have persevered after winning that writing competition at nine years of age."

"Life sometimes gets in the way. Often when you least expect it. You married young, had two beautiful children who kept you busy and then -"

"And then came the broken dreams," Kate interjected, a

bitterness in her voice. "I always expected Charlie and I would happily grow old together. I keep reliving that last argument we had before he stormed out. And then it was too late. He was gone."

"It's been ten years, Kate. None of it was your fault. Let it go and move on."

"You're right, Mary. I just wish I knew the truth. It haunts me still."

"In the meantime, there are so many other things to celebrate. You've nearly completed your first novel. I know it will be a best seller. And how lucky am I? I can boast I knew you before you became famous!"

"You're my biggest fan. Well, actually, my only fan so far," Kate chuckled. She'd told no one at Possum Walk about her literary ambitions. "Of course you can boast anytime." Kate glanced at her watch. "I'd better unpack. Then I'm looking forward to sitting at the computer with a cup of tea and review my notes."

"I need to finish this weeding and visit John after lunch."

"Would you like some company? I'd love to see John if he's up to visitors."

"But what about your unpacking and writing?"

"It can wait!"

***

Late Morning

Kate was struggling. She admitted it. She was so excited to log on to her computer and continue her novel, her mind brimming with ideas she'd developed during her holiday break. Now it just wasn't coming together. She glared at the computer screen as the mouse pointer flashed back at her. Waiting for her to continue typing.

"You and I aren't friends at the moment," she said to the screen. It remained silent. "I'm the one who was on holidays," she added, "not you!"

Clenching her teeth, she pushed away from her desk and picked up the always reliable stress ball for good measure. She paced around the study, stretching her body, trying to kink out the stiffness in her bones. Squeezing the hapless ball, she tried to think her way past the current sticking point in her story.

Her gaze fell on the shelf above her monitor. Her inspiration. On it were many items neatly lined up next to each other. The sight never failed to delight her. Yet to the casual eye, the shelf with its motley collection made no sense and was quite bizarre.

She recalled the day Mary entered her study just after she'd finished setting it up.

"Oh my goodness!" The sight of the shelf and its contents stopped Mary in her tracks. "Why do you have rat poison in here? You should store it away safely in the garage."

Her fingers slid across the shelf. "Oven cleaner? Painkillers? Insulin? Kate, what are you up to?"

Kate stood proudly in front of her collection and couldn't resist teasing her.

"Do you know there are hundreds if not thousands of everyday items that can kill a person if used in high enough quantities?"

Her friend's expression was priceless. Kate quickly told her about her writing a murder mystery novel.

"I'm researching how to kill people without getting caught. These items give me inspiration."

"I had no idea." Mary's initial shock turned to surprised delight. "What fun!"

Kate's enthusiasm must have rubbed off on Mary because the very next day she brought Kate a bottle of anti-freeze.

"I sneaked it out of John's garage," she said. "For research purposes only, you understand." With those words, she deposited it next to the rat poison and left, leaving Kate gazing after her, speechless.

Kate picked up the same anti-freeze bottle, hoping for a miracle to cure her own brain freeze. The story took on a life of its own two chapters ago and wandered off in a new direction. She loved the change for the female lead character. It absolutely made sense. But Kate couldn't work out how to get her back to the main plot and the looming second murder scene – which now required a whole new context and rewrite. Apparently she had fallen into a common trap most first time writers fell into. She didn't like it and it hurt her head right now.

The early morning flight home must have finally caught up with her. For the creative part of her brain was not in gear at all. To make matters worse, the folder which contained most of her research and background information for her plot and murder scenes was missing. It was invaluable material and represented many long hours of work. The various and interesting poisons she'd discovered were fascinating and enriched her ideas.

She relied on that material. She looked everywhere in the house for the folder and couldn't remember where she'd put it. She'd last seen it well before her holiday. That was over two weeks ago. She sighed. It would turn up eventually, in the most unlikely place no doubt.

She needed a break. The room felt like it was closing in around her. If she didn't do something, fast, to get herself under control, she'd explode. She was wasting time, getting nowhere, too wound up to be productive. Inspiration would not make an appearance today.

A quick swim in the heated pool before visiting John would relax her. She loved soaking in the spa afterwards. It sounded perfect. Just the solution to give her renewed energy.

Glaring back at the computer screen, she noted it was in 'sleep mode'.

"Traitor!"

She left the room, slamming the door behind her.

***

Early Afternoon

"How do you plan to kill Rhonda Kavich's character?" Mary asked as Kate drove them both to the hospital.

"Just working on it. Chocolates with Valium syringed into their soft centres."

"The cherry chocolate ones you and John love so much?" Mary giggled at the suggestion. "I don't think Adrian will find that amusing," she added.

Adrian Kaufman, a retired police officer, was a close friend of the Robbins who lived in the same street. Kate waited for the inevitable each time Mary mentioned him.

"I don't understand why he's never married," Mary said. "I've seen women fawn over him. He's tall and handsome with silvery blonde hair. And those blue eyes are to die for." Mary sighed dramatically, giving Kate a sideways glance.

"But he's emphatic romantic relationships are not for him. I'm still in love with my husband, otherwise I might have been tempted over the years if I were a few years younger," she chuckled. "You're single, Kate. And very attractive. Your auburn hair alone is a beacon to men. It's about time you started dating again."

Kate rolled her eyes at her friend and laughed. "You know I'm not interested in men, Mary, so give it up."

She couldn't deny how thrilled she was when Adrian was first introduced to her and she found out about his police background. What an amazing resource to tap into. Research gold right on her doorstep. Genuine experience beat the internet every time. But they'd barely crossed paths and exchanged only a few words since. She didn't fail to note his good looks either, but only as a passing thought.

"Adrian was a highly decorated agent," Mary persisted. "He was part of an international task force many years ago that brought down one of the biggest international drug cartels."

That impressed Kate. She wondered how he landed that role from being a local police officer.

"He never talks about it, of course." Mary added. "It was initially big news in the United Kingdom. The judge presiding over the case suppressed any media reporting. Mostly because of its political sensitivities."

"Do you remember the name of the task force? And how long ago it was?" Kate asked.

"Adrian's a good man. Best you don't involve yourself in his doings."

"I'm curious. Imagine getting inside the minds of people

who've lived and breathed crime. For research only, of course. It might help my story."

Mary shook her head and laughed. "He won't discuss it, Kate. Take it from someone who knows."

They travelled for a few minutes in companionable silence when Mary abruptly turned to Kate, a worried expression on her face. "Kate, I must warn you that John is not quite himself these days. Even in the short time you've been away, his mental health has deteriorated." Her eyes filled with tears.

"What do you mean?"

"His memory is failing and there's a chance he might not recognise you. Sometimes he says things that make little sense. It's as if he goes into his own private world and I can't reach him."

"I think I understand," Kate said. "It must be difficult for you both. Perhaps he'll settle down once he's home in familiar surroundings."

"If only it were that simple." Mary's sadness hung heavily in the air.

***

When Kate and Mary entered John's room on the tenth floor of St Ignatius Hospital, they found John and Adrian Kaufman laughing together. John's face lit up at the sight of his wife.

"Mary, my darling!" They embraced warmly.

Kate acknowledged Adrian with a smile and a nod. "Hello Adrian." She extended her hand out to him, which he clasped briefly but remained silent. His easy laughing demeanour from moments earlier with John was gone. Neither spoke. Kate looked away, feeling herself start to fidget under his unwavering gaze.

"Good to see you Kate!" John waved her towards him, a big smile on his face.

"How are you feeling?" she asked.

"Never better. Doctors say I can go home soon."

Kate handed him a bag of his favourite chocolates. John immediately popped one into his mouth.

"Mm. You know my weakness, Kate," he chuckled. "Thank you. Better hide these before Rosie arrives," he continued. "She will be along shortly. That woman looks after me so well. I admit to being lost without her."

Kate wondered who Rosie was. Perhaps a nurse.

"Have you been sleeping well?" Mary asked, sitting close beside him on the bed. "I brought you some crossword puzzles."

"Thank you, darling." He gazed at Mary adoringly as he held her hand.

John then turned to Kate and nodded towards Adrian, who stood at the foot of the bed. "Where are my manners?" he said. "Kate, have you met my friend, Adrian Kaufman?"

"Yes, I have."

"He's a good man. He knows all our truths, our secrets," John continued in a conspiratorial tone. "I honestly don't know how we would have survived all these years without his friendship. He stood by us from the beginning, steadfast and loyal."

"I think Kate knows we are friends with Adrian, darling," Mary quickly stepped in.

"I'm honoured to be your friend, John," Adrian replied calmly.

Suddenly, John sat upright, appearing nervous. His eyes wide, he scanned the room with jerky movements, as though looking for someone or something.

"Rosie told me to be careful. To be quiet." He grabbed Mary's arm. "She turned our lives upside down. It wasn't her fault but she should have stayed silent."

Mary placed a gentle hand on his shoulder, despite his fierce grip. "You're safe, John," her voice soothing. "No one will hurt you here. You've been ill. But you are getting better now."

"Nothing will ever be the same again." He shook his head vehemently. "Rosie is gone. Gone forever."

Mary glanced at Kate before turning her attention back to John. "Rosie is dead and buried, John. That's where she needs to stay."

"I've seen the eyes," he continued, an urgency in his voice. "I'll never forget them as long as I live. They haunt my dreams. Pure evil they are." He shuddered. "And now they are back. How can that be?"

"That's not possible," Adrian reassured his friend. "There is no danger. You are safe."

"Be especially careful, my darling," John said to Mary. "These are dangerous times. It's not over yet." With that, he released his grip on her and slumped back on the pillow, closing his eyes.

Kate stared at John for a moment, then, bewildered, looked from Adrian and Mary. Her mind tried to grasp the change in John in only a few weeks and felt an acute sense of sadness coupled with disbelief at what she'd witnessed. She saw the stricken look on Mary's face. Her heart went out to both of them, two friends who she'd grown to love.

"He's deteriorated since the last time I saw him a couple of weeks ago," she murmured. "You warned me but I had no idea just how pronounced it has become. I'm so sorry, Mary."

Mary sank into the empty chair beside John's bed. She regarded him sadly. Kate realised his dementia was progressing at a faster pace than before they admitted him to the hospital. It wouldn't be long before he required a high level of care beyond living at home.

"It's unfortunate you had to witness that, Kate." Adrian said quietly. "He is having these episodes more often now. Sometimes it's easier to just agree with whatever he says, even when it makes little sense."

"Of course," she replied.

"The other place. That's where he goes during these episodes." Mary's tone was bleak.

Adrian looked from one woman to the other. "I think it's time for a coffee," he said, his tone brighter. "Tea, Mary?"

She nodded.

"I'll come with you, Adrian," Kate quickly offered.

Kate and Adrian were silent as they went down the lift to the hospital cafeteria on the ground floor. Seeing John's mental deterioration upset Kate. She didn't expect it. Only a few weeks earlier, before he became ill, he was well, high functioning. Ever the joker, making people laugh with his stories. Sometimes he forgot names, or what he'd done in the last few hours or days. But nothing compared to what she'd witnessed today.

"Penny for your thoughts." They exited the lift and Adrian smiled down at her. His face was even more handsome with that smile. "I think I understand what you must be feeling," he continued. "I still find it difficult to watch him go through these lapses."

"It's just the speed at which he's declining that shocks me. I admit to having no first hand experience with people suffering from dementia and can't comprehend what Mary must be going through on a daily basis."

"She's coping well, under the circumstances, but she will need a good friend in her life as time goes on."

Kate agreed. In that moment, she vowed to be that person, no matter what it took.

***

Mary sat next to John for the longest time, staring down at his beloved face. It was getting harder to cover up his ramblings as his illness progressed. Thankfully, most people saw what they wanted to see – a man whose memory was failing, who had delusional tendencies.

Kate was a dear friend and Mary cared about her. She was like the daughter she never had, even though there was only a ten-year difference between them. And she was also astute. Would she wonder at Mary's constant rush to cover up his comments? Would she look deeper into what he said and ask questions? What would she, Mary, reply if she did?

John talked about Rosie more often these days. After all this time. Mary was grateful he had not yet mentioned Peter. It was a matter of time and she feared the consequences.

She felt more alone as John's illness progressed. For the first time in many years, she wanted to unburden herself. Her urge to confide in Kate was becoming stronger. She trusted her. As a friend who would not judge them. Kate was the one person in a long time who she felt would understand and care. They had a special connection and she knew Kate felt the same.

But old habits were hard to shift. After many years of secrecy and lies, it was a big step for Mary. She would discuss it with Adrian first. He would know what to do. Yet, as she sat there biting her lower lip with worry, her one regret was mentioning the task force and Adrian's connection to it. And the drug cartel.

He would not approve of her telling Kate - or anyone. Not a smart move. She was slipping. What did it matter after all these years? There was no danger now. Living a more normal life was a relief at last.

Three

Day 1 – Evening

Rhonda Kavich started off on her usual evening walk. This was her favourite part of the day. Tonight, the air was crisp and the sky clear. Winter was fast approaching, but not this evening. Walking was healthy for the body and soul. And keeping the mind active was very important. In her late fifties, Rhonda prided herself on the discipline she practiced.

Unfortunately, she inherited a solid build together with her above average height thanks to her Polish background. She appeared physically imposing to others. But she worked at keeping lean and healthy by going to the gym every day. Then aqua aerobics three times a week.

Keeping herself busy was the key. Because then she didn't have to think about her children who she rarely saw or heard from. Nor the loneliness that often crept in. She refused to let her mind go in that direction and firmly pushed the thoughts away.

Still, she admitted to feeling a little tired of late. Today was a full day. Aqua aerobics was always enjoyable. Afterwards she attended a meeting of the Social Committee. But that Cathy Eldridge was getting on her nerves. How dare she talk to Rhonda that way! All she did was ask if her male friend was going to move in. What was wrong with that? Cathy got angry and snapped at her, telling her to mind her own business and not be such a busybody.

"Well, of course I'm busy. All the time." Rhonda shot back.

Cathy didn't like that response. Some people were so touchy. Cathy's 'friend' often showed up at dinnertime and left after breakfast. Rhonda's house was only three away from hers. Everyone knew what was going on. Why didn't the woman just admit to it?

Anyway, Rhonda wasn't sure if she would continue as a member of the Social Committee. It was losing its appeal. That afternoon's meeting was disappointing. Things seemed tense. Rhonda puzzled over it.

"We need to finalise our winter and spring program, ladies," Julie French, president, announced. There were no men on the committee. Despite the committee's best efforts, they never ever volunteered or nominated to join. Even the unfortunate husbands of some committee members refused to take part. Only once did a member get her husband to attend a meeting, but he soon disappeared, never to return.

Of course, everyone had different ideas about the upcoming social calendar.

"How about a night at the races?" someone suggested.

"No, it's too cold at this time of year."

"A pizza night here at the clubhouse?" Some liked that idea.

"What about a night at the opera?" Rhonda offered.

Her one genuine passion was opera. She had season tickets too. And didn't mind going on her own. She preferred it. That way she wouldn't have to make small talk which would then detract from the beauty of the performance.

"It's a little expensive don't you think, Rhonda?"

Julie French was always so negative. How she became the President was beyond her.

"Yes, it is a little expensive but such a wonderful and cultured experience."

"Not everyone can afford the Opera, Rhonda." Julie French persisted.

"It's better than throwing your money away on gambling," Rhonda shot back pointedly. They didn't speak for the rest of the meeting. And the opera idea disappeared from the discussion. Oh well, their loss!

As she glanced at the house opposite hers, she wondered how Paula Vincent was settling in. No lights. She must be out again. They met a few weeks ago when Paula moved in. Rhonda saw the moving truck pull up in front of her house that day and went over to introduce herself.

"Hello, I'm Rhonda and live at the corner house across the street. Welcome to Possum Walk."

Paula had her back to her and was directing where to put the furniture. She must have been startled at Rhonda's words for she visibly jumped.

"Er, hello," she replied. She was softly spoken.

"Aren't you a tiny little thing? There's nothing of you." Laughing, Rhonda continued. "Possum Walk will fix that in no time.

There's a constant stream of social activities with mountains of food and drink."

Paula gave her a tight smile. "Yes, well – as you can see, I'm busy. Thanks for coming over but I must keep going. Please excuse me." With those words, she turned away, dismissing Rhonda.

"How rude!" Rhonda muttered under her breath.

Weeks later, she changed her mind. In observing Paula, she realised perhaps she was shy rather than rude, someone who found social networking a little difficult. Whilst Paula was happy to sit with various groups of people at the clubhouse, she did very little to contribute to the surrounding conversations. Rhonda must invite her soon for afternoon tea and find out all about her. She estimated they were both of a similar age. The difference was that Paula worked a few days a week and Rhonda didn't need to.

Adrian Kaufman lived next to Paula. He was single and a tad mysterious. An ex-police officer with a poker face and eyes that gave nothing away. Not surprising. Very handsome man too for his age, which she estimated to be mid to late sixties. She tried to engage him in conversation several times when she saw him at clubhouse functions. But he always conveniently found an excuse to remove himself from her presence. She decided he was rude and not worth her effort.

Next door to Rhonda was yet another single man, Diego Santo. He migrated to Australia from Italy with his parents when he was a teenager and still carried a slight accent. For a foreigner, he had settled into Possum Walk life very well. Alas, the man liked his vino a little too much, she suspected. She smelt it on his breath sometimes. People seemed to like him. And his food too apparently. He often brought home cooked Italian food to share at the weekly happy hour.

"I'm not sure what the fuss is all about," she said to Paula one evening as she stared down at a plate of fried peppers. Rhonda always tried to sit near her to give her support. "I think his food looks rather rich. He fries a lot of it. This is not healthy."

Paula mumbled a brief response Rhonda couldn't hear with all the surrounding chatter. Once she was alarmed when he offered her a piece of walnut and apple cake.

"No, no, no! I'm allergic to nuts!" She was scathing. "That dish is venom to me!"

Rhonda walked past his house tonight and, like Paula, he didn't appear to be home. She wondered whether there was a developing friendship or something more between Paula and Diego. They spent a lot of time together. He was so gregarious compared to her quiet reserve. Sometimes opposites were attracted to each other. She would continue to watch the two of them over the coming weeks. Her instincts were never wrong.

Nearing Kate's house, she frowned at the state of her garden. It just wasn't up to standard. Kate should take greater pride and plant a few more flowers. Rhonda decided she would ask Mary if she had any spare orchids. They would brighten up Kate's garden. And then Mary would not have to put up with looking at that sorry excuse of a garden as she worked in her own patch.

Poor Mary, she thought. She had a lot to deal with these days. Her husband was ill and losing his mind. How embarrassing it must be for both of them. Many residents wondered about his odd behaviour. She noticed Mary repeatedly try to cover up his failings. And she had the upcoming Winter Orchid Show to finalise in the next couple of weeks. It was too much. She decided to offer her assistance with the show. That would surely ease some of the pressure.

Rhonda didn't immediately detect anything unusual as she strolled. Her gaze was still on Kate's pathetic garden. Then everything happened so fast.

She detected a whiff of smoke. Before she could wonder about it, a loud thumping noise to her left distracted her. She glimpsed movement near Mary's side fence.

That was when she saw the fire. Flames licked up against the front window inside Mary and John's bedroom. The blinds and curtains melted before her eyes. She froze in shock. Suddenly, the glass of the window shattered with the heat, jolting her out of her inertia. Acting on instinct, she turned towards Kate's house.

"Kate! Kate! Help! Anyone!"

She saw a light inside Kate's house. Moving as fast as her arthritis would allow her, she was relieved when Kate rushed out. The look of shock on her face as she saw the fire said it all.

Fortunately, Kate had her mobile phone in her hand. "Emergency!" she yelled down the line. "Fire! At Possum Walk!"

By the time Kate finished making the emergency call, several neighbours had gathered outside, alerted by the shouting. She hurried to Rhonda, who couldn't stop shaking.

"A fire at Possum Walk!" Kate said to her. "A potential catastrophe with all these timber houses."

They both watched Adrian Kaufman push through the crowd as he made his way towards it.

"Mary!" Rhonda heard the panic in Kate's voice. Mary would have smelled or seen the fire if she was home.

Rhonda's thoughts were racing. "Maybe she's fallen and is unconscious inside!"

"Adrian! We have to get inside. Mary may be hurt." Kate stopped him as he passed. His face reflected his fear.

"I'll try." His voice was strained.

The two women watched Adrian swiftly secure Mary's garden hose to her tap. Other men joined him. He handed the hose to one of them and hurried towards the front door, shouting out Mary's name.

Rhonda watched him try to enter the house but the fire had become too fierce, forcing him back. He looked around to find another way in. The side gate entry was blocked as it was too close to the fire in the front bedroom.

"Can someone check if Mary's at the clubhouse?" Kate shouted to the gathering crowd.

Paula Vincent came forward from the crowd. "I just came from there and didn't see her." Rhonda's heart sank and her worst fears grew as she slowly turned once again towards the burning house.

The heat was intense and people pulled further back. However, the glow of the fire mesmerised Rhonda, its flames seeming to draw her closer. She inched towards the burning house.

"Rhonda, what are you doing? Move away from there."

Rhonda heard Kate's voice but ignored it. She couldn't take her eyes off the flames as they greedily engulfed the whole front bedroom. It was a raging inferno. She felt dazed, taking everything in as if in slow motion. She inched a little closer and stared at the now gaping hole that once was the bedroom window. Her gaze moved inside.

"Kate, is that..?"

"Rhonda! Kate, get her out of here!" Adrian shouted. The fire had singed his clothes with his attempts to get inside the house. By now, hoses from neighbouring houses were also being used to battle the blaze.

Rhonda ignored everyone, her gaze fixated on the burning house. "There's something inside..." The smoke was getting thick. "I can't quite make out..." She felt Kate grab her arm, pulling her back to a safe distance just as the fire brigade arrived, sirens blaring.

There was chaos everywhere. Firefighters spilled out of the truck with their equipment. One directed the crowd away to a safer distance. Adrian and others stopped hosing the house, pulling away, making room. The smoke looked dark and ominous. The fire seemed relentless.

A strange grinding sound came from the garage adjoined to the burning house. As one, Rhonda and Kate turned towards the sound. Like a bizarre horror movie, they watched the Robbins' aluminium garage door start to warp and collapse into itself with the heat of the fire. Behind it was Mary's car, parked in its usual space.

Rhonda wrenched her arm out of Kate's grip. "No! I saw something through the window!" she screamed at Kate, her heart pounding so hard she couldn't breathe.

Time seemed to stop as the two women stared at each other, panic and shock reflected across their faces. Rhonda felt overwhelmed, her mind spinning. She couldn't figure out what bothered her about the fire. Panic gripped her as she tried to think through the fog in her brain. Something about the bedroom. What was it? Her mind was in overload, struggling to process what was happening around her.

An instant later, terror ripped through her body as Rhonda understood what was gnawing at her, what she had seen through the window of the burning house. Somewhere, she heard someone let out a blood-curdling scream. Just before she fainted, she realised it was her.

***

Kate caught Rhonda before she hit the ground.

"Paula!" She was the closest. "Help me get Rhonda inside." Adrian quickly moved to assist.

Together, they carried the unconscious Rhonda to Kate's living room sofa. They heard more sirens. Relief washed over Kate when she saw the paramedics and police vehicles arrive. Residents directed two paramedics to her house.

"I'll get back out there and see if there's anything I can do." Adrian was gone.

It wasn't long before Rhonda returned to consciousness. Initially disorientated, she tried to push away the paramedics hovering over her.

"No - no - no - no," she murmured over and over, shaking her head, slumping back down on the sofa. Rhonda's gaze turned to the burning house and tears welled up in her eyes.

"It was awful," she whispered. Her eyes locked with Kate's. "She's dead."

"What are you saying, Rhonda?" Kate's heart sank and she

felt tears well up in her eyes. She didn't want to believe what Rhonda's words implied, but she feared the worst too.

"I saw her in the bed. The fire engulfed her. It was Mary. I know what I saw. I'll never forget it."

"Your vitals are good, Rhonda," the paramedic reassured her. "But you've had quite a shock. As a precaution, it's best we take you to the hospital for further examination."

"There's nothing wrong with me!" Rhonda snapped back. Her colour had returned to her cheeks. "I know what I saw. Ask them out there." She waved towards Mary's house.

Kate sighed as she too looked in that direction. She forgot Paula was still in the room, standing at the front window, observing what was unfolding. Kate joined her. Paula barely acknowledged her as she stood seemingly frozen to the spot. Her gaze fixated at what was happening across the street.

"The fire seems under control now," Paula whispered. "It's almost out."

"What a relief. Thankfully, it didn't spread to the adjoining houses."

Two firefighters advanced into the burnt-out house. It was almost dark outside but the light from the torch on their safety helmets led the way. They placed a tarp across the front of the house, blocking the view from curious and worried residents. Yellow police tape already surrounded the property. A few police officers and firefighters were in deep conversation in the garden. Kate could just make out the crushed and trampled orchids around them from the soft glow of the streetlight a few meters away.

"Mary will be upset at the state of her beloved garden," she said to no one in particular.

"It won't matter. She's dead." Rhonda stood behind them. "The image is forever etched in my brain."

Kate opened her mouth to say something when one firefighter emerged from the house, distracting her with his urgent manner. He addressed the group of officers in the garden, Adrian moving towards them. Whatever they were told, their reaction was swift. They all scattered in different directions. Two accompanied the firefighter back into the house and the others went to their respective vehicles. Kate watched as they spoke on their phones. Adrian remained where he was, a lonely figure amid the turmoil surrounding him. His face was grim.

"I'm going out there. They've found Mary." Rhonda made a determined move towards the door.

"Do you think that's a good idea, Rhonda?" Kate blocked her from the door. "You've had a shock. Let the police do their job. We'll find out more in good time."

"Look! More police." Paula called their attention to a police vehicle coming to a halt in front of the Robbins' house. A man and woman, both in plain clothes, stood before the house. Several firefighters and police officers joined them and all appeared to have an intense conversation.

A few minutes later, the plain clothed officers moved towards the growing group of residents. After a brief conversation, one resident pointed to Kate's house. Adrian, stony faced, joined the two as they met Kate at her door.

"I'm Detective Michael Abbott and this is my colleague,

Detective Joyce Penrose." He had a commanding voice and appeared in his mid-fifties.

"Kate Trellow," she said, feeling a sense of dread.

"A deceased female has been found at the scene. She is yet to be identified, but we believe it is Mary Robbins, owner of the property."

Kate felt her chest tighten with overwhelming grief. She was stricken and thought her legs would buckle from under her. Her eyes stung with tears, but she brushed them away.

"I knew it!" Rhonda sobbed, collapsing against Kate. Adrian eased her away.

"What happened?" Kate asked, her throat tight, her breathing ragged.

"I can't say at this stage until we undertake a full investigation," continued Detective Abbott. "I understand you raised the alarm, Mrs Trellow?"

"Yes, but only after Rhonda saw the house burning and alerted me."

"I'd like to ask a few questions of both of you." His gaze moved between them.

Kate nodded. She was numb with grief.

Rhonda continued to sob quietly.

***

It was a long night. Kate was numb from exhaustion, her body weary. Her mind refused to accept Mary was dead. Detective Abbott directed endless questions at her in quick succession for nearly an hour. It was gruelling. All she wanted to do was crawl into her bed, pull the covers over her and sleep for hours until the pain of Mary's death left her.

"When was the last time you spoke to Mary?"

"Can you describe what happened tonight?"

"What kind of person was Mary Robbins?"

"Was Mary Robbins happy with her husband?"

What kind of question was that one, she wondered.

"Where is John Robbins now?" the detective continued.

"In the hospital, recovering from pneumonia," she replied. Her voice was hoarse from exhaustion.

"Pneumonia?"

"And dementia," Kate replied.

"We'll follow that up as soon as possible. Did the Robbins get along with residents in Possum Walk?"

"Yes, I think so." Kate frowned at the growing implication of the questions.

"What do you know about the Robbins' background? Friends? Family?"

"They've been in Australia for over 20 years."

"Children?"

"No children."

On and on, he shot the questions.

"How did the fire start?" Kate asked at one point.

"It's early stages yet." Detective Abbott appeared to choose his words carefully. "We believe the electric blanket on her bed caught fire while Mrs Robbins was sleeping."

Kate shuddered at the image of those words. "Mary felt the cold well before winter this year. She just couldn't get warm enough."

"Did she always use an electric blanket?" the detective asked.

"No, I don't think so. Mary and I were with several residents in the clubhouse one day. She said she had an old electric blanket from years ago that she was going to unpack and try out. Thought it was about time she and John enjoyed it."

What a fateful decision that had turned out to be. Kate felt a deep sorrow physically inside her, like a lead weight anchoring her down. Any remaining energy or will to answer the detective's questions were quickly depleting. What a horrible situation. With Mary's death, John was suddenly left on his own with deteriorating health. He had limited options moving forward.

"She didn't deserve this," Kate murmured. "It was a horrible way to die."

***

"I asked how Mary died," Kate said to Rhonda later after their respective interviews. "The detective told me it was likely a faulty electric blanket."

She snorted her disbelief. "Rubbish! Mary didn't have an electric blanket on her bed. Less than a week ago, Mary told me she threw it out after trialling it. She didn't like it at all."

Kate stood there for a moment, completely stunned. "Then how did it turn up on her bed again?"

"Exactly." Rhonda's eyebrows lifted as she gave Kate a knowing look.

"Surely, you're not suggesting what I think you're implying? She must have changed her mind. Or purchased a new one. Simple."

"Believe what you will, Kate Trellow. There's more behind this fire. You mark my words. The police believe it too. They asked me odd questions that sound like something suspicious took place."

"Detective Abbott told me several other residents were interviewed tonight," Kate continued. "Mary's death is going to hit residents hard."

Kate noted Adrian immersed himself in assisting the emergency services where he could. He also had several conversations with various police officers and firefighters. It had fallen to him to identify Mary's body, Detective Abbott told her.

At one point that night, Kate saw Cathy Eldridge standing at a distance from the other residents. She was visibly shocked and refused to be comforted, telling people who approached her to leave her alone. Many residents were overwhelmed by the tragedy of one of their own dying in such circumstances. Everyone's reaction and shock would be different. Poor Cathy.

It wasn't long before reporters and their cameras arrived in their news vans.

Four

Day 2 – Early Morning

*BREAKING NEWS * BREAKING NEWS * BREAKING NEWS*

This is Rick Lewis reporting from Robinwood, an outer suburb north of Melbourne. An elderly woman has died in a fire at a local retirement village. Residents of Possum Walk Over 50s Community alerted the Fire Brigade last evening after one of the housing units caught fire.

Fire Inspector Greg Davis said it was a tragic situation because a woman in her 70s had lost her life.

"Given the proximity of the weatherboard units to each other," he said, "it was fortunate firefighters contained the fire to just the one house where the deceased lived. Damage was primarily to the front of the house."

He indicated from preliminary investigations that the wiring of the electric blanket was faulty, which may have caused the fire. The deceased woman, who cannot be identified at this stage, was asleep in her bed when the fire started and the fumes overcame her.

Following this tragedy, the Inspector shared an important message with the public.

"This is a chilling reminder to replace your electric blanket every ten years, even if you think it's working fine and doesn't appear to be damaged. If you have an old electric blanket that's sitting in the cupboard for ages, think about how long ago you bought it before you plug it in. And never ever buy a second-hand one. The exact age may be uncertain."

***

The coroner's office attended the scene in the early hours of the next morning and removed Mary Robbins' body. Hidden behind the wall of canvas, the house with the yellow police tape surrounding it was a confronting reminder that something terrible had occurred. The lack of damage to the neighbouring properties astonished residents. Many went further and called it 'a miracle'.

The freakish nature of the accident deeply shook some residents, causing many days and weeks of sleeplessness and anxiety. Others couldn't wait to replace their existing electric blankets fast enough and did so the very next day. A few stopped using their electric blankets altogether. The ones who didn't own or use an electric blanket merely shrugged. They never understood the fuss about those blankets anyway. Nonetheless, the tragedy touched all.

Poor Mary...

Poor John...

There was, however, one person who slept soundly that night.

***

Afternoon

Rhonda felt agitated and off colour since last night. She had a migraine that reverberated inside her head every time she moved. Her mind was numb and normal tasks felt sluggish. Even washing up after breakfast was painful. The noise was deafening to her hyper-sensitive ears and her hands trembled.

She was astonished that she fainted at the scene. It was not like her to resort to such dramatics. But the image of Mary burning in her bed would remain etched in her memory forever. Tears sprang into her eyes and she impatiently brushed them away. No time for nonsense like this.

Voices coming from outside distracted Rhonda and she looked out the front window. She immediately saw the police car parked in front of Diego's house next door. Intriguing. Why were they there? Diego stood on his porch chatting with two police officers. She moved closer to the other side of her window, where she could better hear what they were saying.

"I was asleep," Diego said to one officer. He sounded anxious, defensive. "I went to bed early and didn't hear a thing. Can't believe Mary is gone!" He looked at the burnt house next to him and shook his head. "I'm so sorry, so sorry."

"What time did you go to bed, Mr Santo?"

"I don't remember," he sobbed.

"So you're telling us you slept through the whole incident last night? The sirens of the fire trucks and police vehicles? The surrounding commotion over the next few hours?"

"Yes, sir." Diego hunched over as though in pain.

"We rang your doorbell and banged on your door and you heard nothing?" The two police officers glanced at each other.

Diego remained silent.

"May we come in, please?"

They entered the house together and Rhonda heard nothing more. Of course, Diego didn't hear the chaos of last night. He was undoubtedly blind drunk and fell asleep. She would bet her life on it! She felt frustrated and annoyed at Diego's lack of self-respect. Drinking was the curse of the devil and he should practice more restraint. The stupid man was not reliable, even to save himself. What would have happened to him if his house had caught fire? He'd probably be dead like Mary! Waking up to the horror of the Robbins' house burnt down must have been quite a shock for him.

The migraine intensified and Rhonda groaned. She was tough and she'd become used to them over the years. It would ease soon enough. But this was by far the worst she'd suffered in a long while. The ones that frightened her were where she lost time. It happened only a handful of times, thankfully. She remembered nothing between the onset of the migraine and her waking up. Finding a half-eaten sandwich she didn't recall making or eating, or a letter she didn't remember writing, was terrifying.

She pulled her shoulders back, determined to get on with her day. No more would she worry about the fire, the suspicions that persisted in her head. She'd avoided them all morning. But they niggled at the back of her mind, insistent.

She trusted her instincts. Something was wrong. She just didn't know or understand what it was.

Five

Day 3 – Afternoon

Kate couldn't focus on writing. She sat in front of her computer screen, hoping for distraction away from the pain and sorrow of Mary's death. But it didn't work. She was at the same impasse in her storyline and didn't have the mental stamina to push through it.

For the hundredth time, she wished she could find her missing research folder. It was a bright purple colour, which made it easy to spot. She remembered reading about fires caused by faulty electrical appliances. She'd printed the article because it intrigued her. And for future reference, of course.

A couple of media vans were parked around the clubhouse as she went to pick up her mail at the letterbox station. It was three days since the fire but the media interest hadn't waned. She saw Cathy Eldridge talking into a microphone with a female journalist, a cameraman shooting it all.

"I've known poor Mary for nearly three years," she heard Cathy say. "A beautiful and kind woman."

Kate gave them a wide berth. She wasn't prepared to answer questions about Mary or the fire. It was still too raw.

She groaned inwardly as she approached her street when Rhonda hurried out of her house towards her. She'd been waiting for her return evidently.

"Kate, it is truly a puzzle. I can't believe Mary's gone!" Tears welled in her eyes. "Why was there an electric blanket found on Mary's bed? It wasn't supposed to be there."

"Mary must have changed her mind because the cold weather was unbearable for her. That's the only logical explanation."

"I'm not convinced, Kate. It makes little sense. Mary was adamant about how much she disliked that electric blanket."

"It seems a little odd," Kate agreed. "What I don't understand is why she didn't wake up when the fire started."

"Perhaps she took a sleeping pill?" Rhonda replied, frowning.

"I read about a case in the United States where a husband drugged his wife before killing her with a tampered electric blanket. After initially thinking it was an accident, the police charged him. Luckily, the court convicted him and sentenced him to life in prison."

Kate immediately regretted her words when Rhonda's eyes widened in shock, only to be replaced by a speculative gleam.

"How bizarre that a similar incident has occurred here at Possum Walk," Rhonda said.

"Thankfully, in Mary's situation, there is no menacing husband in the background attempting to murder his wife. Just a horrible accident," Kate quickly added.

Rhonda stared at Kate intensely. "That's an interesting story," she remarked, her eyes narrowing.

"You surely don't think John killed Mary! From his hospital bed?" Kate challenged Rhonda. "You're actually entertaining the thought?" When Rhonda didn't immediately deny it, Kate added, "That's preposterous!"

"Honestly, I don't know, but something isn't right. Things are odd. I know people don't take me seriously sometimes, but this situation worries me."

"If there is anything suspicious about the fire or Mary's death, the police will find it. There's nothing we can do about it for now," Kate said firmly.

She should never have fed Rhonda's suspicions by telling her about the case in the United States. The woman would become even more unbearable. If that were possible! Regrettably, the damage was done. Somehow, she had to downplay the situation.

"You protest too much, Kate. Maybe you harbour your own doubts and are afraid to voice them."

"Don't be ridiculous Rhonda.!"

"Why did you mention the case about the murderous husband? Or why Mary didn't wake up when the fire started? Things are on your mind, even if you don't want to acknowledge them publicly."

"Perhaps the grief of Mary's death has affected my thinking. It's all been so surreal."

"I don't believe it was an accident," Rhonda persisted. "I believe the fire was deliberately lit and someone killed her! There! I finally said it out loud."

"Why would you think that?" Kate was stunned. "Who would want Mary dead? It's ridiculous and you know it. You're looking under rocks!"

"I know people here talk about me behind my back," Rhonda said dispassionately. "I sense it more so now whenever I bring up the fire and Mary's death. I see the rolling of the eyes."

Kate knew it was true. She often felt frustrated with Rhonda's constant opinions and disapproving nature. She understood how others would react to Rhonda's latest obsession.

"I'm sorry you feel hurt, Rhonda." Kate didn't know what else to say.

"No one ever takes me seriously. But I watch people. I see things, how others behave when they think no one is looking. Take Diego Santo for example."

"What about Diego?" Kate asked, a little bewildered at the unexpected turn of the conversation. Diego lived next door to Rhonda.

"Well, everyone knows he's an alcoholic. He likes his wine. A little too much. And he sings all the time when he's drunk. I hear him from my house. Harmless, right? But is he? Where was he the night of the fire? The house next to his was on fire and he was nowhere to be seen. Neither did he answer when the police did a door knock that night."

"How could you possibly know that? You were at my house with the paramedics."

"I overheard him talking with the police on his porch the day after the fire. He told them he slept through the whole thing."

"Well, how lucky for him that the fire didn't spread," Kate replied drily.

"Yes, but there's more. It was an instant before I saw the fire. A noise distracted me and then I glimpsed movement near the fence between Diego's and the Robbins' properties. I'd forgotten that detail with all the commotion. At first I thought it was an animal, a possum maybe, scaling the fence. But now I've had time to reflect on it. It was too big for a cat. It was definitely a person. I think it was Diego. Who else could it be?"

Kate's stomach did a deep dive and her eyes widened in stunned disbelief.

"Rhonda! Are you sure? Have you told the police?"

"No. I only just remembered it. But what if I'm wrong?"

"You need to leave that to the police to follow up. It might be important information. Or nothing at all."

"But if Diego was drunk, it couldn't be him, could it?"

Rhonda's hesitation surprised Kate. The other woman was usually so quick and smug to find the negative in others, highly critical with no insight into how offensive she could be. She had absolutely no filter. Which is why Kate was astonished at her behaviour now.

"Would you like me to accompany you to the police?"

Rhonda shook her head vehemently. "No, I need time to think it through," she said firmly. "I warned you, Kate. Things don't add up with this case."

Kate stared at Rhonda for the longest time. So many emotions spilled over her. Confusion, curiosity and frustration all battled to rise to the surface. For the first time since Mary's death, she started to seriously consider what Rhonda had said. Was she right about the fire? The thought frightened her.

"If Diego was indeed the person you saw, then he lied about his movements that night. Why?"

"I don't know." Rhonda frowned, a pained expression on her face,

"And what if Diego was indeed drunk and it was someone else jumping the fence? Rhonda, you must go to the police! They need to investigate this further."

Kate felt a sudden tremor run through her body. Her hands became clammy and her chest was heavy with each breath she inhaled. No! It was an all too familiar sensation. Not now! Not in front of Rhonda Kavich! She heard Rhonda's voice as though from a distance. She had to get home.

"I'm sorry, Rhonda, but I have to go." Kate quickly turned away. "Remembered something urgent."

She knew her behaviour was rude, but she had little choice. She practically ran to her house, desperate to get inside the safety of her home. She collapsed against the front door as she shut it behind her. Paralysed with fear, she stood rooted to the spot. Her heart raced, her muscles tensed and her body trembled uncontrollably. Heat radiated under her skin in every pore.

She experienced her first panic attack after her husband passed away. At the time, she didn't understand what was happening to her and actually thought she was having a heart attack and dying. Numerous tests finally gave her a diagnosis. Over time, she learned to accept the attacks. The fact they were unpredictable was a challenge. It didn't matter if she was upset or calm, happy or stressed, they just happened.

The last episode was a few months ago after her son-in-law passed away. Regardless, they were a curse to live with. She refused medication and instead practiced relaxation and meditation exercises, listened to podcasts and took classes.

On rare occasions, she'd been able to control them up to a point, but sometimes nothing worked. Sometimes they were fleeting, lasting a few minutes, perhaps a day. Other times, they lasted several days. These were the tough ones.

She willed herself to move further into the house, slumped into the soft warmth of the sofa, fully clothed, and closed her eyes.

"Go away," she groaned. She prayed this time it would be a minor episode.

Six

Day 4

Kate woke the next day feeling refreshed, with no lingering symptoms of the previous night's episode. A mild one this time. As always, she was determined the disorder would not control her life. Sometimes during the night, she changed into her pyjamas and snuggled under the doona in her bed.

Her conversation with Rhonda the day before came crashing back and she felt her heart pound. Rhonda had certainly dropped a bombshell about Diego. Could it be that he was involved? She didn't know Diego very well, but they were on friendly terms and often interacted socially through activities at Possum Walk.

Kate felt horror and confusion at the possibility that Mary's death and the fire were deliberate acts of crime. She felt overwhelmed. She cursed Rhonda for getting inside her head with her wild theories.

Mary may have changed her mind and given the electric blanket another try. Being old, the wiring sparked and caused the fire. The fumes of the fire may have overcome her before she woke. Further, it might have been an animal that caught Rhonda's attention the night of the fire, not a person.

She sighed. She missed Mary. Missed her wisdom and advice. She loved their chats together. Equally, if the whole incident had indeed been an awful accident, she was upset at her friend's lack of care. The fire could have been avoided if she'd not unpacked that old electric blanket from how many years ago! Of course, there was always going to be a high risk the wiring would be faulty after all this time. Why didn't Mary take more precaution? She should have known better.

She wouldn't let what Rhonda said about Diego consume her. She wouldn't! Of course, the police should know about it. But it was up to Rhonda to do that. And in her current frame of mind, it didn't seem likely anytime soon. She appeared un-characteristically reluctant to follow through with what she saw. Kate needed to convince her to do so. Any bit of information was important until it wasn't.

Kate, and everyone else, would just have to be patient and wait for the police investigation to be completed. That's what Adrian had said. The truth would come out soon enough. In the meantime, she would orchestrate a friendly chat with Diego as soon as possible.

Kate was also keen to speak to Adrian for an update on John. She was concerned for John, how he was coping with the news of his wife's death. Perhaps she could share her confusing thoughts with Adrian. Discuss the possibilities of foul play, what Rhonda may have witnessed the night of the fire. She dismissed the suggestion instantly. She didn't know the man. And he was best friends with the Robbins. Intuitively, she knew he would not be receptive to discussions like that.

Regardless, it wasn't long before Kate rang Adrian's doorbell. She heard voices coming from inside the house, but no one came to the door. She was about to ring again when she heard Adrian's voice raised in anger.

"We have to protect him! At least until we know for sure."

Someone else replied, but she couldn't make out the voice or what was said.

"If what we suspect is true, he's a sitting duck! It's not safe!" Adrian's voice again. This time, frustration and anger combined.

The other voice replied, but again she couldn't hear the words. Male, she thought.

Were they talking about John? Kate backed away slowly, not wanting to alert Adrian, and whoever else was inside, to her presence. She glimpsed movement to her right near the shrubs planted along the front wall of the house, she turned towards the movement and saw a man emerge from the side of the house. She didn't recognise him.

"Who are you?" she demanded. "And what were you doing back there?"

He put his finger near his lips in a motion to stay quiet and nodded towards Adrian's house. Listening unashamedly to the voices coming from within the house. He must be a journalist, snooping around for a story, Kate guessed, as she watched him in disgust.

"How dare you eavesdrop on private conversations!" Kate couldn't believe anyone would so blatantly behave this way. "Who are you?"

"Don't be so self-righteous. You were doing the same thing," the man replied, his tone smug. "My name is Rick Lewis, a reporter with the Melbourne Times newspaper."

Suddenly, the front door was flung open. Detective Abbott emerged with Adrian. Both looked startled to see Kate and the reporter.

"I – er – rang the doorbell," she shrugged feebly. Kate felt like the kid who'd been caught with her hand in the cookie jar.

"And I'm Rick Lewis, reporter with the Melbourne Times." His arrogance was at another level and Kate disliked him instantly.

Adrian recovered first. Ignoring Kate, Adrian turned to the reporter. "What do you want?" His words were harsh and demanding.

"It's alright, Adrian," Detective Abbott said beside him. "Rick Lewis and I are old friends." His voice told another story. "What are you doing here, Rick? Looking for another fake scoop?"

Rick laughed. "That hurts, detective. I'm here like everyone else, trying to get the real story behind the fire and the woman who lost her life."

"By spying on people?" Adrian interjected. "Isn't that what you were doing?"

"No less than this lady here," Rick Lewis replied smoothly. "She was listening at the door."

Kate's face turned bright red. She looked guilty as charged.

"It's alright, Kate," Adrian said. "Thanks for dropping by Detective." He extended his hand out. "And take your *friend*," he emphasised the word, "with you."

Detective Abbott looked like he wanted to say something

more to Adrian. His expression was mulish, but then he returned the handshake, nodded to Kate and dragged the reporter away with him.

"What can I do for you, Kate?" Clearly distracted, Adrian watched as the men disappeared around the corner.

Kate wondered at the tension between Adrian and the detective.

"Is everything okay?" she asked, following Adrian's gaze down the street. "I heard shouting. And I wasn't eavesdropping," she added tightly. "I rang your doorbell and no one answered. I was about to knock on the door and hesitated when I heard raised voices."

"I'm sorry about that. Detective Abbott was following up on John's welfare, specifically if there were any plans for his discharge. They want to interview him as soon as possible. It's going to be a little tricky, especially with the dementia. He needs ongoing support now that Mary's gone. In a safe facility. And crucially, away from prying reporters."

His explanation sounded reasonable, but Kate's instinct warned that there was more to it. Why such animosity between the two men? She mentally chastised herself because, after all, it was none of her business. However, she was curious to know more.

"I was concerned for John, after he received the news about Mary."

Adrian looked solemn. "He's taken her death hard. It's to be expected. After all, they were together for a long time. Thankfully, his recovery is going well. The doctors hope to discharge him in a week or so."

"That's encouraging news. But where will he go?"

"I've requested that he remain in the hospital as long as possible. He can't live on his own. And returning to Possum Walk is out of the question regardless. The house is uninhabitable. The hospital's Social Services team is looking at permanent care options for him."

"Something suitable will come up," Kate reassured him. "He deserves the best. It's such a tragic situation. I don't know how he'll cope without Mary."

Adrian nodded in agreement but remained silent. He still seemed preoccupied.

"And what about the cause of the fire? Have they released any further information?"

"Investigations are ongoing and police say little until it's done. But they confirmed that the wiring in the electric blanket was faulty. It sparked the fire."

"I've replayed what happened that night over and over in my mind," she said sadly. "How did Mary not wake when the fire started? I pray she didn't suffer. So many questions haunt me."

"Going back and forth to the hospital, worrying about John's health, she was exhausted. It's hard to know. A toxicology report will clarify if she took something to help her sleep. And the smoke would have been deadly."

Adrian's sorrow was clearly visible as he continued. "All will become clear after they complete their investigation, Kate."

Of course, he was correct. She just had to be patient. "Thank you, Adrian. So grateful that John has you. You're a good friend."

"We've known each other for a very long time, over twenty-five years. I would do anything for John and Mary. But I couldn't save Mary."

"What happened was a horrible accident."

"You can't imagine..." He struggled to compose himself, his grief tangible.

"I guess there are no relatives or other close friends you could call upon?"

"No one."

"It *was* an accident, wasn't it, Adrian?" She couldn't resist asking, despite her earlier resolve.

"Why do you ask?"

She squirmed under the sudden intensity of his stare. He looked and sounded annoyed.

"I feel uneasy but don't know why," Kate replied. "Mary didn't like the artificial sensation of the electric blanket, according to Rhonda, and told her she'd removed it from her bed. And yet there it was! On fire!"

Adrian watched her keenly. "Go on."

"The fumes of the fire would have choked her. She might have taken sleeping pills. I didn't know she even took sleeping pills."

Adrian raised an eyebrow at her.

"Not that it matters," she added hastily. "I don't expect to know every detail of her life, do I?"

"No, I guess you don't," Adrian replied drily. "The police investigation will provide the answers. We'll know soon enough. In the meantime, the funeral will have to be delayed until the coroner releases the body."

"Of course." Kate's research had been useful for more than her novel. "At least two weeks."

Adrian looked at her in surprise. "How do you know that? It's not exactly common knowledge."

Kate flushed under his scrutiny. "It's just something I read recently." Her reason sounded lame, but it was literally the truth.

Time to lighten the mood before he questioned her further. She couldn't mention what Rhonda told her that morning.

"I was planning to visit John again. Do you think it's too soon?"

"Thank you, Kate."

"For what?"

"For persisting after your first visit with John, which was a tough experience."

"It's not something that is negotiable. Mary was a special lady in my life. John is my friend, too."

"He could do with familiar company. Maybe you should check with the hospital before you visit, just in case he's not having a good day."

"I'll take him some of his favourite chocolates once again. Mary used to chastise him about his 'addiction', as she called it. *'You'll get an ache in your belly'* she would lament."

"And John's reply was always the same," Adrian added. *"'I don't care. I'm here for a good time, Mary, not a long time.'* And then they would laugh together."

Kate and Adrian both grinned at the bitter-sweet memory. Their gazes locked. Somehow, the light hearted moment was gone. Kate felt an all too familiar breathlessness but this time it was different.

It wasn't a panic attack. Instead of the trademark heaviness in her chest, she felt nervous knots in her stomach. And a sense of awareness. She caught a whiff of Adrian's cologne, a pleasant mix of sandalwood and musk. His eyes were blue, but so much deeper.

Confused by her reaction, Kate abruptly turned away. Adrian stepped back. That awkwardness between them was unmistakably present again.

She didn't understand it.

She didn't like it.

Not at all.

Seven

Day 5

Kate waited until the next day before calling the hospital and received reassurance that John Robbins was indeed allowed visitors. Nevertheless, it was with some trepidation later that afternoon that Kate rode the lift to John's room. She didn't know what to expect as she gently opened the door. What she didn't expect was Rhonda Kavich and Paula Vincent leaning over his bed with concerned expressions on their faces.

"Kate! We were just visiting with John." Rhonda and Paula exchanged a relieved look before turning towards her.

"These ladies are delightful!" John waved her into the room. "So good to see you again, Kate."

"How are you, John?" Kate watched his face intently. He appeared well, his usual self. "I've brought you some more chocolates."

John grasped the bag and eagerly popped a chocolate morsel into his mouth. He was ready for another one when he stopped.

"Where are my manners? Would you ladies like a chocolate?" He waved the bag in front of Rhonda and Paula.

Kate and Rhonda declined but Paula took one. "For later," she smiled as she placed it in her handbag.

"I'm sorry, ladies," John continued. "I forgot your names and where you are from." He looked at both Rhonda and Paula expectantly.

Silence. Awkward.

Rhonda glanced at Kate helplessly. Paula looked uncomfortable. Neither woman knew what to say.

"Paula and Rhonda have come to visit you today, John," Kate explained. The two women appeared tense, their expressions worried, as they attempted weak smiles back at John. "They are both from Possum Walk where I live."

John seemed to accept Kate's explanation and grinned back at them all. "Decent of you to visit."

"Have you been here long?" Kate asked the other two women.

"About ten minutes," replied Rhonda. "I took Paula to the opera. Matinee session."

"Love the opera, especially Italian opera," John said in between bites. "I introduced Mary to the opera years ago. She didn't much care for it."

"It puzzles me why anyone wouldn't enjoy opera." Rhonda sniffed her disapproval. She'd recovered quickly. "It's about the emotional experience and one can't help being swept up in the performance."

Kate caught Paula's quick, pained expression and wondered if she felt the same as Rhonda about opera. Perhaps not. How could

Rhonda be so passionate and in tune with something like opera whilst simultaneously be so insensitive to people's feelings?

"Not everyone likes the same things," John chuckled. "Otherwise, the world would be a boring place, wouldn't it?"

"I suppose so," Rhonda said reluctantly.

"Take my Mary, for example," John continued. "She took an instant dislike to kingfish. No one could convince her otherwise. And she never forgave Rosie for what she did to us."

Kate didn't know how to respond. Rosie? Maybe Rosie was not a nurse after all. And fish? Well, she didn't know many people who ate kingfish anyway.

"John was telling us about his trip to Italy. He went there yesterday," Paula said, giving Kate a meaningful look.

"It was wonderful," John exclaimed. "I thoroughly enjoyed it. And the food. My goodness! The architecture, the history." He frowned. "But something terrible happened there. I didn't know what to do."

"Really?" Kate kept calm, her face carefully blank. "Was Mary with you?"

"I don't remember. Maybe she was busy at home." Confusion replaced his frown. "Rosie was there. She doesn't like Mary."

Kate was just about to ask who Rosie was when John abruptly sat up in bed, the bag of chocolates flying off his lap, scattering the contents across the floor.

"Mary killed Rosie," he said, deadly calm. "She had no choice." His gaze was fixed somewhere faraway.

Kate glanced at Rhonda and Paula, shock reflected on their faces. Quickly, they turned away, fumbling as they retrieved the scattered chocolates back into the bag. Neither spoke. She moved closer to them.

"Mary warned me John made little sense these days," she whispered as she glanced back at him. His eyes were closed and he appeared to be dozing.

"He remembered who we were when we first came in," Rhonda hissed, a little agitated. "How could he forget so quickly?"

"This was a mistake, Rhonda." Paula turned to the door. She was visibly shaking. "We should leave now."

Without waiting to see if Rhonda followed, she left the room quickly.

"Did you go to the police, Rhonda?"

"No, I didn't." Rhonda's response was defiant as she handed her back the bag of chocolates. "He's quite mad, you know," she said, giving Kate a last glance before exiting as well. She never looked back at John.

Kate sank into the chair beside John's bed, her mind spinning. She regarded him sadly then closed her eyes for a moment. Mary and Adrian were both right. His dementia had progressed at a faster pace than anyone expected. Particularly since he'd been in the hospital. Mary must have felt such profound sorrow with each passing day, watching her husband's declining health.

"I'm sorry, Kate." She was startled out of her thoughts. John's gaze was clear. "Did I go to that other place?"

Kate nodded, not trusting herself to speak.

"Mary told me I go to 'that other place' sometimes. I remember nothing much about these setbacks but they must be dreadful. I could tell by Mary's reaction the first few times they occurred."

Kate squeezed his hand. "You will be fine, John," she re-assured him.

The episode had tired him, for his voice was weak and his breathing unsteady. "You...must be careful," he whispered. "Mary and I trust and care deeply for you, Kate. She worried so and wanted to tell you. You can trust us. And Adrian. But don't trust anyone else. I'm begging you. I don't care what happens to me. But Mary," he teared up, "she must be kept safe."

There was an urgency in his voice as he continued. "I've seen the eyes. I'll never forget them as long as I live. They haunt my waking hours and my dreams. Evil they are." He shuddered. "And now they are at Possum Walk. How...can that...be?" Kate saw him struggle to remain awake.

"Don't talk now John. Try to rest. I'll come by again soon."

His eyelids fluttered into sleep. Kate stared down at her dear friend for several minutes. Her heart went out to him. He looked so vulnerable lying there. A lonely figure with a mind betraying him at every opportunity.

She felt overwhelmed and confused with all he'd said. What was real? What was delusion, as Mary and Adrian described it? In his mind, it all made sense. But not for everyone else. Especially not for Kate. Others saw a man who rambled about nothing, didn't make much sense. But likely made sense to his wife and friend at some level. His fear of danger. Keeping his wife safe. Rosie. In isolation, they meant little. Harmless tales. But she'd overheard Adrian tell Detective Abbott that John wasn't safe, that he needed protection. All appeared straightforward on the surface. Yet, a disturbing picture was starting to emerge.

She moved towards the door as the nurse came in.

"I'm Kate Trellow, a friend of John and his wife Mary." The nurse gave her a sympathetic look. "How is John progressing? His dementia seems to have worsened since I last saw him."

"Expected. But he has good periods too." The nurse's name badge said "Libby." She gave Kate a thoughtful look. Then, she continued with a chuckle. "He tells wonderful and fascinating stories, you know. Did he tell you about his trip to Italy?"

Kate was startled.

"He watched a documentary on the television yesterday," Libby continued. "About Italy." Before re-entering John's room, she added, "And his wife seems to dislike kingfish!"

She shrugged and smiled her goodbye.

Eight

Day 6 – Morning

Six days after the fire, there continued to be an endless presence of police officers and firefighters at the Robbins' house. It played havoc with Kate's nerves, with everyone's nerves, particularly those residents who lived in the immediate vicinity. They couldn't avoid the constant reminder of what had taken place in the burnt house. There was no reprieve.

She knew other residents felt the same. Even the walking groups avoided the area. And those who accessed the Creative Centre in the next street went the long way around instead of cutting through the pathway near the Robbins' house. Mary's accident and the fire were all everyone talked about.

Bothered, Kate wondered if there was indeed a mystery surrounding John and Mary, their lives and 'secrets'. John's warnings, keeping Mary safe, not trusting anyone. Were they truly ramblings? Regardless of his state of mind, John's words made sense if there were suspicious circumstances surrounding his wife's death.

Detective Abbott's visit interrupted her thoughts. He wanted to ask her "a few more questions".

"I don't know how much more I can tell you, Detective," Kate said, as they both took a seat in her living room. She speculated once again about the conversation she had overheard between Adrian and the detective a few days earlier.

"This is routine, Mrs Trellow," Detective Abbott reassured her, pulling out a notepad. "Did Mrs Robbins get along with everyone here?"

"Yes, of course. She was the kindest, most gentle person I know."

"Could she have had an argument or conflict with anyone here?"

Kate shook her head. "Not that I'm aware of."

"Did the Robbins have close friends in this community or regular visitors?"

The detective's line of questioning surprised Kate. "Adrian Kaufman is a longtime friend, practically family. Everyone liked Mary."

She thought for a moment about visitors she may have seen. It occurred to her she rarely saw anyone visit in all the time they had lived at Possum Walk.

"If they have visitors, I've not taken any notice," she replied.

"Can you please recount exactly what you did the day of the fire?"

That day left a lasting impression in Kate's brain. She had no difficulty recalling everything, including her conversation with Mary that morning and the visit to John in the hospital. The detective made copious notes of her answers.

"She was worried about her husband's illness and how he was getting forgetful. She was looking forward to him coming home soon. I drove her to the hospital in the afternoon to visit John." She told him about their visit and John's deteriorating health.

"Did you and Mrs Robbins discuss anything else that day?"

"Er - yes," she replied reluctantly. "I'm writing a novel and I was chatting to her about the storyline and characters."

His expression didn't change. He would be an excellent poker player, she thought.

"What is the novel about?"

"Why is that relevant to this investigation?" Was he mocking her?

"Nothing is out of bounds, Mrs Trellow."

"It's a mystery about the murder of a resident." Kate gave him an outline of her story and how it was about people in a similar community to Possum Walk.

She saw a flicker of surprise in the detective's eyes. "And the murder? How did it occur?"

"Poison." She coughed, her throat constricted. Why did she suddenly feel like an insect under a microscope?

Detective Abbott stared at her for the longest time. "Interesting. And the rest of the day?"

"I tried to do some writing but couldn't concentrate, so I went for a swim and spa instead."

"Did Mrs Robbins ever mention an electric blanket to you?"

"Not directly," Kate answered, "but about a month ago, she mentioned how cold she was feeling this winter. She said she was going to pull out one from storage they'd bought years ago."

The detective continued to scribble on his notepad.

"I'm curious, Detective, as to your questions. You said initially that there was faulty wiring in the electric blanket. Is there any reason to doubt that it was an accident?"

He didn't reply immediately instead giving her a piercing look. "Investigations are ongoing. Until then, we are not at liberty to say anything further. We will know more very soon."

He rose. The interview was over.

***

Later

Kate's head was spinning. She went over and over the interview after Detective Abbott left. His questions were confusing. Had he cast doubt about the accidental nature of the fire? Or was Kate overthinking it? She was afraid, yet fascinated by the genuine possibility that both she and Rhonda might be on the right track after all. That obnoxious woman, relentless in her pursuit of the truth, may be onto something.

It meant that someone did indeed want Mary Robbins dead. That dear, sweet person wouldn't harm anyone. Who would do something so monstrous?

Detectives Abbott and Penrose were the lead officers of the investigation. She heard they were systematically interviewing every resident, manager and staff member, including contractors who were on site the day of the fire. She thought it was overkill. Now she was not so sure, given the investigation may have taken a different turn.

It was time she acted. She needed answers. Mary was her friend and she owed it to her. First thing on her list was to speak with Adrian. He was the Robbins' close friend. Maybe she could share her concerns with him and he would shed some light on what was going on. Did he even suspect anything? She'd try to catch him later in the day.

Next, she must speak to Diego. She didn't know exactly how she would tackle it, but it would happen. Rhonda had to be convinced to go to the police with her new information as well.

It wouldn't be easy in her current state. The panic episode she experienced two days ago had left her unsettled and anxious. Her instincts were super heightened and she had a nervousness that was difficult to shake. Detective Abbott's visit had left an indelible mark of fear that was difficult to ignore.

More than ever, she became convinced that all was not as it was being portrayed. The nagging suspicion that something ominous had happened at Possum Walk could not be silenced.

Nine

Day 7 – Late Morning

Kate's opportunity to speak with Adrian had to wait till the next day. This time when she rang his doorbell he answered promptly.

"Kate!" His expression was warm. "Everything alright?"

Kate hesitated, suddenly not so confident about broaching the subject.

"May I please come in for a few minutes, Adrian?"

"Of course."

"I visited John a few days ago. Rhonda and Paula were also there. We- "

"Rhonda and Paula visited John?" Adrian was taken aback. "I didn't realise they knew him that well."

"Well, I'm not sure about Paula, but Rhonda knows the Robbins well. They moved into Possum Walk almost at the same time. We're all shocked at how quickly his mind is deteriorating since we last spoke to him. He didn't seem aware of Mary's death."

"It's certainly a difficult time for him. He knows it deep down. When his mind is clear, he remembers. He shed tears when I told him. He mentions her often when I visit. You might have caught him on a day when he was not quite himself."

"You're probably right. I hope you can enlighten me." Why was she so nervous under his scrutiny? Her hands were clammy and her heart raced. He waited patiently for her to continue.

"Do the police believe there are suspicious circumstances surrounding the fire and Mary's death?"

"Why would..."

Kate held up her hand to stop him. She inwardly cringed at what she was about to say.

"It's just that Detective Abbott has been asking some strange questions that hint rather strongly of something that is more than an accident. Of course, people here at Possum Walk are talking. I initially believed that interviewing all the residents was excessive. But now I'm not so sure."

Adrian's eyes widened with every word Kate uttered. She felt a mix of embarrassment and anxiety at the same time. Her instinct screamed all was not as it seemed and she tried to quell it. But with each silent moment that passed, with Adrian's gaze locked on her, she didn't know what to think. His hands clasped and unclasped almost in a nervous gesture and his lips pursed into a tight line. Kate wondered what was going through his mind.

She wanted desperately to cover the awkward moment and continued hastily. "I overheard you and Detective Abbott arguing the other day. You were angry with him. Something about not being safe and someone, I presume John, being a sitting duck."

Silence. It was deafening.

"Well – er – Kate." Adrian finally said. "My goodness. That's quite a story. Forgive me for saying this but you certainly have a vivid imagination." His tone was mocking.

"Please don't insult me, Adrian." Kate bristled at his patronising tone. "There's here's something more going on. Just what it is I can't figure out. Don't you sense it too? You are a former police officer, surely you must be querying things? You're practically family to both John and Mary. John told me you know all his secrets. Don't you want to uncover every rock to get to the truth?"

"The truth!" Adrian practically spat the words. He took a deep breath. Kate sensed he was trying to gain control over his emotions. It seemed to work because he continued more calmly.

"The police are still investigating the matter. They will ensure all the evidence is scrutinized. The coroner is involved and it takes time. We just have to be patient for all will be revealed soon."

"Why the questions about anyone potentially wanting to harm Mary, or if either she or John had any conflict with other residents?"

"Due process," he replied promptly. "It's standard procedure to check every angle of a case like this."

"Detective Abbott said the same thing." Kate said.

Adrian was being too slick with his responses, his eyes guarded at the same time. He rose, clearly trying to get rid of her, Kate suspected. But she held firm and stubbornly remained seated.

"Rhonda said that Mary didn't have an electric blanket anymore. Yet it was on her bed," Kate persisted.

Adrian shook his head. "There must be a reasonable explanation. As I said, the police will get to the bottom of it. Now if you will excuse me..."

"No Adrian." Kate was annoyed at his dismissive stance. "I read about a case where a husband killed his wife with a faulty electric blanket and tried to make it look like an accident."

"You think John killed Mary?"

"When I visited John last time, he said something about keeping Mary safe. That it was all Rosie's fault. He also said Mary killed Rosie because there was no choice."

Kate thought she saw a spark of surprise in his eyes, but it was gone as quickly as it came.

"John's illness compromises his mental state. You've seen it first hand."

"Who's Rosie, by the way?" Kate refused to back down. "He also warned me to be careful, as though I too am in danger. Why would he say those things?"

"You believe a man who suffers from dementia? Who is confused most of the time? And can't distinguish between fact and fiction? Come on, Kate! Listen to yourself!" Adrian didn't bother to hide his scepticism.

Whilst Adrian's attitude annoyed her, she was most annoyed with herself. This conversation had not gone the way she expected. She'd handled it badly. Of course she sounded like a crazy person. Deflated, Kate rose to leave.

"Thank you for your time, Adrian. I'm sorry to have bothered you." She couldn't get out of there fast enough. Why did she naively think she could extract any information or gain his support? She had no chance pitted against him. He was a seasoned police officer with years of experience in handling all kinds of people and situations. She was a rookie by comparison, totally out of her depth.

"I'm sorry if I've offended you, Kate. That's the last thing I wanted to do." He sounded sincere. "It's just that you surprised me. And rarely does anyone surprise me. You were a good friend to Mary. It's natural that you care."

"Thank you." She moved to leave.

"Why are you pursuing this? The police have it in hand."

"Honestly? I don't know. There are too many questions floating in my mind that won't go away. And no rational answers."

"Or you may be too emotionally involved you can't be objective."

"Likewise, Rhonda believes something is wrong," she said lamely. Perhaps Rhonda's claims influenced her more than she realised.

Adrian stopped her at the door. "Kate, a word of caution if I may. Don't believe everything you hear or see. Especially from people like Rhonda. Sometimes, things are not what they appear to be. They're better left alone." He hesitated before adding, "It's safer for all that way."

"You're talking in riddles, Adrian. My former husband did that constantly for months before he died. He was hiding things from me. I didn't pick up on it at the time. But I learnt. Too late.

That's what you're doing now. I won't go through that again. I just can't."

Kate felt tears well up in her eyes and she brushed them away impatiently. She felt horrified at how much she had revealed to Adrian. But he pushed her the wrong way.

"Mary was my friend," she continued. "I care about what happened to her. And if there is anything at all suspicious about her death, I won't stop until I find out the truth."

"I didn't mean to upset you. And it's admirable that you should want to validate Mary's death. But this is an impossible situation." She felt his intense gaze go right through her soul. "And what you experienced with your husband is not what is happening here. I've never lied to you."

Before Kate could respond, Adrian shut the door, leaving her alone on the porch.

***

Late Afternoon

How much longer would the investigation take?

Kate felt wretched, disturbed by the possibility that someone killed Mary and might get away with it. The constant troubled thoughts were taking their toll on her nerves. She remained uptight and uneasy a lot of the time, filled with misgiving about something she couldn't control.

She didn't understand why the investigation was taking so long, why Adrian was so tight-lipped about – everything. His cryptic words earlier did nothing to reassure her or dispel her concerns. A week had already passed since her friend's death. Surely the police would know by now if there were any suspicious circumstances surrounding the fire? If they did, they weren't sharing either.

Rhonda's story about someone jumping the fence needed checking out. If Rhonda didn't tell the police soon, Kate felt she had no choice but to do it for her. It might be important information and neither she nor Rhonda should withhold it. At the first opportunity, she would examine the fence between Diego and the Robbins' properties for any incriminating evidence. Unless the police already found it.

She must be cautious, find the right time to enter the Robbins' property. Investigators were on site all day. The blue and white Police tape and canvas covering the front of the house was an ominous reminder something had taken place behind it.

The last of the emergency services vehicles left by late afternoon. The street was quiet, with no one in sight. Now was the perfect time to slip over to the Robbins. It took a few seconds to duck under the police tape and make her way down the side of the Robbins' property along the fence line. The side gate, usually shut, was fire damaged and lay on an angle, useless. She stopped for a moment, listening. No sound came from Diego's house. Not even the singing Rhonda earnestly complained about. So far, so good.

She didn't know what she was searching for as she scanned the grassed area sprinkled with a few plants in clusters here and there. The area was water damaged, the plants trampled, no doubt by the firefighters. What hope was there to find anything incriminating in this quagmire? Still, she moved forward slowly, her eyes focussed down.

Towards the back of the house, she saw long wooden planks

stacked against the fence. There were two neat piles, four planks high. Kate studied them for a moment. The thick wood was deep enough to make a high makeshift step. If Rhonda did indeed see someone jump the fence that night, could they have used this stack of wood as a step up to escape? To access Diego's property?

Gingerly holding onto the nearest fence post, Kate stepped onto the wood panels. They felt sturdy enough. She placed her entire weight on the stack. The fence was a good height and she saw over the top of it into Diego's backyard. However, she knew she would never have the strength or fitness to hoist herself over it. Would Diego be able to scale that fence? She tried to picture it in her mind. No, she really didn't think so, not with his stocky build and short stature.

Frowning, she stepped back onto the ground. Maybe not a good theory after all. She continued to scan the ground, looking for anything, something, that might give a clue. It was nigh on impossible, with so many people having trampled over this area since the fire.

"Kate! What are you doing here?" Rhonda hissed behind her.

Kate felt her heart thump against her chest, startled by the sound of the other woman's voice. She quickly swung around. Rhonda was half crouched, battle style, watching her. If the situation wasn't so serious, it was almost comical seeing Rhonda like that.

"Rhonda! You scared me half to death!"

"Did you find anything?" Rhonda glanced behind her.

"Not really," she said, "except for these planks of wood." She waved to the stack nearby. "What do you think?"

Rhonda studied the stack for a moment. "You think the

person I saw that night used this as a springboard to get over the fence?"

"Maybe," Kate said, not really convinced. "It's pretty high. If you really saw someone that night, whoever it was is fit and agile to scale this fence."

"I see what you mean. Did you find anything else?"

"No, I just got here a few minutes ago. How did you know I was here?"

"I saw you come out of your house and cross the street. I know why you came here. You believe what I said about someone jumping the fence that night?"

"I'm not sure, but it's worth following up. Did you tell the police about it?"

When Rhonda's mouth pursed in that stubborn way, she had her answer.

"Rhonda, you must say something. It should be the police here, not us. I don't even know what to look for."

"I will, I promise," Rhonda replied quickly. "You really shouldn't be here, Kate. It's against the law!"

Kate gave her a disbelieving look. The nerve of the woman! It was because of her she found herself here!

She was about to tell her so when Rhonda added, "But now that we're here, let's seize the moment to examine this area quickly and then leave."

Kate couldn't answer. Shaking her head, she turned away and continued to study the ground, ignoring the other woman. She knew Rhonda followed behind her, equally vigilant in examining the ground.

Kate was about to give up when her eyes fell on something

peeping out from under a trampled plant nearby. It was a small metal object, half buried under the mud and debris.

"What is it, Kate?"

"An earring," Kate said as she picked it up, wiping away the mud stuck to it. It was blue, in the shape of a crescent moon with tiny gemstones embedded along one edge.

"It looks familiar. I've seen it somewhere before," Rhonda said beside her. "Mary must have dropped it. Easy enough to lose with all the time she spent in the garden."

Kate put the earring in her pocket and both women turned to leave.

"Well, well, well. What do we have here?"

Rick Lewis, the snoopy eavesdropping reporter, stood before them. He blocked their exit. Whether deliberately or not, Kate couldn't tell. He had a grin on his face and shook his head as he tut-tutted at them. They'd been caught! By the worst person.

"Who are you?" Rhonda demanded.

"Rick Lewis, reporter with the Melbourne Times, at your service." He gave her a mocking bow.

"What are you doing here?" Kate felt deep in the pit of her stomach he couldn't be trusted. She was wary of him, especially after his performance at Adrian's house a few days ago.

"Same thing as you, I suspect. Looking for answers. You really should be careful, Kate. People might think you're following me."

His arrogance was unbearable. Kate refused to stay one more minute.

"Excuse us, please. We must leave." Kate made to move past him, but he didn't budge.

"Not until you tell me why you're here," he replied.

"I don't owe you any explanation, Mr Lewis. Besides, it's none of your business," Kate snapped back. "Come along, Rhonda."

She pushed past the reporter, Rhonda right behind her.

"You ladies know that it's illegal to be on these premises whilst there's an ongoing police investigation?"

Kate didn't bother to answer. He didn't deserve one nano-second more attention. She heard him chuckle as they hurried away.

"I'll be seeing you soon, ladies. That's a promise."

Ten

Day 8 – Before Daylight

Kate couldn't sleep that night. Her conversation with Adrian played over and over in her mind like a bad record. And that reporter Rick Lewis! What an odious man. She glanced at the bedside clock. It was going to be another-tossing-and-turning-in-bed kind of night.

She felt frustrated that she'd not had the chance to speak to Diego the day before. Even though she knocked on his door twice, he wasn't home or at the clubhouse all day.

Could he be capable of jumping over that fence? He was short, but she wouldn't exactly describe him as agile or fit. But desperate people do desperate things, especially under the influence of alcohol or other drugs.

Sighing for the umpteenth time, she flung the doona cover to one side and made her way through the silent darkness of the house to her study. She might as well keep pushing her novel along.

As she passed through the living area, she saw the street

lighting filter through the semi open shutters of the window. She must have forgotten to shut them before bed. She looked out. There was not even the whisper of a breeze. The frost forming on the lawns was the only hint of a chilly winter's night.

All was quiet and an eeriness hung in the still air. She tried to avoid looking at the Robbins' house, but she couldn't resist its pull, like a moth to a flame. In the harshness of the night, the building looked even more macabre. It appeared wounded, pathetic, and in need of resuscitation. The life was sucked out of it the day Mary died.

She was about to turn away when a flash of light caught her attention. Was her mind playing tricks on her? Frowning, she watched in the direction she had seen it, inside the Robbins' house. And waited. There it was again! Towards the back of the house. She made out a wavering beam of light. From a torch? Someone was in the house. Who and why? They'd pushed aside the canvas that hid what once was the front door, now a shell of unrecognisable timber.

Without thinking about the wisdom of it, Kate quickly pulled on a dressing gown before leaving her house. She probably should call the police but decided there was no time. Whoever was in there had no business being there. Not at this early hour of the morning. They might be gone by the time the police arrived. And the only exit was through the front door and no one had come out in the past few minutes.

Taking a deep breath, more to stem her nerves and sudden anxiety, she pushed past the police tape and entered the house. She stood still, straining her ears for any noise. Silence. No sound of anyone moving around. Her eyes adjusted to the gloom. She couldn't see any movement but her instincts screamed she was not alone.

She continued quietly down the hall, barely breathing, her heart racing inside her chest as though it would burst through any second. She approached the living area with caution. There was a strong smell of smoke and dampness in the air, almost making breathing difficult because of the heaviness in the air. A lot of work would be required to restore this section.

Kate didn't have time to grasp what happened next. She heard a sound behind her. As she spun around towards the noise, she felt someone push her forcefully against the wall. Stunned, Kate collapsed to the floor, gritting her teeth against the sudden pain searing through her body. She squeezed her eyes shut against the flood of hurt. She heard running footsteps as the intruder escaped through the back door.

She lay there stunned for a few minutes, struggling to catch her breath. She'd disturbed someone who shouldn't be in the house, who was determined to hide their identity. What were they looking for?

She groaned against the pain as she tried to roll onto her side to haul herself upright. But she didn't have the strength, realising she'd have to lie there for as long as it took until she did. And then cursed as she remembered her mobile phone on her bedside table.

She froze in fear as she heard more footsteps running towards her from the hallway. Had the intruder returned? She held her breath, her heart suddenly pumping hard against her chest.

"Kate?" Adrian's voice, loud and unmistakable.

"I'm here!" Her relief was overwhelming. She tried again to get up but to no avail.

The light from a torch reached her seconds before Adrian rushed into the room and to her side.

"What happened? Are you alright?"

Kate nodded, leaning heavily against Adrian as he gently helped her up from the floor. She bit her lower lip against the shooting pain with every movement she made. Her bones screamed in protest. It took all her willpower to slow her breathing and quell the fear that lingered. Kate wasn't sure if it was from the shock of the attack or from the attack itself.

"How did you know I was here?" she finally asked, scowling at the agony as she straightened.

Adrian held her a moment longer until she steadied herself. "I saw you cross the street and enter the house. I was curious what you were up to at this time of night?"

"I saw a light and came over to check it out. Someone was in here, Adrian. They - pushed me before running out the back door," her voice quivered slightly, "and then you showed up."

"What possessed you to come here alone?"

He sounded angry, his tone harsh, and not a little annoyed. She deserved that. She realised she'd been foolish.

"Did you see who it was?" he continued.

She shook her head, exhaustion washing over her. Adrian must have noticed, for his tone changed, became more soothing. 'Any broken bones?"

He watched her carefully as she tried to stretch her muscles and limbs. But nothing seemed out of place. Just badly knocked about and bruised.

"Come on, let's get you to a hospital."

"No, please. There's nothing broken. Just help me get home. I'll be alright."

"Are you sure a doctor shouldn't examine you?" He sounded doubtful.

"I just want to get into bed." Her body trembled and she felt chills racing up and down her spine.

He held her steady as he gently guided her back to her house. He didn't stop till she was lying in bed with the covers up to her chin. She sighed. She felt better already and the trembling was subsiding. The shock of the night was gradually lifting.

It felt like hours later when Adrian shook her gently awake, urging her to swallow painkillers with a glass of water. But it must have been mere minutes.

"Who was in the Robbins' house, Adrian? And what were they looking for? Please tell me what's going on."

He gazed down at her, an uncertain gleam in his eyes. "I can tell you one thing. You must be more careful, Kate. I have enough to be concerned about in this case without worrying about you getting into trouble." He rubbed his hand across his forehead looking weary.

"That bad, eh?"

"That bad," he replied. "Now get some rest. We'll talk later."

Eleven

Morning

Kate woke, her body ached everywhere and she felt like a truck had hit her. She groaned as she sat up in bed, willing the pain to go away. Perhaps she should have taken herself to the hospital last night.

Last night! The intruder at the Robbins' house. Her memory flooded back. The violence of the attack affected her deeply and she still felt shaken. Yet something about it bothered her. She tried to remember every detail that led up to the moment someone shoved her hard against the wall. A sound behind her. Perhaps a footstep?

Adrian came to her rescue almost immediately after the attack. He'd been wonderful and supportive. They irritated each other but seemed to have an odd connection that made little sense. It could be their mutual concerns for the Robbins that drew them together.

She would not get any answers staying in bed. She still had a lot to follow up on. Her to-do list was growing longer. She could now include uncovering who her assailant was. Glancing at her watch, she felt surprised it was after ten o'clock. She ignored the aching pain that rippled through her body. The push into the wall had been brutally hard and her body screamed in protest today. No doubt bruises would also appear as a result. A long, hot shower sounded perfect.

A knock on her bedroom door startled her.

"Are you awake? Can I come in?"

Adrian. How did he get into her house?

"Just a moment." Ignoring the shooting pains, she quickly got out of bed, slipping into her dressing gown and opened the door. Adrian stood there looking refreshed and relaxed.

"How are you feeling this morning?" He gave her a quick inspection before adding, "Any pain or injuries?"

She shook her head, frowning up at him. "How did you get in here?"

He gave her a sheepish grin. "I slept on the couch last night, just in case."

"In case of what?"

"In case you woke up during the night and needed anything, of course," he replied. "I made you some breakfast. You up for it?"

Kate's stomach rumbled loudly in response. She smiled ruefully at him. "I think my stomach definitely is."

The eggs on toast were delicious and they ate, making small talk. After they finished, they settled on the sofa, each sipping on a mug of steaming hot coffee. Neither spoke for a few minutes.

Kate had so many questions, yet she sensed Adrian would not be easily forthcoming in giving her the answers. She caught

him glancing several times out the front window to the Robbins'
house across the street.

"Why did you really stay over last night? Can you just keep it
simple for once and tell me the truth, please?"

Adrian gave her a half smile but didn't immediately respond.
He seemed to ponder on her words for a few moments.

"Alright," he said finally. "Simple, you say. I can do simple."
Kate held her breath, suddenly anxious at what he might say. "I
was worried whoever attacked you last night might come back
for you."

Her stomach took a nosedive with alarming force. She had
never considered the possibility. "I thought I was in the wrong
place at the wrong time. Should I be worried?"

"I don't know," Adrian replied. "But we can't dismiss any risk.
Who was in the Robbins' house at that time of night? And why
were they there? What were they looking for? These questions
are obvious. The answers are more challenging."

"So you think the fire was arson?"

Adrian paced the floor, unable to remain seated. He hesitated,
seemed to struggle with what to say. His anxiety was palpable.

"I'm not sure – yet. But I admit I have my suspicions."

His admission startled Kate. "What troubles me more," she
said, "is that someone may have tampered with the wiring of
the electric blanket that it sparked a fatal fire. This suggests pre-
meditated murder, that someone wanted Mary dead. Why? Who
would want to hurt her?"

Adrian remained silent, but Kate noted his jaw tighten, as if
trying to control his expression.

"I overheard you describe John as a 'sitting duck' and telling

Detective Abbott that he needed protection." She looked to Adrian for an explanation. "Why?"

The single word hung in the air between them like a heavy mantle. Once again, Adrian hesitated and appeared to struggle with an inner turmoil.

"I'm not at liberty to discuss the Robbins. I'm working closely with the police to scrutinise every detail and all evidence that will help uncover the truth about the fire and Mary's death. I will say this, though. I don't believe in accidents, at least not in this case."

"The key is finding the identity of whoever was in the Robbins' house last night," she said.

"Do you recall anything at all about the person?"

Kate thought Adrian seemed less tense, but back to business. Familiar territory for him. She frowned, thinking about her attacker, trying to capture those few fragmented moments. The sound behind her as she automatically turned towards it. The push forcing her against the wall.

"I think the person is strong," she said, digging deep in her memory. "A male. It was a powerful push. But maybe it just feels that way because I was taken by surprise."

"That's a positive start. Anything else?"

"The person was shorter than me, maybe average height."

"What makes you say that?"

"I felt the attacker push upwards from the middle of my back as though the person reached up." Kate shrugged. "I'm not overly confident but I can't recall anything else. It happened so quickly."

Could her attacker be the reporter, Rick Lewis? He was

snooping around earlier. Maybe he came back. But why attack her? He was a tall man, but not as tall as Kate. How could Kate say anything to Adrian? He wouldn't be too happy to be told she'd been at the Robbins doing her own snooping around.

"You've done very well, Kate. I'm astonished you remembered anything. In many cases involving trauma, one blocks the incident and the minor details till later."

"Thank you." She felt herself flush under his gaze. She hated keeping information from him. Or the police.

"Until then, you are not to put yourself at unnecessary risk like you did last night. Is that clear?"

"Yes, I'll be careful." Kate stood to stretch her screaming muscles and release the aches in her body.

"Oooh!" She couldn't help her reaction as she moved.

"Maybe you need to be checked out by the doctor," Adrian suggested. "And a police report will have to be made about last night too."

Kate groaned, this time not because of her body's aches and pain. "I guess so," she reluctantly agreed. "But I don't think Detective Abbott likes me."

Adrian looked surprised. "Really? I can't imagine why."

Kate shrugged but didn't enlighten him. She didn't know for sure, anyway. Just a gut feeling.

"Are you worried about John's safety? Is that why you and Detective Abbott quarrelled the other day?"

"No, of course not," he said sharply. "We don't even know for certain if Mary's death was anything but an accident."

"But you're worried enough, aren't you? You said you didn't believe in accidents. Don't deny it."

"I won't," he replied, quietly.

"Thank you for at least admitting to your concerns."

"I'll leave you to make a doctor's appointment and contact Detective Abbott about last night. In the meantime, take it easy, Kate. And be careful."

After Adrian left, her house suddenly felt empty, no longer a sanctuary. Someone attacked her without provocation last night. The viciousness of the attack played over and over in her mind that it overwhelmed her. Adrian was worried enough to stay over last night. Now, for the first time, she felt vulnerable in her own home.

She no longer felt...safe.

Twelve

Day 9

Adrian called her in the morning to ask after her welfare and to advise her he would be away for a couple of days following up on business for the Robbins. Kate made a statement to the police about the intruder and the assault.

She spent most of the previous day attending several tests, including x-rays, ordered by her doctor. He reassured her that the bruising and aches would eventually disappear and prescribed medication to give her some relief.

It was late afternoon when Kate visited Diego.

"I apologise for disturbing you, Diego." Kate smelt the alcohol on his breath. He swayed a little as he led her inside. She'd decided her excuse for the visit was to check up on Diego's welfare following the fire and Mary's death.

"Everything okay, Kate?" He still had a trace of an Italian accent even after all his years in Australia. Sometimes it was quite charming.

"Yes, under the circumstances. I can't bear to look at the

Robbins' house. It's like we've all been dropped into a horror movie. How are you coping? It must be difficult for you living right next door."

Tears instantly formed in his eyes. "It's so terrible. I can't stop thinking about it. About Mary. Is there a date for her funeral yet?"

"No. I believe there will be a delay of a few more days. Adrian will let everyone know when it's confirmed. We have to wait for the coroner's office to release her body."

He stared at her, a look of dread on his face, when he suddenly collapsed in tears. "I'm afraid, Kate."

"What are you afraid of?" She was stunned at the rapid change in his demeanour.

"I have to tell someone," he sobbed. "It's the dreams. I don't know where reality starts and ends anymore." Diego rocked back and forward on the sofa. "I think I did something bad but I can't remember."

"Tell me what it is. We can work it out together," she reassured him gently. She kept her voice steady, but inside alarm bells were ringing. What had Diego done?

"That's just it! All I know is that on the night of the fire, I think I was inside Mary's house. I have an image of her sleeping in her bed. But I'm not sure. I see flames. It's all a blur in my mind. Why would I be in her house?"

Kate's pulse raced. "Have you told anyone else about this, Diego?"

He shook his head. "I don't think so."

"Diego, were you, by any chance, drinking that night?"

He avoided eye contact and mumbled something under his

breath. The rocking ceased. He clasped his hands together, probably to stop them from shaking.

"Diego, if you want my help, you have to be honest with me."

"I never want to touch another drop again! It's affected me so badly this time. I hear voices, soft and whispering in my ear. And have visions. Of eyes, so frightening that they look evil." His words were full of torment. "I remember nothing after I drink anymore. About that night? Bits and pieces are coming back slowly. But nothing makes any sense."

"Let's assume you were in the house, as you say. Do you remember jumping the fence to get back home?"

"No. I don't think I'm physically capable of it."

He was probably right, Kate surmised. "Maybe you drank more than usual?"

"I have never blacked out like this! Even after my worst binges. And I've had a few in my lifetime. I recall everything afterwards. It's as if..." he struggled to find the words.

"Yes?" Kate prompted him.

"It feels like my memory has been erased. Not from the effects of the drink. But from - I just don't understand it. I slept through the fire, the sirens, everything."

"Do you remember anything at all?"

"Nothing much. I woke the next morning and felt different. Not the usual hangover. The police came to see me that day. They said they tried to contact me on the night of the fire. Rang the doorbell several times, even tried knocking. But I heard nothing."

Kate wasn't sure what to make of his story. Diego sounded genuinely distraught. Perhaps the simple explanation was that

Diego's drinking was affecting him more than he realised by causing black outs. He just dreamt it all in his drunken state and nothing really happened as he told it.

"I wasn't a drinker once," he whispered almost to himself. "My family was wonderful and I grew up happy. My cousins and I were close. Until they were caught up in the local drug wars. The lure of easy money. One by one, they died." He shrugged heavily. "I got lucky but it was never the same after that. I was never the same."

Kate wondered if his family and the anguish surrounding it were the reasons behind his drinking. Alcoholism was complex and who was she to judge what she didn't understand?

"What should I do, Kate?" Diego looked at her with hope in his eyes, seeking a magic answer. She didn't have one.

"I don't know, Diego," she replied. "Perhaps you should go to the police and tell them about these visions."

"How can I?" He cried again. "What will I tell them? I don't want them digging into my family's background. It's buried. In the past."

"Why is your family an issue? You said your cousins were involved in drugs, not you."

He hesitated, still quietly sobbing. "Because they worked for the Mafia. And the Mafia never forgets. My parents moved to Australia to get away."

"I see," Kate replied, but she didn't, really. Anything she said would sound inadequate. No wonder he drank.

"That's why I can't go to the police. Besides, they'll think I'm crazy."

"No, Diego," she replied firmly. "Perhaps they will see a man who drinks too much and dismiss the story about your visions. Or maybe they will investigate further. Either way, you owe it to Mary and her family, to yourself, to assist in any way you can to resolve this case."

Diego gave her a startled look, then relief. "You're right," he said calmly. "It's the honourable thing to do. I have no choice."

"I can accompany you if you like," she said, immediately feeling a strong sense of Déjà vu. She'd said the same words to Rhonda a few days earlier.

"Thank you, Kate but I have to face this on my own. I know deep in my heart I would never harm anyone. Especially Mary, who has been nothing but kind to me. But I'm afraid. Worried that I'm going crazy."

"You can get professional care. There are therapists who can help unlock your memories, the visions, from that night."

"Do you really think so?"

"It's a good start."

She left Diego in a less agitated state. His sobbing had ceased and he had a look of resignation, yet some hope, about him. He would not find this easy.

Kate wanted to believe Diego's anguish and fears were genuine. If he was lying, then he was a great actor. What an absurd thought to pop into her head! No one was that clever. Not in the real world.

Her cynical side, the one which had taken a big hit at the other end of a man's lies, refused to be so trusting, so naïve, ever again.

Regrettably, she found herself at an impasse.

And it couldn't be at a worse time.

Thirteen

Day 10

When Kate visited John the next day she found him sitting up watching the television. This time there was no welcoming smile or greeting, just a glance and nod her way. He returned to watching the screen, totally focussed.

"Hello John." No response.

"I brought some of your favourite chocolates again." She offered the brightly coloured box of goodies to him. John's gaze fixated on the screen. Not even a flicker that he heard her. And he didn't reach out for the chocolates either.

Kate's heart sank. He was in 'the other place.' She sat near him and, together for the next twenty minutes, they both watched the program in silence. She felt sore and stiff sitting there after a while. Her body was healing and the aches and pains were slowly subsiding. There were blueish purple bruises in several areas, battle scars, but they didn't bother her too much.

Kate turned to gaze at John. This disease took its toll on the individual and their family. To witness the ravages of it firsthand was overwhelming. Mary must have struggled to watch the man she loved slowly disappear. Deciding to stay a little longer, she tried to get as comfortable as possible and returned to watch the television screen.

"Kate! When did you get here?" John was back from 'the other place'. She gave him a warm smile and handed him the chocolates. Again, as last time, he reached out with pleasure and started eating them.

"Are you well, John?"

"Never better," he replied in between bites. "I'm leaving here soon. Adrian said a change will be beneficial to me. Especially after all we've been through."

"That's wonderful." She wondered if he sometimes remembered that his wife was dead.

"Did you see Rosie outside?" he asked. "She went to get me some water." Kate glanced at the full jug of water on the bedside table.

"She's been gone a long time. Probably shopping." He chuckled. "She's always ducking in and out of the shops, down alleyways looking for bargains. And I'm forever following behind like a puppy. I don't know why but it seems the right thing to do. I worry about her. She isn't always in good health, you know."

Kate wondered once again who Rosie was but didn't ask. She nodded, encouraging him to continue. It was wonderful to see traits of the old John she knew and cared for.

He was silent for a few minutes, happily chewing on his chocolates.

"You know," John's mood shifted. "It was on one of those shopping trips that our lives changed forever."

"Italy?" She recalled his story from the previous visit.

"Yes. How do you know that? I can't say too much. Sworn to secrecy. Mary would have my head if I told you," he chuckled. "Rosie was never the same afterwards. She was terrified. She couldn't sleep, she fell ill. I was so worried about her." He started getting agitated. "We couldn't stay. I lost her that day. Rosie was gone."

"John, who is Rosie?"

He looked at her in surprise. "Why do you keep calling me John? You know who I am."

"Who are you?"

He laughed. "I can't say. It's a secret. Only Adrian knows, of course. We trust him implicitly. Mary has her secrets too." He came closer to Kate and whispered, "She never cared for kingfish."

"And where is Mary?" she dared to ask.

"Mary? My mother? God rest her soul. Did you know her? A formidable woman, that one. Took no nonsense from her four boys. But a heart of gold."

She wondered where in the deep past he was in his mind.

"Adrian said I need protection. Protection!" He scoffed.

Kate recalled the conversation she overheard between Adrian and Detective Abbott. Adrian was worried about protection for John. Why?

"Why do you need protection?" She was curious.

"I don't need it! Adrian fusses over me like an old woman."

He grew silent for a moment. "Mary needs to hide for a while. She's the one who needs protection, not me. It's not safe. She's seen the evil too."

Kate smiled gently. "John, there is no evil. You are safe."

"Evil. It's all around us. I told you to be careful, Kate."

"Who is trying to harm you?"

No answer. Kate was confused. She couldn't be sure what was fact or fiction in John's mind. One thing she knew. He didn't remember Mary was dead. Not in that moment at least. He looked tired. Kate probably stayed a little too long this time.

"I'll let Mary know you're looking for her, John." She stood to leave.

"Mary is gone. Rosie is gone. My poor love." He closed his eyes but not before Kate saw a tear slip down his cheek.

She patted his hand softly, offering some comfort before whispering, "Rest now John."

John said Adrian knew their secrets and that intrigued her. What was Adrian's relationship with the Robbins that they entrusted him with their 'secrets'? There was more than friendship binding them, she was sure of it. It was difficult to sift through all he spoke about. But it made sense if it was a memory and not fantasy. Those secrets might be the motive that put the Robbins at risk.

What were they all hiding?

Fourteen

Day 11 - Morning

No one at Possum Walk knew about the intruder at the Robbins' house nor the attack on Kate. The proof came when Kate attended the weekly chair aerobics class. Rhonda and several other women were there as well. That Rhonda never mentioned it was significant. It meant she didn't know. Which was a good thing. Attracting the attention of concerned or curious residents was the last thing Kate wanted.

"Raise your left leg and hold." The instructor worked through her usual program.

Kate's normally smooth movements were absent today. She was still sore from the attack and her body felt stiff, unyielding to the shape shifting being demanded. Even sitting on the chair hurt. She probably should have stayed home.

"Stretch those calves, ladies!"

Kate sighed and stretched.

"A bit out of sorts today, Kate?" Rhonda sat in the chair next to her. That woman didn't miss a trick.

"No, just tired. Not sleeping very well."

"I know that feeling all too well," Rhonda replied. "That's why I take an evening walk. Helps me relax."

Except for the night of the fire, no doubt. Kate grimaced with the pain of the next stretch.

"Did you go to the police, Rhonda?" she whispered.

Rhonda ignored her.

Several residents sought Kate out when they gathered in the clubhouse for a warm drink.

"How are you feeling since that horrible night of the fire, Kate?"

"So sorry about Mary."

"How is John?"

"Have the police given you any more information?"

"Those nice detectives interviewed me the other day."

So much for not wanting any attention, Kate sighed, as she politely engaged with them all.

"How could such a tragedy happen here at Possum Walk?" someone asked.

"Extraordinary things happen to ordinary people every day," Kate said.

She spent endless hours on the internet reading cases about this very thing. Had Mary found herself in an extraordinary situation? Mary and John were wonderful people. There were never any signs the Robbins' lives were anything other than normal, no red flags or behaviours that she ever wondered at. Till now.

"Mary was just a normal person, like the rest of us," Rhonda said.

There were murmurs of agreement from the group. For the

first time since she'd met them, Kate thought that maybe John and Mary Robbins were not who they appeared to be after all. The implication terrified her.

She felt a slight tremor sliver down her back and twist inside her body. The familiar clammy hands and shortness of breath began. They were coming on frequently since her friend's death. Not surprising, as her emotions were raw. Quickly excusing herself, she exited the clubhouse. Her legs were already trembling with weakness. So far, they had been minor episodes, but enough to unsettle her and put her out of action for a while.

She went straight to bed.

***

Rhonda watched Kate leave. Kate's behaviour was strange at times. Like now. She cut everyone's conversations short and left suddenly, without an explanation. She suspected Kate was a little on the wild side. Rhonda saw the largish tattoo on her upper thigh one day when the wind blew her dress about, despite Kate trying to hide it by quickly pushing her dress back down. Tattoos were filthy habits. Rhonda didn't understand why people abused their bodies that way.

Other times, Kate was warm and caring. But occasionally, there was a distance about her that Rhonda didn't understand. Like now.

"Where's Kate?" Paula Vincent came to sit next to her with a cup of tea.

"She left."

"Is she feeling alright? She didn't seem to have the usual enthusiasm at class."

"Not sure. Maybe she has a lot on her mind."

Rhonda glanced around the room to check if anyone was nearby. She leaned towards Paula and whispered "I saw someone jump the fence from the Robbins' house to Diego's house the night of the fire. I think it was him."

Paula gave her an alarmed stare. "Are you serious? Why didn't you tell me before now?"

"I'm not sure what I actually saw. I told Kate about it and she said I should tell the police."

"You can't say anything to the police unless you're sure."

Rhonda noticed they were drawing attention and stopped the discussion. Both women rejoined the conversations with the rest of the group for the next little while. It was while the group was clearing the table, ready to leave, that Rhonda saw the earrings.

"Those earrings are just like the one we found in Mary's garden!" Rhonda exclaimed, pointing to Cathy Eldridge. She realised the moment she made the mistake and put her foot in it.

The other woman stopped and stared at her, confused. "We? What are you talking about, Rhonda?" Cathy always had it in for her, she was sure of it. Didn't seem to have the patience with Rhonda like she did with others.

"Those earrings. They're beautiful. Same half-moon shape but another colour. The one in Mary's garden was blue. Yours are a deep emerald green. I was just admiring them. They are beautiful," she finished lamely.

"Yes, a few women bought the same design at the jewellery presentation last month." Cathy frowned. "I thought Mary bought nothing that night. Maybe she did, after all. Didn't you attend that event?"

"No, I didn't. Must have been busy that day." Rhonda wanted to end the discussion about the earring. Fast.

"What happened to Mary's earring?" Another woman piped up.

"Nothing," Rhonda quickly replied. "I found it in her garden the other day."

"What were you doing over there, Rhonda?" Cathy was like a dog with a bone. "You have no business being there, not while the police are still investigating."

"No, it was before the fire," Rhonda hastened to correct her.

She hated lying, but she had no choice this time. Wishing she'd said nothing, take the words back, she swiftly said her goodbyes and left.

Fifteen

Day 12

Kate thought about Adrian. A lot. He had all the answers she wanted. Unfortunately, he wasn't very forthcoming with them. What she knew about his background was from Mary. He was an enigma and shared nothing about himself. She determined to find out who the real Adrian Kaufman was.

Mary told her he was a highly decorated police officer involved in taking down one of the biggest international drug cartels. There would be information about that on the internet. She looked forward to uncovering the story.

She admitted her feelings towards him had shifted since the night she was attacked and he took care of her. Exactly what those feelings were was too early to say. He intrigued her and she felt a connection between them she didn't really want to face just yet. She was afraid. The hurt of ten years ago still haunted her.

With a hot cup of tea, she made herself comfortable at the computer and started. She searched his name but had no luck. Not even a mention of his career in the police force or any other law enforcement agency in the State of Victoria. She widened her search to include every state in Australia to no avail.

She was about an hour into browsing the many websites and public government archives that she didn't at first hear the doorbell ring. A loud knock on the door captured her attention. She felt intense irritation when she saw Rick Lewis standing at her door.

"What do you want, Mr Lewis?" She refused to be civil.

"And a good day to you too, Mrs Trellow." He grinned and bowed like he had in the Robbins garden. The arrogance of the man!

"May I come in, please? I promise not to take up too much of your time." He smiled, appearing genuine.

"I'm very busy and don't have time to spare," Kate replied and started to close the door. He put up his hand, stopping her in mid action.

"Please don't do that," he said. "I truly have a dilemma and hope you can help me."

Reluctantly, she opened the door wide and within moments they were sitting at her dining table.

"Several residents mentioned your name. They think you have insider knowledge in this case." Rick said.

"That's absurd! Why would anyone say that?"

"Maybe because of your friendship with the deceased and her husband?"

"That's a long bow and you know it! I have no more information than what the police have said publicly, which isn't much at this stage." Her frustration must have shown because the reporter raised his eyebrow at her. She ignored it.

"Yet, you were snooping around the Robbins' property the other night. What were you looking for?"

"As I told you that night, it's none of your business."

"Okay. I'll back off. For now."

"So what's your dilemma, Mr Lewis?"

"Please call me Rick. May I call you Kate?"

"If you insist." She sounded sullen and didn't care. He got under her skin and she didn't appreciate his probing.

"Just a few questions. I'll come straight to the point. Do you believe the fire that killed Mary Robbins was deliberately lit? Or do you think it was an accident?"

Kate was stunned at the audacity of his question. She may well harbour her own suspicions but she wasn't about to share them with a reporter!

"I beg your pardon – er – Rick. What sort of question is that?"

"Just what it appears to be. There are a few rumours circulating at Possum Walk and residents are talking about arson."

Kate kept her face expressionless. No way was she going to share her suspicions with this guy. She felt the familiar tension snaking inside her body. The beginning of another panic attack was the last thing she wanted to occur in the presence of Rick Lewis. She forced with all her being to quash the feeling down. Her breathing became shallow as she tried to gain control.

"What do you think happened, Rick?" Good. Her voice sounded normal. And the tension seemed to be easing.

"I'm the one asking questions, remember?"

"I'm very interested in your view," she persisted.

He gazed at her for a long moment. "It depends which way you look at it. Some suggest that your friend unpacked a very old electric blanket and the faulty wiring caused the fire. But the police are asking strange questions that imply a potentially sinister occurrence."

"Well, like everyone else, you'll have to wait for the police to conclude their investigation and release the findings. Don't reporters have a direct line to the police?"

"It doesn't always work that way, unfortunately. Detective Abbott is saying very little, which adds to the peculiarity of this case."

"Well, I'm sorry Rick, but I don't think I can enlighten you."

The doorbell rang – again. Who was it this time?

"Adrian!" A warm feeling rose inside her when she saw him. She'd missed him over the past few days and that surprised her. He looked equally happy to see her. They both grinned at each other.

"How are you feeling?" he asked.

Just then, he saw Rick behind her sitting at the dining table and stopped in his tracks.

"What is *he* doing here, Kate?" he scowled at the other man.

"Mr Lewis was just leaving," Kate replied, hoping Rick would take the hint.

"Good to see you again, Mr Kaufman." Rick extended his hand to Adrian. "We haven't had a proper introduction. I'm Rick Lewis from the Melbourne Times."

Adrian kept his hands by his side. "What do you want from Kate?"

"Oh, we were just having a friendly chat. But I'm glad you're here. I wanted to speak to you, too."

"I can't imagine why, Mr Lewis."

"You're a very interesting man," he said, glancing at Kate. "Kate, Mr Kaufman is a bit of a mystery." She felt rather than saw Adrian tense. "I can't find any information about Adrian Kaufman anywhere. Not his police career, his family background. Nothing. It's as though he doesn't exist."

Adrian didn't react. He stared at the reporter, his stance ominous. Kate froze, her stomach twisted into knots. She didn't dare breathe. Admittedly, her own search on Adrian found nothing so far.

"I think you'd better leave now, Mr Lewis," Adrian said through clenched teeth.

"Be careful, Kate," Rick said. "You know nothing about this man you're spending time with."

With those parting words, he ignored Adrian and left.

A deafening silence followed the slamming of the door. Kate and Adrian stared intensely at each other. He looked a little nervous and his body remained tense. She felt numb, not understanding, afraid to jump to conclusions. She'd lowered her guard with Adrian. Something she'd not done in a long time. Her insecurities threatened to spill over once again. She couldn't risk another man hurting her again. But she felt compelled to find out what was going on.

"Is there any truth to what Rick Lewis said, Adrian?" She wanted desperately for him to deny it, all of it. To tell her it was a malicious lie.

"It's complicated Kate."

Her heart sank. So he was hiding something after all.

"Let me put it this way. Is your name, your real name, Adrian Kaufman?"

He hesitated. Her stomach churned with nerves.

"I know this must be difficult, Kate. We hardly know each other. But I'm asking you to trust me. Just for a while longer," he said. "It's hard to accept, but there are things, other people's lives, at stake. The less you know for now, the safer it will be for you."

"Please, just answer the question. Is your name Adrian Kaufman?"

"Yes. And no."

Kate was confused. She wanted desperately to believe Adrian, to believe in what he said. But her innate warning bells refused to be silenced.

"I don't know how to feel, how to react."

She turned away, not sure of her own judgement anymore. A part of her really wanted to give Adrian what he asked. But another part, the one which still hurt deep inside, wanted to run. He asked too much of her. How or why should she trust him? The best thing for her was to walk away and have nothing more to do with him.

She turned back towards him and opened her mouth to tell him so when she hesitated. He gazed out the front window at the Robbins' house across the street. In that instant, his expression was bleak, defeated. He quickly shut it down when he saw her move.

"Alright, Adrian. No questions for now."

"Thank you, Kate." He sounded relieved.

"You've asked a lot of me. But I'm the least of your problems." He frowned at her. "You have a bloodhound on your trail. And he will not be easy to get rid of."

"Rick Lewis is arrogant and ambitious," Adrian replied. "A lethal combination, for sure. He might become a problem. But I can handle his kind."

Sixteen

Day 13 – Early Hours

John was dreaming. He dreamt of Rosie. And Mary. They were in happier times and laughing together as they walked along the Thames River in London. In the distance was the tall figure of a man watching them.

"Don't go yet, Rosie." John tried to catch her as she pulled away. But she giggled and disappeared. He turned towards Mary who stood silently next to him. Suddenly she wasn't laughing anymore. She had tears in her eyes.

"Why did you leave me?" she murmured.

He puzzled over those words. "All good, my dear," he said, looking around. "I'm right here. Dry your eyes and let's go buy an ice cream."

She shook her head. "Remember our secret. Your life depends on it."

Secret? Yes, he remembered. It was a whisper of a memory somewhere deep in his mind and he couldn't quite grasp it. Mary's image faded.

"Please don't leave!" But she too disappeared. The man in the distance continued to watch him. But now he saw him clearer. He looked familiar. Who was he? It was slowly coming to him...

A noise in his room startled John awake, pulling him from his dream. It must be night, for darkness engulfed him. There was a sliver of muted light from the corridor filtering under the door and it filled the room with dim shadows.

He lay quietly, waiting for whatever or whoever had woken him to become clear. He wanted to get back to sleep so he could continue dreaming.

A nurse appeared by his side. He couldn't quite make out the face, which was in shadow. John chuckled. Of course. His four hourly medical observations, or 'obs', as the nurses called it. It must be time.

"I was having such a wonderful dream when you woke me," he said to the faceless nurse. His eyes adjusted to the dim lighting.

The nurse didn't respond. Instead, he was handed a bag of chocolates. Did the nurse bring them to him? Or were they the ones Kate brought him on her last visit? He thought he finished them. What a lovely surprise.

"Thank you," he said. "I look forward to enjoying them tomorrow."

But the faceless nurse took one chocolate out of the bag and pressed it into the palm of his hand, closing his fingers over it.

"Really? Right now?" He grinned. He felt less sleepy suddenly. What a treat! The chocolate smelled wonderful. He placed it in his mouth with anticipation.He quickly finished the chocolate when another one was placed in his hand.

"Jolly good stuff." He chewed in between the words.

The fifth – or was it the sixth - one he pushed away. "I want to go to sleep now. Tired." He struggled to keep his eyes open.

He felt the quick stab of a needle. Did he usually have injections he wondered? His mind was foggy, his thoughts hazy. Seemed to experience that a lot lately, remembered little these days to be honest.

"Sleep. Soon you will join your wife," the nurse whispered in his ear. He barely registered the words. But he saw the eyes close to his face, malevolently gazing down at him. He struggled against the horror of the burning green brilliance. His worst nightmare. Devil eyes.

"No!" John tried frantically to raise himself off the cushions, to get out of bed. He had to escape. He knew the devil eyes would hurt him. But to no avail.

"No-o-o-o-!" he cried desperately, slumping back heavily. What was wrong with him? He was so sleepy, so tired. His body felt unusually heavy. What little strength he had was gone. He closed his eyes, unable to fight against the exhaustion.

Abruptly, he heard the nurse move away and leave the room. Confusion slammed against his mind, trying to understand what just happened. Was it real? Did he have a nightmare?

So tired.

Blessed sleep beckoned...

Seventeen

Afternoon

Despite everything that had occurred since her friend's death, writing kept Kate's mind occupied. Every spare moment she devoted to it was one more moment she lost herself in her fictional world. Since the tragedy, she worried she would never write again, at least not for some time. Thankfully, she was wrong.

With renewed vigour, she successfully resolved the sticking point in her novel and was about to pen a second murder scene. This scene called for the murderer to inject poison inside chocolates to kill the victim. She was excited to get it down.

Mid-afternoon, she took a break. And wondered. If there was little to no information about Adrian to be found on the internet, perhaps she could go around the problem. Uncover clues about the taskforce.

It seemed information on relevant taskforces was equally impossible to uncover. And she'd spent over an hour on it. She was about to give up when a minor news item caught her attention. It was an English newspaper article dated May 1995, relating to a notorious Mafia Queen named Lidia Ciambella. Authorities recently arrested her for murder in Italy, alleging that she headed up a drug cartel with ties across Europe, the United Kingdom and Australia.

Kate instantly became intrigued. The power of the Mafia in Italy was a widely recognized fact. Some Mafia families migrated to Australia decades ago. She watched movies and television series about Mafia families. But she never heard of a Mafia 'Queen'. Nor of Lidia Ciambella.

Several hours later, she knew considerately more. Lidia Ciambella was famous for her remarkable green eyes. Some referred to them as 'devil eyes'. She was ruthless in her climb to power, surviving a male dominated world of crime at a young age. A fascinating life.

After her arrest, several of Lidia's minders and key people turned state's evidence and testified against her and her organisation. There was enough proof of drug trafficking and other related criminal activities to bring down the cartel. Law enforcement agencies made many successful arrests coordinated across multiple countries over an intense twelve-month period.

Kate felt the adrenalin race through her veins. Finally, a breakthrough. This must be the case! It made sense.

Immersed in her findings, Kate lost track of time. She forgot to eat dinner, having ignored the rumbling of her empty stomach for the past hour. She couldn't ignore it any longer.

It was midnight.

Eighteen

Day 14 - Afternoon

Kate suspected neither Diego nor Rhonda had taken their stories and suspicions to the police. On the one hand, she didn't blame them. Both were reluctant to take action. Both had different reasons to doubt their recollections of the night of the fire. So many questions with no answers. The autopsy report was due soon. That would shed light on the case once and for all.

Mary's funeral was scheduled to take place in a few days' time. John was still in the hospital and permanent care accommodation was not too far away. The funeral would be tough on John. For his sake, she hoped he was well on the day and not in 'the other place' so he would have the chance to mourn his wife properly. Kate's heart went out to him. How tragic it must be to grieve a loved one when suffering bouts of dementia. It would be a living hell. She decided to visit him again in the afternoon.

When she arrived at the hospital, she headed straight to his room. When she opened the door, there was no one there.

Instead, the bed had been stripped down and none of John's belongings were in sight.

Initially taken aback, she recovered, thinking the staff must have moved him to another room. Or perhaps the hospital had already discharged him after finding permanent accommodation. She dismissed that thought instantly because Adrian would surely have told her if that was the case.

She found the nurses' station where three nurses were busy going about their tasks.

"Excuse me." Kate approached one nurse, who looked up and smiled at her expectantly. Realising it was Libby, the nurse she spoke to at the last visit, she gave her a brief smile and nod of acknowledgement.

"Hi. I'm looking for John Robbins. He was in room eighteen last time I visited."

The other two nurses stopped what they were doing and turned to stare in her direction.

"You're looking for John Robbins?" Libby hesitated and appeared nervous.

Her behaviour startled Kate. All kinds of unsettling thoughts raced through her mind. Had something happened to John? Did he have a relapse?

"Is John alright? Did you move John to another room?"

"I met you the other day," Libby said. She seemed to have recovered somewhat. "Your name is...?"

"Kate Trellow. I visited him a few days ago. You told me he'd watched a documentary about Italy. Remember?"

"Yes, of course, Kate. One moment please." Libby turned to her colleagues and they quietly exchanged words. Kate was becoming more suspicious by the second. Something wasn't right. The nurses were on edge, which made Kate on edge. Where was John? And why would no one give her a straight answer?

One nurse left and Libby returned to Kate.

"Kate, would you mind going to the waiting room down the hall? Someone will be with you shortly." She seemed more composed now, less nervous. But there was a tension in the air that Kate couldn't comprehend.

"Is everything okay? Where's John?" She heard the frustration and mounting unease in her voice and tried to steady her breathing. Anxiety threatened to spill over and she needed to remain calm until she found out where John was. There might be a totally simple explanation.

Nodding to Libby, she made her way down the hall. Asking any more questions would be useless. Worried, she made her way to the empty waiting room near the lifts. A doctor arrived a few minutes later.

"Ms Trellow. I'm Maggie Stone, medical registrar on this ward. You enquired about John Robbins?"

"Has something happened to John? Where is he?"

She forced her voice to remain calm. The unexpected turn of events shook her. No one was forthcoming with information. She'd grown even more alarmed before the doctor arrived. Perhaps the hospital discharged John after all. Why had the staff not told her that?

"John Robbins is no longer on this ward."

"Has he been transferred or discharged?"

"I'm sorry. Unless you are family, I can't divulge any further information. Privacy rights of the patient. You might wish to check with his family. I'm not at liberty to say more." With those words, she turned to leave.

"Wait! Why can't you tell me where he is? Has he taken a turn for the worse?"

The doctor gazed steadily at her. "I'm not at liberty to say any more. The matter is out of our hands now."

"What matter? Where's John?" Her face felt hot and panic was rising. Breathe in, Kate, she told herself firmly. Stay calm.

"I can't tell you anymore. Excuse me, but I have patients to see." She was gone.

With no hesitation, Kate rang Adrian's number. The call went to voicemail and Kate didn't leave a message. She hadn't seen him for a few days. He'd rung her though, every day to check on her welfare. Because of the attack, he told her. Which she thought was sweet. Now, however, she felt bewildered and not a little resentful. If Adrian knew anything at all about John's situation, why hadn't he told her?

Adrian rang her back as she drove home.

"Adrian! Where is John?" She sounded loud and panicked and immediately felt foolish. She pulled the car to the side of the road so she could concentrate on the call.

She softened her tone, consciously slowing her breathing as she continued, "I went to visit him and he's not in his room. The hospital staff won't talk to me because of privacy laws and told me to get information from John's family." Her voice was getting louder with each word. Her anxiety levels were rising. "So here I am. I'm asking. What is going on?"

There was a slight pause before he replied. "It's complicated."

"Have you moved him? Has the hospital transferred him to other accommodation?"

"Unfortunately, I can't say anymore for now. I have to finalise the funeral arrangements. I'm not sure when I can see you. Hopefully soon."

He hung up. Kate stared down at her phone. She was completely puzzled, and confused, by the turn of events.

Where was John? More importantly, was he alright? What information was Adrian withholding? She suddenly realised his behaviour towards her just then had been decidedly cool, so different from their last encounter. Something had shifted. And it had to do with John, she was sure of it.

She slumped down in her seat, feeling deflated. When would she ever get straight answers from Adrian, the police? Mary's death was becoming more and more enshrouded in mystery. The cause of the fire was a pivotal clue she still had to work out. It seemed as though she was trying to get through a thick forest and at every turn she came to a dead end. Only they knew the way out. It was a secret they seemed to deliberately keep from her.

She sighed, confused more than ever.

Secrets...

Nineteen

Day 15 – Early Hours

It was too easy. No one suspected a thing.

Kate Trellow's research came at an opportune time. The file was open on her dining room table and – curiosity prevailed. The overwhelming urge to snoop won out. It turned out to be illuminating. The snap decision to slip away with it took little effort whilst Kate was distracted.

It was astonishing that Kate Trellow wrote about crime and murder. It appeared growing numbers of people held secrets at Possum Walk. Her research was thorough. It was irresistible. The actual story was unfolding before her very eyes and she didn't even know it. How comical! Kate Trellow was now a valuable pawn to be manipulated at will. It was going to be such fun!

The electric blanket scenario was enticing. The case of the husband who killed his wife was pure genius. Sloppy work, for the reckless fellow got caught! The air of drama about it appealed. A truly golden opportunity not to be wasted. Precise timing was crucial. It was worth it and very satisfying to watch the house go up in flames. With Mary Robbins in it! Orchestrating it in reality took a bit of effort, more than expected, to make it the perfect murder.

That stupid woman, Rhonda Kavich, caused some initial bother. She persisted in telling everyone Mary Robbins hated electric blankets, that the fire was suspicious. And the earring found in the garden? Mary's earring, she concluded. The woman clearly didn't mean to say anything about it and regretted it. What was she doing snooping around the Robbins' house, anyway? Her mouth could get her killed one day. Ironic. And funny. Like everything and everyone, the woman had an expiry date. She was, after all, quite dispensable.

Gaining access to the hospital in the early hours of the morning and to John Robbins' room was a satisfying surprise. No one stopped to ask questions. In fact, a couple of staff nodded as they walked past. The uniform helped no doubt. And the hospital face mask. By now, John Robbins was dead. Suspected heart attack. Thank you once again, Kate Trellow!

The last act of this play required perfect staging. The remaining pieces of evidence must be planted in the perfect setting. Overhearing one innocent comment had been pure luck. It led to everything falling into place so easily and made clear what needed to be done next.

Now for the final scene. Slipping into the house was risky. But there was confidence that nosey neighbours were tucked up asleep in their beds. Memorizing the layout of the house made it easy to navigate in the gloomy hours of the morning. Many social visits over the past few months had ensured that.

A grin escaped. The Robbins had no idea their nemesis was

living amongst them at Possum Walk. In plain sight. Patiently waiting for the right time to strike. They had all passed time chatting and laughing. What a sham! Any time now, the police would announce John Robbins' death. That would be a beautiful moment.

The gloved hand held up the earring. The gems in the crescent moon shape gleamed eerily as they caught the faint light peeping in from the window. It was almost hypnotic to behold.

Now, where to put it so it would be easily found. Nowhere too obvious. Turning slowly about the room, the ideal spot was straight ahead. Wedged between two cushions on the sofa. Reverently, the solitary piece of jewellery was laid just so.

Now for the second piece, *the* masterpiece. Ah, just there. Perfect. Discreet. Unremarkable at one level, but sheer gold.

Let the fun begin!

Suddenly, the face became serious. The pretence fell away. The painful years of suffering and anguish had been such an immense burden, sometimes an overwhelming weight to carry. A constant dark shadow.

Now, it all fell away and instead, freedom reigned. There was only piece to look forward to. Overwhelming and intense emotion welled up inside. Finally, it was over. Both of them gone.

May they rot in hell!

Twenty

Day 16

It was the first day of the Winter Orchid Show weekend. The Possum Walk Garden Club regularly did the rounds of the flower and garden shows locally and sometimes travelled to Melbourne for the big ones. Many residents wanted to join them for this particular one, given Mary Robbins had been such a big part of it as President.

The Northern Orchid Society management committee named one of their awards in the President's honour. The inaugural Mary Robbins Beginner Display was to be presented at this weekend's show.

The outing was just what Kate needed right now. Following the last few days of police interviews and strange interactions with Adrian, she was ready for a break. And this would be the perfect solution.

Over thirty residents from Possum Walk made their way to the show. Many got a lift in the community bus driven by Cathy Eldridge. Others car pooled to get there. Kate drove Rhonda,

Paula and Julie French to the venue. The conversation in the car was light hearted, much of it around families, particularly grandchildren and their shenanigans.

Rhonda looked a little tired. At one point, Kate saw her in the rear-view mirror, trying to hide a yawn.

"Not feeling well, Rhonda?" Paula asked, concern in her voice.

"I haven't been sleeping well the past few weeks. You know, after the fire, it's been difficult." The others murmured in agreement.

"It's been a difficult time for all of us," Kate said. "But today, it's a celebration about Mary and what she loved. Her orchids. Let's make sure we all have a good time."

"A great time!" Paula chimed in.

Once inside the venue, residents moved about in small groups exploring the many beautiful and creative displays. The winners of various categories were all at the front of the hall on stage, with the name of each owner next to their plants.

Kate wandered around on her own, absorbing the atmosphere. She felt nostalgic, almost expecting Mary to pop up behind one of the many pots of orchids for sale. The show catered to the novice right through to the well-established orchid lovers and experts. The event was extremely well organised and coordinated with no little effort from Mary over the years.

The saddest moment was when she realised that Mary's own entries in the show were missing. Burnt, trampled, dead. She'd nurtured and protected them inside her house for months in anticipation of the show. And her entries often won a prize or two.

In the next aisle, out of sight, a child loudly asked her mother what the flower was called. As they came into view, she recognised Libby, the nurse who had looked after John. Mother and daughter didn't notice her.

Libby replied to her daughter, "An orchid."

"An awkward?" Her daughter frowned. She looked about seven years old.

"No, an *orchid*."

To which the little girl said, "But it's leaning over and it looks a bit awkward. Are you sure you've got it right, mummy?"

Kate chuckled to herself. She must remember to share the story with the ladies later.

Their voices grew distant and Kate saw them stop at another stall further down the aisle. She was reluctant to call after them. She didn't want to think or talk about John. Neither the way the hospital had handled her concerns. Nor the way Adrian had fobbed her off afterwards. Today was Mary's day.

After a while, she sat at a table inside the makeshift café and ordered a cup of tea and scones. She didn't mind when Rhonda and Paula joined her with their own refreshments.

"It's just marvellous!" Rhonda looked animated.

Her face had a glow and her eyes were sparkling. She didn't appear tired now. Kate realised it wasn't often she saw Rhonda smile or happy.

"Enjoying yourselves, ladies?" she asked both women.

"What a testament to Mary," Rhonda replied, nodding. "All the hard work she and the management committee put in to create this marvellous event twice a year. The Spring show is coming up in the next two months!"

"I love it too," Paula chimed in. "So many colours. I've never really taken notice of orchids before. The flowers are so beautiful. And each one is different. I really love the Mary Robbins' award winner. Stunning display."

They conversed for a few minutes. Finally, Kate shared the story about the little girl and her mother. They had a good laugh. She didn't bother to add that she'd already met Libby at the hospital. It wasn't really relevant.

"Hello ladies." Kate heard the all too familiar voice behind her. Rick Lewis. Gritting her teeth against the inevitable showdown with this man, she saw him move around the table, facing her. He smiled at Rhonda and Paula.

"Hello Kate. We meet again." He glanced at Rhonda, acknowledging her with a nod. "How is everyone enjoying the exhibition? What a wonderful show of support for your friend, Mary Robbins."

The words appeared complimentary, but to Kate, they sounded patronising and insincere. She didn't waste any time with niceties. "Why are you here, Mr Lewis?"

"I'm writing a piece on Mary Robbins, the person, not the victim. I heard this show was special to her, being the President of the Orchid Society who sponsors it."

"They do more than sponsor, Mr Lewis," Rhonda replied coldly. "They create, organise and fully fund these events. Hours and hours of tireless volunteer work and a very dedicated group of people."

"My apologies. I didn't mean to offend." Turning to Paula, he said, "I don't believe we've met, Ms...?"

"Vincent. Paula Vincent." Her words were clipped, low.

Good! Rick Lewis would get nothing useful from this group. Let him bother some of the other residents.

"How are you all coping since losing your friend? Do you have any concerns about the police investigation?"

Kate had to give him credit for his persistence, misguided though it was. Silence from the group.

"There's widespread talk of arson. And murder." He watched them keenly. He wanted a reaction, any reaction, from one of them, Kate thought cynically. And then he would pounce. First grade journalism, this one. But no one made eye contact with him. Nor spoke.

At that moment, Kate saw Libby and her daughter enter the café. Libby spied her instantly and, smiling, waved to her. No sign of any unease from their previous encounter. Relieved to be distracted away from Rick Lewis, Kate motioned for them to sit at the table next to them. She introduced Libby to Rhonda and Paula, adding that Libby was the nurse looking after John. The women exchanged greetings. Rick Lewis stood by, silent for once, observing the group.

"And this is Grace," Libby introduced her daughter.

"I couldn't help overhearing you explain the name of the flowers to Grace, who thought they should be called 'awkward'." Kate smiled at Grace.

Libby laughed at Kate's words and the little girl smiled shyly at Kate. "We've sorted it out now," she said, looking down at her daughter. "Haven't we, Grace?"

The little girl nodded happily and said, "They are awkward to look at. But they are called 'orchids' so we don't hurt their feelings."

"That's very sweet," Rhonda said to Grace.

"What a delightful child," Rick Lewis said to Libby. "I'm Rick Lewis. Journalist for the Melbourne Times. My friends forgot to introduce us." They shook hands.

"I'd love to chat to you sometime about John Robbins. How is he coping with his wife's death?" Rick looked expectantly at Libby.

"You know I can't discuss that, Mr Lewis. Patient confidentiality. You must speak with the family. Or the police."

The police? Kate was surprised. Why would Libby suggest he discuss John with the police? She realised the police would have visited the hospital to interview John more than once. Libby and the staff would know that. Except Libby's face told another story. Immediately she uttered the words, *Or the police* her 'oops' facial expression gave her away. Kate watched her with interest. Libby regretted her words. Why?

"Are the police investigating John Robbins?" Rick was quick to pick up on Libby's words too.

Libby recovered quickly. "The police have been on the ward several times to visit Mr Robbins. It's logical to direct questions to them." It was clear she didn't want to discuss the matter further when she turned her back to him, speaking to Grace in soft tones.

"It was worth a try," he laughed. He looked around at the group of women. "Well, I'll continue my tour of the show. Perhaps I'll have better luck with some of the other people who knew Mary Robbins."

Kate was happy to see Rick Lewis leave. She suspected the

others were too. Rhonda confirmed it when she said, "What a horrid man!" and visibly shuddered.

The atmosphere lifted significantly afterwards. Light chatter followed, mainly about the Orchid Show. Kate desperately wanted to quiz Libby about John, but knew the other woman would not say anything. Regardless of her pact to herself not to think of anyone or anything except Mary today, it was tempting to try to prise information from her. But she let it go.

One thing she noticed was Libby glancing at Paula occasionally, a slight frown on her face.

"Have we met before?" Libby finally asked her.

"I don't think so," Paula replied slowly.

"Your face is familiar. Your accent. From England?" When Paula nodded, she continued. "I used to live in the south of England. I trained there as a nurse and worked in one of the big hospitals for a few years before I moved back to Australia with a brand new husband and child."

Paula shrugged but didn't reply.

"You remind me of someone I knew a long time ago," Libby added. "Were you ever at St Stephen General Hospital in London?"

"No, I lived in the far north of England," Paula replied, a little sharply. "Rarely came to London."

"Sorry," Libby said hastily. "I didn't mean to offend you. My mistake."

"No harm done," Paula replied.

Kate sensed uneasiness between the two women and couldn't understand why. Not long after, Libby excused herself, telling the group she was off to order some food and drinks.

"Libby and her daughter seem nice," Rhonda said, appearing oblivious to Paula and Libby's exchange. "She's chatty, isn't she?"

Libby and Grace didn't return to their table. After a while, Kate looked around for them but they were gone.

Twenty-One

❦

Day 17 – Morning

The weather was fitting for a funeral, Kate thought as she snuggled further into her coat. The frosty wind and rain lashed at her as she made her way into the funeral home. Mary would have hated this bleak weather.

Most of the people present were residents of Possum Walk who, like Kate, came to pay their final respects. A handful of others were likely friends from the Orchid Society or past coworkers. Adrian greeted people as they entered.

Kate saw him hesitate before giving her an acknowledging nod. He looked tired, with dark circles under his eyes, like he hadn't slept in days. Which was probably true. It was an immense responsibility taking on John's care and the Robbins' affairs now Mary was gone. And, of course, the funeral arrangements. She should have offered to help, she thought too late. It might have eased those dark circles.

"Hello Kate. You must have a lot of questions but now is not the time."

His abruptness took her by surprise. It was as though he'd rehearsed it and rushed to get the words out. He looked slightly uncomfortable, too. Probably feeling guilty at his dismissive air on the phone the last time they spoke. And his behaviour just now.

Now is not the time. He'd done it again! Made her defensive. As if she would make a scene today of all days. He must think very little of her. Annoyed and disappointed, she tried not to let her emotions show.

"Will John be here today?" She suspected the answer but asked anyway.

"No, he's not well." His response was unmistakably cool.

Kate's anguish over what may have happened to John resurfaced. That Adrian refused to discuss it at all, or give her the expectation he would do so, was unacceptable.

"I don't know what's going on," she whispered. People were milling around them. "Why your behaviour has suddenly changed. But we need to talk!"

Surely Adrian couldn't have missed the depth of her emotions as she flung the words at him. He searched her face intently for what seemed like ages. Kate held her breath and felt nervous at his scrutiny. What did he expect to find? His expression softened for a moment and then toughened. Swallowing hard, he nodded and turned to the next person.

Kate had no choice but to move along. Where did the caring and supportive man from the night she was assaulted in the Robbins' home disappear to? Or the man who made breakfast for her the next morning? She was way too sensitive when it came to Adrian Kaufman. She needed to take a chill pill because he was a most infuriating man.

She acknowledged both Detectives Abbott and Penrose with a tight smile. Their presence was a thoughtful gesture under normal circumstances. Police attended funerals not just out of respect for the victim but sometimes for other reasons. Kate guessed that if there was any suspicion around the fire and Mary's death, they would watch with interest those who attended her funeral.

Why? Because there was a high likelihood that a Possum Walk resident was the offender if there had indeed been a crime committed. An offender with the means and the added advantage of knowledge of the Robbins and the wider Possum Walk community.

Kate stopped in her tracks, stunned. Someone bumped into her back and she hastened out of the way to an empty seat. Who else could it be other than a resident living in Possum Walk, a secure gated community? At a house where she had never seen outsiders visit?

A chill went down Kate's back. She felt dazed. She never connected someone at Possum Walk being responsible for the fire and Mary's death. But it made sense. The shroud of mystery surrounding Mary's death, the fire. Regardless of due process, the police had acted strangely from day one. Something was decidedly off. A potential arson and homicide case fit far better into the confusing picture than a terrible accident did.

Kate's thoughts swirled in freefall inside her head. Her chest tightened. She couldn't think beyond the revelation that shook her to her very core. Her body felt pinned to the chair, unable to move, except to breathe. Slowly...in and out. Did someone murder her friend? It was the only logical answer to explain the madness of the past few weeks since the fire.

"Hello, Kate." Rick Lewis took the seat next to her.

"Are you joking?" Kate scowled at him. "I can't believe you have the audacity to show up at Mary's funeral. How dare you!"

"Just doing my job," he replied in a low voice.

"Why are you the only reporter still hounding Possum Walk? Everyone else left days ago. There's no story here."

"Well, I beg to differ. I think something big is going down. And I'm going to uncover it."

Kate scoffed at him. "You're delusional. Go back to wherever you came from and leave us alone. Haven't we been through enough?"

"I actually agree with you. I'd like nothing better than to leave the place. But I have a nose for these things. I smell a rat."

"You're the rat!" Kate replied, her voice getting louder.

They were attracting attention as people sitting around them turned in their direction. Kate had to get her temper under control. It was not like her to be so rude. She made this man the exception.

"What if I told you that the police believe someone at Possum Walk is a murderer?" Rick whispered as he leaned close to her.

Kate kept her expression neutral and stared straight ahead, deciding the best strategy was to ignore him. She'd only just come to the same realisation moments earlier. How did he gain information of this nature?

As was his usual style, he persisted. "I overheard an intriguing conversation between your friend Adrian Kaufman and Detective Abbott you'd find very interesting."

The music started. Saved by the 'bell', a relieved Kate thought.

When Adrian rose to give the eulogy, the room grew silent. He was a man of few words.

"Thank you for coming here today to pay your respects to a dear friend, Mary Robbins. Unfortunately, John Robbins, her husband, can't be present. He is still unwell and recovering from pneumonia in the hospital."

A murmur rippled through the crowd. He briefly described Mary's teaching career, her love of orchids and her retirement life at Possum Walk alongside her beloved John. It was a beautiful and simple service. There was no coffin. In its place was a mounted display of orchids, in every colour and shape. A fitting and breathtaking tribute to a kind and wonderful person.

After the service, people gathered for refreshments at a local function centre. Adrian mingled but kept away from where Kate sat with Rhonda, Paula and Diego at a corner table. It was almost as though he evaded her. At one stage, she saw him speak for some minutes with Detective Abbott. Interesting, she thought. Both had their poker faces on. She caught them glance towards her several times and wondered why.

Rick Lewis' last words haunted her as she watched the two men. She admitted curiosity to know more, but the reporter was the last person she would seek information from. He was obviously dangling that piece of carrot to gain her attention and possible cooperation. Isn't that how it worked with reporters?

"It was a lovely service." Rhonda's lips trembled slightly. Paula nodded in agreement. Diego remained silent but he was teary.

"I'm surprised John was not present," Rhonda continued. "He looked well enough when we saw him a few days ago in the hospital. You agree, Paula?"

Paula started to respond but Rhonda continued on. "Anyway, it's probably for the best. The poor man was not himself. Couldn't take the risk that he would make a spectacle of himself today of all days."

"A spectacle of himself?" Kate couldn't believe it. Her nerves were frayed enough today without Rhonda's foolish commentary.

"Rhonda, you can be so insensitive!"

She kept her voice low, not wanting to draw attention from others close by. The other woman's lack of insight didn't surprise her. Yet there was no excuse for stupidity. She wanted to reach across the table and shake some sense into her.

"Now is not the time or place, ladies." Diego glared at Rhonda pointedly. He too had been keenly watching the interaction between Adrian and Detective Abbott.

"John must be unwell," Paula said quietly, "or else he would surely be at his wife's funeral."

"Just as well he wasn't here!" Rhonda was unforgiving. "Anyone for a drink?" She left the table without waiting for a reply.

Kate shook her head as she gazed after her. "She can be one hard woman."

"She has a good heart underneath that bluster," Paula said. "I'll go check on her."

Kate turned to Diego. "How are you, Diego?"

He shrugged, not replying.

"Have you spoken to the police yet?"

"No. I have nothing to say to them."

"It's the right thing to do. Your memory from that night may return with some help. You might hold valuable information relevant to the case."

Diego looked anguished, in pain. "I was drunk. It was a little frightening for a while. Now I've eased back on the wine and already feel much better."

"How can you be sure it wasn't real?" Kate was alarmed at his casual dismissal.

"I was confused, had a little too much to drink. When I thought about it, I realised it was just my mind playing tricks on me."

"How can you know?" she asked, less forcefully. "Is there any shred of doubt in your mind?"

Diego hesitated. There were beads of sweat on his brow and he clenched and unclenched his fists. He refused to make eye contact with her, instead looking around the room. She sensed he was barely maintaining his control. That was enough for Kate to know.

"Leave it alone Kate! I'm sorry I told you!"

He stormed off.

Twenty-Two

Late Afternoon

Adrian finally approached Kate as she attempted to leave the building later that afternoon. Many had already left. It was a long day and she felt drained. There were things between them that needed to be said but she wasn't in the mood right now. She wanted to get home and into a hot bath, dissolve the tension out of her aching body. And reflect on the day. There was a lot to absorb. Her conversations with Diego and Rick Lewis for a start.

"A moment of your time, please, Kate."

Adrian followed her out the door. "I'm tired. I'll see you later."

"We need to talk," he persisted. "It won't take long."

"It can wait till tomorrow."

"No. It's deadly serious," he replied, not elaborating further, a grim expression on his face. She noticed the tight lines of tension around his mouth.

Her eyebrows shot up at his words. And admittedly, she was curious to hear what he had to say.

He led her to a quiet room off the foyer.

"Who are you, Kate Trellow?" His unexpectedly harsh tone caught her unawares. "I know very little about you."

"I could say exactly the same about you!" she fired back.

Undeterred, Adrian continued. "Why the keen interest in Mary and John Robbins? It's unusual and a little amplified. You haven't known them for very long. Why do you care so much about John and what happens to him?"

"What questions are these? I refuse to defend my actions to you!"

His suspicions baffled and floored her. Strangely, she felt total betrayal by this man. It had come to this so quickly. She thought she was connecting with him, yet a stranger stood before her. It took enormous effort not to cry and to quell the mad thumping of her heart. Her emotions were raw and her hands trembled. She knew she was close to the breaking point.

He stopped her as she tried to leave. "Can I trust you, Kate?" His voice was filled with anguish. "I desperately want to trust you. What game are you playing?" Kate's face burned under his intense scrutiny. "I can't figure you out. And now..." He dragged his fingers through his hair in an agitated movement. "It might already be too late."

"You're not making any sense. Stop talking in riddles. If anyone has secrets, it's you. What's your problem?"

"You!" he shot back. "I gave you advice once before, Kate. Remember it every time you stick your nose where you don't have any business to. Am I being clear now?" His irritation was palpable. "Let me put it another way. Stop with your meddling. It's making you an easy target and a liability in this investigation."

"A liability?" Kate was bewildered and exhaustion overtook her. She felt her legs weaken and, thinking she was about to collapse, gripped the table beside her. "I don't understand. I loved Mary. We were friends. Good friends. And now she's gone. Under suspicious circumstances. You know it too. I just want to find out the truth."

She felt deflated. The roller coaster emotions of the past weeks had left their mark. Humiliating tears rolled down her face. She brushed them aside impatiently as she continued.

"Since she died, my world has turned on its head. My life was simple and relatively normal. In fact, a little boring to be honest. Now, so many crazy thoughts constantly run through my mind. If this case was straightforward, why am I tortured by so many unanswered questions? I can't help but wonder at the discrepancies, like a jigsaw puzzle with a missing piece."

"Hell Kate! Why don't you just leave it alone? Let the police investigation see it through. Someone attacked you the other night. Don't you get it?"

"I'm no dummy, Adrian. Whoever attacked me wasn't waiting for me. I was in the wrong place at the right time." It was useless trying to convince him. "I'm done talking and leaving. Don't try to stop me."

"Wait!" Adrian's tone softened. "I don't have the authority to discuss the Robbins or the fire. I'm just trying to protect you against yourself."

"Who made you my protector? You don't have the authority to protect me." She threw his own words back at him. "And I don't need protecting."

"You're right. I'm sorry you feel that way. But you have no idea about the complexities and layers of this case."

More riddles. She'd had enough. Kate fled the room and this time Adrian didn't follow. Her body slammed into a man coming through the door. Detective Abbott. Pain radiated throughout her still tender body and nearly knocked the breath from her. What more could she take today? The detective held her steady as she regained her balance. And her breath.

"Sorry!" She tried to move past him. He held fast, not letting her go.

"Just one moment please, Mrs Trellow."

"I was just leaving," she said, desperation in her voice. "And it's Kate."

"You need to accompany me to the police station for more questioning, Kate."

"Another interview, detective? What more can you possibly want from me?"

"Someone tried to murder John Robbins."

Twenty-Three

John Robbins was D.E.A.D. Dead.

Why was there no broadcast yet? Adrian Kaufman announced John Robbins was still in hospital recovering from his illness. Obviously stalling for time. The fools believed him! If only they knew the truth about the Robbins!

Surprising to see so many people from Possum Walk at the funeral. Didn't think the old bag had that many friends. But then again, they were just going through the motion. No one really cared about Mary Robbins. They only cared about themselves. They liked to meddle in each other's business, not wanting to miss out on the latest gossip. How shallow their lives were.

It was unbearable living at Possum Walk! Now that the work was done, it was time to move on. Or was it? It was the biggest stage ever played to date. The biggest role. The adrenalin rush was powerful.

Of course, the police must be waiting till *after* the funeral to release the information of John Robbins' death. Too much tragedy in one day, eh?

Must remember to fake a suitably shocked face when the news breaks. And a glint of tears. That always worked.

John Robbins was D. E. A. D.

Dead! *"How terrible."*

Dead!! *"Who would do such a thing?"*

Dead!!! *"Both of them? They didn't deserve this."*

It would be easy to pretend to care. Evil eyes glowed with hate. A maniacal laugh escaped and echoed in the empty room.

Twenty-Four

"What? Murder John?" Kate's heart jumped, her skin crawled with shivers of shock. First Mary. Now John. The room spun for a moment as she fought against the impact of Detective Abbott's words. He kept a painful grip on her arms and wasn't about to let go. Her brain was frazzled, trying to make sense of it all.

"Is he alright?"

Detective Abbott didn't respond. With a determined look on his face he led her out to his car.

"Wait one moment, Detective." Adrian followed them. "Do you think that's necessary right now?"

"Yes I do, Adrian." You know better than anyone how this works. There's no time to waste."

"I'm coming with you both." She was grateful and relieved, nodding to him, because she couldn't speak. Her throat was tight and she felt a choking sensation of panic rise up. Mary's death was no accident. Someone had threatened John's life. What was it about the Robbins that made them such high risk? Kate thought she knew her friends. She realised now that she never did.

Suddenly, so many things about the Robbins' lives didn't add up. It was as though the veil of blindness lifted from her eyes and she saw everything in a different light. Their unusual lack of visitors. Barely any mention about their lives in England before they came to Australia. That look of sadness she caught in Mary's eyes from time to time. John's reference to keeping secrets. Was it really all in his head? Or something more?

It seemed mere minutes passed before she took a seat in a cold, sparsely furnished room across the table from Detective Abbott. Detective Penrose joined them. Adrian waited outside. She found comfort in knowing he was close by. The mirror along the wall of the room was surely a one-way viewing panel. She felt like a fish in a tank full of sharks. By now, the initial shock had worn off. But she couldn't shake the implication of what it meant.

Kate felt the clamminess of her palms as she clasped her hands. Screaming was a genuine possibility. It welled up inside her like a tightly wound coil about to spring out. Her body trembled against the tension and she didn't think she could bear another second. She was nervous that a panic attack was imminent and worried some more.

Outwardly, she appeared calm as she sat quietly in that cold room facing Detective Abbott. How did she possibly fit into all this madness? She suspected, no - she knew - in the depth of her soul she was in a grim situation and mentally braced herself.

"Mrs Trellow, we are about to - "

"I told you to call me Kate." She snapped, showing the first sign of nerves. Control. Breathe slowly. The grip on her hands tightened.

Detective Abbott outlined that the interview was about to

begin officially and told her it would be recorded. Ominously, a red light on the camera in the corner flickered on. Her face paled when he advised her she could call a solicitor at any time to represent her. Her body remained ramrod stiff and upright. She couldn't bend if she tried.

"Should I be worried, Detective? Do I need a solicitor?"

"That depends on you and what unfolds in the next hour."

It took all her resolve not to react.

"First, how are you recovering after the attack the other night?" The detective seemed genuinely interested.

Kate shrugged. "A few aches and pain. Nothing serious."

Nodding, he then asked several questions about her movements from the previous week since she last saw John Robbins in the hospital. Both he and Detective Penrose alternated between questions, sometimes interjecting with each other and her responses.

She told them everything. Except about her conversations with Rhonda and Diego. And she didn't mention her research on Adrian Kaufman either. The former were not her stories to tell and the latter was too embarrassing to tell. The thought of Adrian discovering that she was investigating him mortified her. He was likely on the other side of the mirrored wall, watching and listening.

"So what did you do on the day of the fire?" Detective Penrose interjected.

"The day of the fire?" Kate felt rattled. Why were they questioning her about that? "I arrived home on an early flight after visiting my daughter in Queensland. Had a quick chat to Mary outside. After unpacking, I caught up on emails, bills and other things. In the afternoon, Mary and I went to see John in the hospital. We arrived and Adrian was already there with John. Afterwards, I spent the rest of the day at home. Until Rhonda's shout for help drew me outside. And that's when I saw the house on fire and called ooo." She shuddered at the memory. Weeks later, it was still raw.

"Did you see or hear anything suspicious during that day?" Detective Penrose continued.

"No. How could I? I was mostly in the study, which is at the back of the house."

"Did you notice anything unusual once you called emergency services? Anything at all?" This question from Detective Abbott.

Kate thought for a moment, concentrating on how the events played out that night.

"No. Everything happened so fast it was chaotic. Rhonda fainted. Paula and Adrian helped get her inside my house. I didn't really see anything more other than through the window."

"Anything else, Kate?" Detective Penrose prompted her.

"I recalled thinking how quickly the crowd gathered, that they were in the way of the emergency services."

"Did anyone or anything in the crowd stand out?"

"Not really. A couple of people stood alone on one side. Like Cathy Eldridge. Paula stayed inside with us the whole time and I didn't notice when she left. Other than those two, the rest were a sea of blurred faces." Detective Penrose nodded and pulled back, signalling Detective Abbott to take over.

"When is the last time you saw John Robbins?" Detective Abbott asked.

"About a week ago. I tried to visit him again the day before yesterday but he wasn't in his room and the staff refused to tell me anything." The tight-lipped behaviour of hospital staff made sense now.

"Did you take him any gifts?"

"Cherry chocolates. His favourites."

"I see. Where did you purchase them from?"

"I – er – didn't. I had them at home."

Both detectives exchanged glances.

"Those chocolates are my favourites. I introduced John to them," she clarified. "I keep a steady supply."

"Where were they purchased?"

"From one of the local shops." They were readily available on the market.

"Did you bring him chocolates on all your visits?"

"Yes. They cheered him up."

"They certainly did, Kate." The harsh sarcasm in his voice took her aback.

"When was the attempt on John's life?" she asked, desperately needing answers. No one had said anything about John's condition.

"Three nights ago," Detective Abbott responded.

"What happened? Was he badly hurt? Is he going to be okay?"

"You mean you don't know?" The detective's gaze remained fixated on her, his expression one of disbelief.

Kate grimaced at his noticeable insolence. Why did he dislike her to the point he didn't bother to hide it? She felt bewildered and lost. And then it hit her. The police were treating her like a criminal about to be exposed. They were fully interrogating her.

She was a serious suspect in the murder of Mary Robbins and the attempted murder of John Robbins.

It was too ridiculous and Kate nearly broke out in laughter. But this was no laughing matter. It was dangerous. She glanced at the two-way window, convinced Adrian remained on the other side watching everything. That's why he'd been so cool in the past few days. He believed the same as the police. That she'd committed the crimes. Nausea welled up in her throat and she suddenly felt clammy all over. She was on the brink of collapse.

"What are you implying, detective? That I am responsible for what's occurred in this case?" Her voice sounded shaky and hoarse even to her own ears. But she used every bit of strength to keep going.

"Do you need a glass of water, Kate?" Detective Penrose asked.

Kate couldn't speak and nodded instead.

"We'll have a few minutes' break," the other woman said.

The water was a welcome relief. There was silence in the room, enabling Kate to recover some composure. She was grateful for the break.

Detective Penrose continued with the questioning. "When did you first meet the Robbins?"

"About two years ago, after we all moved into Possum Walk. They arrived about a month later. We became friends almost instantly. Mary was so easy going, calm and measured. John was garrulous by comparison. He was great fun before his health deteriorated."

"What do you know about the Robbins' lives before they moved to Possum Walk?" Detective Abbott resumed the questioning. He seemed to have recovered from his earlier 'outburst' and had his poker face firmly back in place.

"Just what they told me, mostly what Mary told me really. They came to Australia nearly twenty-five years ago. From England. She worked as a primary school teacher and John as a motor mechanic. They never had children and both of them retired ten years ago. No family in Australia or elsewhere either that they ever spoke of. Adrian Kaufman seems to be their closest friend. He would know more."

"And before moving to Australia?"

"I don't think I ever heard either of them talk about it. Isn't that odd? I never picked up on it till now. It's as if it never existed."

"Did they ever mention or reference specific names of people? Are you aware of anyone other than Adrian who has ever been involved with either of them?"

Kate shook her head. Their whole friendship had been based on common interests through Possum Walk. And Kate's family. The Robbins knew everything about her own family background. She frowned, realisation hitting her too late that she had been entirely oblivious to critical red flags, which in hindsight were right under her nose all along.

"Are you sure, Kate?" Detective Abbott's voice pulled her from her thoughts.

"The only person I recall Mary telling me about was an old colleague in England who died. A woman. I can't remember her name. It was just after we met. She didn't really mention individuals from the Orchid Society either. Mary didn't gossip or speak uncharitably about anyone."

Both detectives glanced across at the mirrored wall. Ah ha! It was a one-way window.

"John spoke about a woman named Rosie a few times when I visited him," Kate offered. "He said Mary didn't like her." She wasn't prepared to tell them about Mary allegedly killing Rosie, according to John. "Not sure how seriously to take what he says now. He doesn't appear to have many good days and his thoughts ramble at times."

Another glance at the mirrored wall. Kate was sure that someone was there on the other side, watching and listening to the interview. Adrian? Other detectives? What did it matter?

"And what did he say about this person Rosie?"

"It's all a little confusing, to be honest. He said everything changed during a shopping trip. Seemed like it was a long time ago. But I think it was just a fantasy."

"Please go on." Both detectives watched her closely, their gazes fixated. Kate barely breathed under the scrutiny.

She let out a deep sigh. "He said Rosie was to blame and he was sworn to secrecy. Mary would be upset with him if he talked but she had secrets too. Apparently she didn't like kingfish. Random I know." She shrugged at both officers. "And by the way, he said there was evil everywhere. Frankly, I thought it was just a jumbled, fantastical mess. Now, I'm not so sure."

Her words fell into a suddenly strained silence, which seemed to stretch on. Was it something she'd said? Abruptly, both detectives stood.

"We'll be back shortly," Detective Abbott said as they both left the room.

Twenty-Five

Kate didn't know how much time passed. The camera in the corner continued to flicker its red light. Watching silently. She was painfully conscious of who might observe her from the other side of the mirror, so she remained still with little expression on her face – as much as humanly possible under the circumstances. Which created a stiff neck and the discs in her back screaming in protest from her rigid posture. Her facial muscles were numb from the tightness of her jaw. She was a mess. And apparently *in* a mess!

Her body was still sore from the assault in several places and this exacerbated her discomfort. She wondered what the police wanted from her. She knew nothing useful about the Robbins but what she had discovered in the past hour was that the police thought she did.

She was such a fool. At least where the Robbins were concerned. Kate was the 'what-you-see-is-what-you-get' kind of person. She thought they were too. But she was wrong. And she felt betrayed by that revelation. Yet another trust broken in her life. Had they lied to her and used her friendship like they must have used others to protect their secrets? For they had secrets. Secrets that someone wanted to kill for.

There was a part of her that wanted to believe her friendship with the Robbins had been genuine, not a sham. She cared for Mary, for both her and John. They spent many wonderful times, laughing together, playing cards, bantering over the latest political story. There had to be some kind of logical explanation for what was unravelling. She had no idea what that might be. She was going to work her hardest to find out. With or without help.

The opening of the door interrupted her thoughts. Detective Abbott and Adrian Kaufman entered the room. Adrian's presence surprised her.

"I have permission to sit in on the interview." Adrian sat on her side of the table. Once again, she glanced at the mirror on the wall and wondered if he had observed the previous session.

"Kate, thank you for your cooperation today," Detective Abbott said.

"Detective, before we go any further, please tell me. How was John attacked?

"I'm not at liberty to say much at this stage, as it's an ongoing investigation." He turned to Adrian. "Is there anything you'd like to say, Adrian?"

"Yes." Adrian watched her intensely. "John had a lucky escape, Kate. Someone tried to poison him with those cherry chocolates you both love so much and then injected insulin into his body. And he's not diabetic."

"Oh my God! Is he going to be alright?"

"Yes thankfully. The night nurse saved him on time."

Kate shook her head and hugged herself tightly, suddenly feeling cold. "I've read about this. Insulin is deadly for non-diabetics. How did he survive that and the poison?"

"As I said," Adrian replied, "the night nurse saved him. Even though he'd eaten quite a few chocolates, the poison wasn't enough to kill him straightaway. And the insulin took longer to react because he had so much sugar in his system from the chocolate."

Kate knew all about the body's response to insulin. She'd researched it as part of her novel. And loved the idea for a murder scene. She frowned as a whisper of fear floated into her mind and floated back out. A fleeting thought.

What if...

But her mind refused to take it any further.

"It's been a big few days for everyone." Detective Abbott abruptly moved away from the table. "We will continue this interview tomorrow. My colleague and I will attend your home in the morning."

"Again?" Jumping to her feet, Kate's shock at hearing about John being poisoned turned to anger. "What more do you want from me, detective? I've given you all the information I have. I just don't understand. Am I missing something?"

Both men exchanged glances. "If it's alright with Detective Abbott, I'll be there tomorrow too." The detective nodded his agreement.

Kate didn't need any support, she told herself. But she admitted to feeling a little comforted knowing Adrian was going to be there with her.

"Well, that's settled," Detective Abbott said. "This interview is over."

Twenty-Six

Day 18 – Morning

Kate woke early. Her eyes felt heavy and swollen. She'd tossed and turned for most of the night and couldn't get Mary and John out of her mind. Someone had murdered Mary. She was sure of it, more than ever now. And then there was John. Poisoned. Who were these people, the Robbins? And who wanted them dead?

By the time Detectives Abbott and Penrose arrived, she felt no better. Adrian was with them. He nodded to Kate but remained silent.

Detective Abbott went through the usual preliminaries but this time he added, "You are currently just a person of interest. No one is accusing you of anything. But we need to examine everything in relation to your involvement in the Robbins' lives. Do you understand?"

Kate nodded, a small measure of relief appeasing her anxiety. Detective Abbott wasted no time in getting back to questions.

"I'd like to discuss the cherry chocolates you gave John on your visits. Do you have any chocolates in the house right now?"

"Yes, of course."

"Would you be prepared to give me your supply to have them tested?"

"You think I poisoned chocolates and gave them to John?" She jumped to her feet. She finally realised what his line of questioning was leading to. Adrian gently pushed her back down in her seat.

"Unfortunately, someone did. John Robbins nearly died because of it," detective Abbott said.

"And you think it was me?" Kate heard a buzzing in her ears and felt sweaty and hot. She struggled to breathe, as if someone had suddenly sucked the oxygen out of the room. Oh God! I'm going to faint, she thought in a moment of panic. She forced the fear down and took deep breaths to calm herself. But she couldn't stop the nervous trembling rippling through her body. She was on the brink of a panic attack, she was sure of it. She had to fight it because she had nowhere to run and hide.

She gulped down precious air, hoping to ease the tightness in her chest. She saw Adrian give her a puzzled look. In a last valiant effort to quash her nerves, she hastily excused herself from the room and locked herself in the bathroom. Splashing cold water on her face, she willed the rising anxiety to ease. She scrubbed at her face vigorously, hoping the coldness of the water would relieve the heat coursing through every pore.

She didn't know how long she was there. It felt like a long time. It might only have been minutes. A gentle knock on the door made her jerk upright.

"Kate?" Adrian's voice. "Everything okay?"

"Yes. I'll be out in a minute."

As she raised her face to the mirror, the sight of her wet hair from the splashing and drained and grey appearance alarmed her. She quickly applied face powder and tied her hair up in a knot. She was relieved the panic attack had indeed subsided. That had never happened before. When she rejoined the others, they simply acknowledged her return and continued where the conversation left off.

"Let's discuss John's attempted murder," Detective Abbott said. "His favourite chocolates were syringed with poison. The same type of chocolates you gave him. Rhonda Kavich and Paula Vincent saw him once soon after Mary Robbins' death. There have been no other visitors, apart from Adrian and yourself."

"This is absurd. Each time I brought him chocolates, John ate them and he never got sick. I would never harm John!"

"Do you know how many convicted murderers have said similar words over the years?" the detective said dispassionately.

"I can't believe what you're accusing me of. It's like I've fallen into a nightmare." Horrified and in shock, she grappled with the genuine possibility of being charged for a crime she didn't commit. She trembled uncontrollably and her voice shook from the effort. She hoped this time, if her panic reared its head, she could resist it.

"A simple gesture of kindness to a friend," she whispered. "Believe what you want. I have no motive, nothing to gain and no murderous intent towards anyone. Why am I under suspicion?"

"You understand we have to undertake a thorough investigation of all leads in this case? Either eliminate or incriminate. The fact is you brought John Robbins chocolates and poisoned chocolates nearly killed him. You have a supply of chocolates in your home. You spent a lengthy period of time with Mrs Robbins the day she died. You had means and opportunity."

"And with what motive?" she shot back. It was unnerving the way her innocence was being twisted into something ugly and far more sinister.

"I haven't figured that out yet," Detective Abbott responded. "But we'll get to the bottom of it, I promise you," he said calmly. "This case has many layers and we are unpeeling them one by one."

He turned and spoke quietly to Detective Penrose for a few moments. She handed him a piece of paper she retrieved from a file in her hand. He seemed satisfied with what he read.

"Do you have any objections to our officers searching your house?" he asked Kate.

Kate was numb. They wanted to search her home for evidence linking her to John's attempted murder. But they wouldn't find anything.

"I have nothing to hide, Detective." Defiance laced every word.

Within minutes, four uniformed police officers entered Kate's house, handing Detective Abbott a document.

"We took the precaution of obtaining a search warrant before coming here." He waved the document in front of her. "It's unnecessary to execute it now that you have given your consent to search the premises, Kate."

This morning's visit was well planned and Kate had no doubt they were prepared to execute the warrant if she resisted.

Adrian addressed her for the first time that day. "You may walk through each room with the police officers. If you do, note what they take away from the premises. I strongly suggest that you avoid making any comments because they could be used against you later."

"They won't find anything incriminating, Adrian." She was frustrated and bewildered. Although still shaken, outwardly she appeared calm, even though her voice probably gave her emotions away.

"Are you okay?" he whispered. "I've been worried about you."

She shook her head but refused to answer. He had the nerve to be worried about her after the way he'd behaved towards her the last few days. It hurt her and she was having none of his concern.

Systematically, Detective Abbott and the police officers searched each room. They took all the chocolates she had stacked neatly in the kitchen cupboards and a few other foods. In Kate's bedroom they stopped to sniff perfume bottles and talc, various tubes of medicines and lotions.

When they finally reached the study, they stopped. Just like Mary did the first time she entered Kate's study. Everyone, including Adrian, stared with the same shocked expressions on their faces. Standing proudly on the shelf along one full wall were many bottles and jars Kate had carefully assembled and labelled with a range of poisons.

Kate groaned inwardly. She could easily explain it, except Adrian advised her not to make any comment. This looked bad, with no help from her right now. She stayed silent.

It was only one agonising, frozen moment in time. Rapidly, the police officers galvanised into action. They moved as one to the shelf of bottles, opening various ones, finding nothing. Sniffing again, finding nothing. Detective Abbott moved quickly to the computer on her desk, unplugged the hard drive and gave it to one of the police officers who then put it inside an evidence bag. Kate bit her lower lip to stop from saying anything to him. Her hard drive held her latest draft manuscript, several articles she'd saved from the internet about poisons. She bit her lip even harder as she recalled her latest search on Adrian Kaufman. They would enjoy that one, she suspected.

Detective Abbott continued his search at her desk. He opened drawers, removed USB sticks, disks and other items. He even took a notepad resting on her desk that she kept for ideas or reminders about follow-up actions.

A few days ago, she printed a draft of the first half of her novel and placed it into a folder. The detective took that as well. She opened her mouth to say something but stopped herself. Instead, she crossed her arms, suddenly feeling chilled and alone.

She firmly believed nothing in her house would implicate her in the eyes of the police because she could explain everything they found. However, observing the contents in her study through the detective's eyes made her reconsider. She breathed a sigh of relief that they didn't find the still missing research folder. That would have been worse! It didn't bode well for her that she was investigating different ways to murder people without being caught, especially because she was convinced she'd now progressed from 'a person of interest' in the eyes of the police.

She received an itemised list of everything taken from her house for her records. Two hours later, when she finally shut the door behind Detective Abbott and his parting words of "I'll be in touch" still ringing in her ears, she was exhausted.

Slowly, she felt the tightly coiled tension which had gripped her release from her body. The past two hours certainly took their toll. For one agonising moment, panic welled up inside her again. She had nothing to hide, yet she felt alone and vulnerable. She dreaded what would happen next.

***

Late Morning

Kate was so distraught and preoccupied with the morning's developments that she didn't immediately see Adrian sitting quietly at her dining table, waiting for her. Their eyes locked for the longest time, his cool and speculative, hers worried.

"So, you have nothing to hide, Kate Trellow?" Adrian's eyebrows rose as he watched her, a grim expression on his face.

"I can explain, Adrian. This is a horrible misunderstanding."

"I want to believe you, Kate. I truly do. Just as I start to trust you, something else happens that makes me wonder if you are genuine or hiding something. Maybe you're brilliant at playing the part, fooling everyone with your innocent manner. Or perhaps you're..." he hesitated, gesturing his arms, seeking the right words, "...just unwittingly caught up in this unfortunate mess and everything is one giant coincidence. Either way, you don't add up."

"I'm exactly what you see," Kate responded wearily. "I'm missing the big picture, something in plain sight but it's intangible. I can't quite figure out why I'm implicated."

She sat next to him. She rested her elbows heavily on the table, putting her face in her hands. It was only morning but she felt drained and tired.

"I'm the prime suspect in John's poisoning, aren't I? And probably Mary's murder."

Kate pulled her hands away from her face. Her body ached, drained of energy. A bitter laugh escaped her.

"Because I gave him some chocolates. Who put the poison inside them is the mystery. I have no idea why the police hounded me since Mary's death with question after question, interview after interview. They must think I know something more than I'm telling them. The funny thing is that I don't know what that is."

"Go on," Adrian encouraged her.

"I think it has to do with Mary and John's past somehow. But I am aware of only the information they shared with me. And you," she looked directly into his eyes, "you are involved too, only I don't know why or how. So you see, I'm really not much use to any of you after all. I have plenty of questions but sadly, no answers."

"Tell me about the bottles lined up on the shelf."

"They're empty. Nothing in them. I have them as props. Research."

"Research for what?"

She hesitated. Should she tell him about her book? After today's police search, it was bound to come out regardless. Surprisingly, she felt embarrassed. Someone who dealt with hundreds of crime cases during his professional life would think her writing interest amateurish.

"A novel," she replied reluctantly. "I'm writing a murder mystery set in a retirement village similar to Possum Walk where several murders take place."

You're what!" Adrian didn't bother hiding his astonishment. "You're researching murders? Let me guess. Poisons specifically?"

She flushed at his reaction but nodded. "It's the preferred modus operandi of the murderer. Specifically, poisons which are readily found in household items that don't require special sourcing. Like rat poison or anti-freeze." Her nerves were frayed.

"I see," Adrian relaxed back and directed a small smile towards her. This was a promising sign, for it was the first one she'd seen all day from him or the police. "I suppose your novel is in the hard drive the police just took away. Including research on the different poisons?"

"Yes. Except for my research folder which I can't find. It's a printout of all my ideas, medical information and scene outlines for the various murders. I know it's not environmentally responsible to print everything, but it works for my brain."

Adrian stared at her for the longest time, a lingering smile giving her hope that he finally believed her. Why that was important to her, she would decipher later. For the moment, she was happy to have someone who didn't watch her with suspicion or plied her with intimidating questions.

"That explains a few things." Adrian's manner had definitely softened.

Kate was relieved. She wanted to clear up any misunderstanding quickly. Her priority was to explain things to Detective Abbott and clear herself of any suspicion. She wondered if Adrian would support her in achieving this now.

An unexpected theory so extreme and unbelievable popped into her mind. She'd felt the beginnings of the idea at the police station when Detective Abbott informed her of the attempt on

John's life with an insulin shot. At the time, she pushed it aside but now it gnawed at her and she couldn't ignore it. Her heart raced at the possibility. It couldn't be. Frowning, she bit on her lower lip and massaged her temple.

"That's odd," she murmured, stunned. Why had she not made the connection before? "Adrian, my research is -" How could she verbalise it? She could hardly breathe. "It's all connected!" She paced across the floor. She was too agitated to sit still. "I came across an article about a husband who killed his wife. Somehow, he damaged the wiring of the electric blanket. Just like in Mary's case, it created a fire and then she died. The husband tried to convince the police it was an accident but he was found guilty and sentenced to life in prison."

"Could be a coincidence." Adrian frowned, but he didn't sound convinced.

"There's another scene where I killed the victim with poisoned chocolate. I thought it was a clever idea and printed it out. That's in my missing folder too." The bewilderment in her voice was evident.

"And your research folder has been missing since -?"

"A month ago. Last time I saw it was before I flew to Queensland to visit my daughter and grandkids." Kate felt nauseous. She couldn't believe what she was thinking. Her theory was so plausible it was chilling. Could it be possible that someone stole her file and was now using her research to kill the Robbins?

"You're right. It's too much of a coincidence to ignore," Adrian replied.

Kate was relieved he didn't dismiss her theory as outrageous. "The facts are glaring. After the attempt on John's life, Mary's death was deliberate. There's no doubt in my mind. There is a connection between the two. What were the Robbins involved in that made them deadly targets?"

Adrian looked away from her probing gaze. He was about to be evasive again. Kate saw it in his stance.

"Don't dismiss me again, Adrian. I think I deserve some answers, don't you?"

"I can't compromise the Robbins' situation. They are caught up in something that occurred a long time ago and has resurfaced in the present. With dire consequences. Your association with the Robbins might also put you in danger and I can't, no, I won't, allow that."

"I'm prepared to take that risk. It's my choice."

"But I'm not prepared to hand it over. I'm sorry. Someone assaulted you once. Probably the same person responsible for what's happened to the Robbins. It's best you know as little as possible."

"Impossible situation! I think we are all in danger, to be frank. We can confidently assume the murderer lives here at Possum Walk. Easy access to the Robbins. And to my research. It gives me the creeps imagining how that person got their hands on my folder. Is it someone who has visited me in my home? Someone I interact with regularly? Or did they break in?" She shuddered. "Someone who is fearless and clever enough to disguise themself as a nurse to get to John. Can you at least give me something?"

"It happened a long time ago. There's nothing to be gained from it now."

"Except my friend is dead and someone tried to kill her

husband. And use my research to implicate me with the chocolates I gave him."

"I'm sorry. I wish I could give you more. The Robbins and I have a long history together. They've been such an integral part of my life that it's difficult to let my guard down, especially now when one is dead and the other nearly died."

He shook his head, a weary expression on his face. "It's been a long few weeks for all of us. But there's one thing I'll agree with you on." Stony-faced, his eyes seemed to pierce her very soul. "Someone living at Possum Walk is a murderer."

Twenty-Seven

Rhonda peered out of her front window for what felt like the hundredth time watching Kate's house. The police cars arrived a little over two hours earlier. The detective who'd interviewed her and her buddy were the first to arrive. They entered the premises followed closely by Adrian Kaufman. About half an hour later, four uniformed police officers also walked into Kate's house. Frankly, Rhonda was intrigued. She had a good instinct and it told her Kate was in some kind of trouble.

After a considerable time, the uniformed officers emerged, each carrying a large bag packed full. The two detectives followed behind. Kate's house had been searched and the police had taken evidence away! This was serious indeed. What could Kate possibly have done to earn that public disgrace?

In Poland, searching people's houses preceded throwing one or more of them in jail, never to be heard from again. The communists were very efficient. At least that was her experience growing up. Here in Australia, she knew it was not quite as dangerous. Nonetheless, this situation brought back memories she'd long buried. She didn't want those ugly reminders to intrude on her life ever again and would do anything to make sure of it.

She noted with interest that Adrian Kaufman was yet to leave. Rhonda continued to watch Kate's house for any further activity. Still no sign of Adrian Kaufman. The story unfolding before her was riveting, better than the movies. She couldn't wait to tell Paula all about it.

Thank goodness for Paula, she thought as she glanced at the house directly opposite her. Paula was out again. She worked three days a week as a teacher's aide. She must ask her where she went and what she did every other day. Maybe she liked shopping because she seemed to buy a lot of things for a woman living alone. What impressed Rhonda was Paula's apology, offered the very week she'd moved into Possum Walk.

"I was rude when you welcomed me to the neighbourhood. I'm sorry. I was preoccupied with getting the furniture organised and felt overwhelmed."

She also brought with her a freshly baked cake as a peace offering. Rhonda felt resentful at first when she opened the door and saw her standing there.

"Any nuts in that cake?" Rhonda asked sharply.

When Paula shook her head and said, "lemon and raspberry cake," Rhonda softened. From that day, Rhonda cautiously started to form a friendship of sorts with Paula. Although a little on the quiet side, Paula's calm demeanour soothed her fractured nerves and excitable nature. What had Paula called her once? Passionate. She liked that description. She liked it very much indeed.

"You are such a good woman, passionate about what you

believe in and I want to support you, truly I do. I don't care what others say about you."

Rhonda was deflated by Paula's last words but then immediately dismissed them. She refused to dwell on small-minded people's opinions of her!

"What's that horrid man doing here?" Rhonda muttered. Rick Lewis walked past her house towards Kate's home. He'd missed the police by a few minutes. She hurried outside to stop him.

"What are you doing here, Mr Lewis?" she called out to him. "You have no business at Possum Walk."

"I heard the police were here," he replied, walking back towards her. He didn't seem fazed at all by Rhonda's words. "Just checking it out."

"Well, leave that poor girl alone. She's not done anything wrong, despite what the police think."

Rick came up to stand on the veranda with her. "Can you tell me what happened?"

"None of your concern. Now, please leave."

"I know a lot more than what the police are telling the residents here. It's a crying shame they are keeping you all in the dark."

Rhonda's curiosity was peaked. "What do you know?"

He paused for a moment before answering, "I know the fire was no accident."

"I knew it!" Rhonda couldn't keep the satisfaction out of her voice. "No one will listen to me. I said all along the fire and Mary Robbins' death were suspicious. The police have been acting strangely around this case. Even Kate and Adrian are up to something."

"I agree and that's why I'm still hanging around. There is definitely something and it's got to do with the Robbins' past."

Rhonda gave him a long speculative gaze. She was intrigued and blatantly curious to know more. And Rick Lewis seemed to have the answers. The temptation was hard to resist.

"Would you like to come in for a cup of tea, Mr Lewis?"

Twenty-Eight

Day 19 – Afternoon

"Mr Robbins? John?"

He barely heard the words. A woman's voice. The sound softly reached him from a distance, washing over him gently. He tried to open his eyes but they felt heavy and he didn't have the strength.

Someone, the woman's voice again, gently shook his arm. "He's regaining consciousness slowly. That's a good sign. He needs to build his strength through natural sleep now."

A beam of light intruded and he squinted against its brilliance, pushing at its annoying presence. Who was John?

"Stop," he rasped in protest.

"John. It's me. Adrian."

This time, he recognised the voice. He tried again to open his eyes but his exhaustion was overwhelming. Sleep took his hand as he drifted off.

The next time he was aware of his surroundings, all was quiet. His gaze moved around the room, cloaked in darkness. He was in a hospital bed, he realised, but didn't know why. The only light came from a machine with a protruding tube going into his arm. He knew it was night. City lights reflected faintly against the glass.

His mind swirled with images, faces, sounds he didn't recognise. A laughing young woman, an older man, familiar scenes - yet not. He experienced a wave of happiness and love. He didn't recognise them, neither the people nor the places, but he felt safe. Frowning, he sensed being safe was very important. It was like he was on the edge of something that was significant but couldn't quite grasp.

His mind suddenly shifted to another swirling scene. An alleyway. The sound of shots being fired. Her beautiful face was fearful, teary. Strangely coloured eyes, full of rage. Devil eyes. He'd just glimpsed hell!

A nurse entered the room, startling him out of his thoughts.

"You're awake, John!" She smiled as she switched on the overhead light. "I'm Libby and am looking after you tonight. How are you feeling?"

The terrible images quickly dissolved, his mind emptied. How was he feeling? He mulled over the question for a moment. He didn't know how he felt. Panic gripped him, threatening to suffocate him. He didn't know!

"Where am I?" he asked, his body shaking.

"You've been very ill," the nurse replied gently as she went about checking his vitals and noting them. "You had a close call. But you're going to be alright now."

Why did she call him 'John'? He didn't feel like a 'John'. The name didn't sound right somehow. He knew that deep down and couldn't explain it.

"I don't remember," he finally offered. "I remember nothing." His panic increased. "Not my name, where I live, my birthday, nothing!" He felt himself struggling to breathe.

"It's to be expected after what you went through." The nurse's soothing tones helped calm him a little, but the panic remained just under the surface.

"What happened to me? How did I end up in the hospital?"

"You had pneumonia. The best thing for you is to sleep. You need the rest. In the morning, you'll feel much better."

He took a deep breath to quiet his anxiety. She was right. He felt drowsy again. In that moment before he succumbed to sleep, a fleeting image of a young petite woman in his arms, laughing up at him, made him smile.

"Goodnight, my love." He closed his eyes.

Twenty-Nine

Day 20 – Morning

Rhonda was impatient to tell Paula all about yesterday's events and was on her doorstep just before nine o'clock. Surely Paula would be up and having breakfast? She was curious too to check out Paula's house. Paula had never extended an invitation to Rhonda to visit, even though Rhonda had welcomed her into her own home many times.

"Paula!" Rhonda pushed past her as the door opened. "You missed a most interesting day -"

She stopped in mid-sentence, a shock wave ripping through her body. The living room before her was the stuff of nightmares. Boxes and baskets covered the floor, some still overflowing and others empty, as far as she could see. Clothes littered every piece of furniture in a haphazard manner. It looked like a tornado went through the house, leaving destruction in its wake. She gaped at Paula.

"I'm – er – still unpacking," Paula signalled towards the room.

In that moment of total astonishment, Rhonda recalled her

mother's words repeated over and over since she was a child. *"Always maintain a clean and tidy house, Rhonda."* Her heavy Polish accent added to the seriousness of her message. *"It's a reflection of your character."* Rhonda believed her. Over the years, her experience proved it repeatedly.

Rhonda looked at her friend, still trying to reconcile what was in front of her with her opinion of Paula. They didn't match. And was that a glimpse of resentment she caught in Paula's eye before she quickly turned away?

"I see," she said. "Why didn't you say so before? I'd be happy to help you sort it out. Would take no time with the two of us." She regretted the words, dreading the possibility that the other woman would take up her offer. "After all, that's what friends are for," she added, more to convince herself rather than Paula.

Smiling her acknowledgement, Paula said, "I missed an interesting day?"

Rhonda spent the next ten minutes describing everything she saw at Kate's house the day before. They both stood the whole time because there was nowhere to sit but it didn't deter Rhonda. She didn't mention Rick Lewis and the conversation they'd shared. He gave her a lot of information strictly in confidence. She respected that.

Paula appeared engrossed. "I think Kate is in some kind of trouble," she said.

"It's to do with the fire and Mary's death, I'm sure of it. The detectives running the case were there. And why did they search and remove items from her home?" Rhonda paused before adding dramatically, "Someone killed Mary! And covered it up with the fire."

Paula's eyes grew large and round. "Kate?"

"No! She's not the murdering kind. But someone sure is."

"Rhonda. You are mistaken. The fire was a horrible accident. Why do you say such terrible things?"

"Kate insists that I'm wrong and counter offers a different version. Don't you think that's a little suspicious? How did an electric blanket get back on Mary's bed? And how could it be so dangerously faulty? I'm not buying it. One way or the other, I'm going to get to the bottom of this."

Paula remained quiet, a frown marring her pale skin. She appeared deep in thought. After a few minutes, Rhonda shook her gently.

"Everything alright, Paula?"

Although she appeared startled, Paula recovered quickly. "Yes, of course. I was reflecting on what Diego said to me once. I want to be certain about what it means because it might become important."

"What are you talking about?"

"Every time I overheard you or others talk about the fire, particularly your suspicions about Mary's death, it disturbed me. But didn't understand why. My instincts told me I was missing something vital, but it always escaped me."

"Go on, Paula," Rhonda urged her to continue.

"A few days after the fire, Diego came to see me, quite disturbed and told me – told me that…"

She struggled to find the words and looked down at her clasped hands. She was nervous and uncomfortable, Rhonda realised. Paula wouldn't look at her.

"Whatever it is, it's going to be alright." She wondered what could be so worrying for Paula. Paula's eyes welled up with tears, which surprised her.

The other woman took a deep breath before continuing. "It was something Diego told me. A few days before Mary died, he helped her carry in a parcel from her car. It was a new electric blanket, one she purchased that very day."

"What! I don't believe it! How can that be?" Rhonda scrambled in her head for an explanation. "Diego was probably drunk as usual and imagined the whole thing. I wouldn't depend on his word."

"I don't know, Rhonda. I thought so initially, but he was sober. Mary told Diego that she regretted dumping her perfectly good blanket. She was determined to get inside and immediately remake the bed. Diego mentioned that she had become fed up with the cold.

"I simply refuse to believe his stories any longer. He told a few of us once that his family comes from Mafia roots. He certainly doesn't act like a Mafioso. Of course, he was drunk at the time. What nonsense."

"The Mafia?" Paula appeared visibly startled.

Rhonda's anger mounted. How dare he tell such outrageous lies? She would confront him and get the truth out of the pathetic man. He was weak and would fold quickly pitted against Rhonda.

"He told you he is part of the Mafia?" Paula repeated.

"Has he never told you his story? In all the time you've spent together?" Rhonda gave her a knowing look.

Paula flushed but shook her head. "Never. He doesn't strike me as the Mafia type."

Rhonda's anger made her churlish and she knew it. "What is a Mafia type according to you?"

"You know. What you see in the movies, on the television. Tough, ruthless, all powerful men."

Rhonda scoffed. "That's such a cliché."

She eyed her friend with renewed interest. There was a distinct aloofness that contradicted Paula's friendly yet quiet demeanour. She was a bit of a loner. And must have had a sheltered upbringing.

"Despite your efforts to the contrary," Rhonda continued, "you don't strike me as being worldly. And yet you have an air of mystery about you too."

Paula's stance stiffened. "I don't understand what you mean."

"Exactly my point. How could you?" Rhonda sighed, letting go of her anger. It wasn't Paula's fault she was gullible where Diego was concerned.

"Thank you for confiding in me, Paula. Diego is a good man, but he battles his demons. His memory as a result is not always reliable."

Paula nodded. "Yes, I see everything clearly now."

"I'll get the truth out of him, eventually. What you told me doesn't change my mind about the fire being deliberately lit." She paused for a moment, deep in thought. "And how does Kate fit into it?"

***

Afternoon

Kate slumped into the chair at her empty study desk. Gone were her computer, files, notes, everything. She glanced over to the empty shelf. The police had even taken her jars of non-existent poisons.

She didn't realise how strongly she would react to the police search. Put simply, it felt like a home invasion. The feeling of vulnerability, her life being exposed to strangers, as the police removed items into those plain paper bags. With each item, they stripped away a layer of all she held dear in her life. She was powerless to stop it and felt victimised.

She was innocent. And she would prove it. But where to start? She stared down at the bare desk where once her desktop computer sat, the copious files and notes next to it haphazardly piled high, threatening to spill over any moment. She had an uphill battle ahead of her without the resources at her disposal. Of course it would be simpler if Adrian confided in her, she thought mulishly.

For over two years, Mary and Kate shared stories about their lives. Mary's dry humour often led to many stories and factoids about her teaching days. There was much laughter over funny comments made by her young students. John's mad passion for vintage cars was the perfect retirement gift from his career as a motor mechanic.

Kate knew a lot about the Robbins' twenty-five years in Australia. She realised how clever Mary had been. For Kate knew nothing about their lives in the United Kingdom. And worse, she'd never really noticed till now. She recalled a conversation between the three of them several months ago, the only time Mary mentioned her younger years. The Robbins invited Kate for a roast beef dinner one evening.

"This meat is so tender, Mary. And the gravy is to die for!" Kate enjoyed Mary's English cooking.

"It's one of my favourite meals," Mary replied. "Mum used to make this once a fortnight. Couldn't afford to have it more often. We all looked forward to it and counted down the days to the next one." She laughed at the memory.

"The anticipation always makes it extra special. Did you have many brothers and sisters, Mary?"

It was at that very moment John's hand shot out over Mary's plate to reach the jug of extra gravy in the middle of the table. He grabbed the handle, only to fumble and spill the contents all over the white linen. By the time everything was cleaned up, the question was forgotten.

When later in the meal Kate asked again, John interrupted with a comment about the social committee and the conversation moved in another direction. At the time, she thought little of it. Now in the cold light of day, Kate suspected John deliberately created diversions to avoid answering the question. And Mary had been careless in bringing it up in the first place. It added up in Kate's mind. Those invisible United Kingdom years were crucial.

Chills ran up and down inside her as she grappled again with the fact that someone who lived at Possum Walk had murderous intent against the Robbins. And that he or she was hiding in plain sight. The real possibility that her research was aiding and abetting their crimes was insane. Inspector Abbott must be told as soon as possible. It might exonerate her and prove her innocence. She desperately hoped this nightmare would end soon. That by some minor miracle the killer would be caught quickly.

Hope! There was a word. Four harmless letters. She clung to them.

Thirty

Day 21 – Early

Something was wrong.

Three days and still no news of John Robbins' death. This morning, a phone call to the hospital enquiring after him was disturbing. Instead of a *"Sorry there is no patient by that name"* the response was *"Please hold."* Perhaps a routine response and therefore nothing of concern. But panic set in and the call abruptly ended. Ringing back might draw unwanted attention.

John Robbins was surely dead. Pumped with enough Valium in the chocolates and then the insulin injection to make him so. No one survived such a chemical onslaught on their body. Especially someone of his older years who was not diabetic. The insulin would have rendered him unconscious, quickly followed by a massive heart attack. The one regret was not witnessing his last moments. Too much of a risk to linger.

Not so with his wife. It had been pure joy to watch the fire lick against her unconscious body. It had all been her fault. Her fault for pushing her nose into other people's business. Her fault for not keeping her mouth shut all those years ago. The family always took care of its own. She had no right to challenge it. Maybe, if she'd just walked away, she would still be here today, blithely living out her twilight years in this godforsaken place called Possum Walk. No more would that woman's traitorous face cause the sickening feeling deep in the pit of the stomach, the constant hatred that was constrained with increasing difficulty.

And then the perfect opportunity. The perfect murders.

Thanks to Kate Trellow, who meticulously researched and recorded every detail. In Mary Robbins' case, a trial run of Mary's old electric blanket she'd disposed of was successful. It wasn't until the spark ignited the flame which ignited the sheets... Well, as they say, the rest was history.

In John Robbins' case, the investigators would inevitably trace the poison and quickly classify his death as a homicide. That was merely a technicality. There was bound to be more intense scrutiny now. Especially after the wife's death.

None of it mattered anymore. What was essential was his permanent demise. With no trace back to the least likely person. No one would ever suspect who the killer was.

But how to be certain he was dead! Deep and dangerous emotions welled up at the possibility he may have survived. Twisted inside like a venomous snake looking for its prey. The pain was almost too unbearable. After nearly thirty years, it was finally over.

Or was it? Being plagued by doubts at this late stage was unacceptable. Adrian Kaufman knew. As did Kate Trellow. But they were tight-lipped, with no outward show of emotion regarding John's current status.

This mission had taken its toll with the constant struggle to maintain a false persona. It sometimes felt overwhelming. But the impetus to see this to the bitter end was powerful. The actor forever on stage waiting until the next scene.

Finally, behind the contact lenses, the eyes glazed over. The pupils dilated to pin points. The mouth salivated and spit spilled down both sides. There were no witnesses to gasp in fear at the madness, at the incoherent mumblings.

"Don't give up. You're near the end." The words were comforting.

"What an obedient child you are. Mummy would be so proud." The ache was intense.

The voices had returned.

Thirty-One

Late Morning

Diego lived next door to Rhonda. She was determined to confront him after the lies he told Paula. The nerve of the man! She knew his drinking would get him into serious trouble one day. And this was the day. Rhonda was not having any of it.

She saw Paula's blinds open. Good! She was home. Quickly making her way to her friend's house, she convinced a reluctant Paula to accompany her. Diego's welcoming smile disappeared when he saw both women on his doorstep.

"Diego Santo, you have some explaining to do!"

Rhonda pushed past him into the house. Paula lagged behind. Rhonda noted he was unsteady on his feet. Drinking again, she sniffed. And also caught a waft in the air of a wonderful smell of spaghetti sauce. She had a fleeting thought of wonder at how he could still maintain his cooking talent under the influence!

"What's this nonsense about Mary Robbins buying a new electric blanket a few days before she died?"

His look of surprise spoke volumes. "I don't understand."

"Did you tell Paula you helped Mary unload it from her car?"

"No! What is this about? That never happened." His bloodshot eyes swelled with tears. Turning to Paula he said, "Why would you say something like that?"

"You mentioned it to me a few days after the fire," Paula replied gently.

"It's not true. You're my friend. We are good friends, I thought. Why lie about something like this?"

The man was insufferable. Cried at the drop of a hat! Rhonda was unmoved. Paula clasped her hands tightly together. She appeared uncomfortable.

"Don't lie, Diego. Why would Paula make up such a story?"

Diego slumped into a nearby chair. He looked bewildered, a frown marring his forehead. He was no tall, good looking Italian man, Rhonda thought dispassionately. At best, plain, stocky and short described him. What did Paula see in him?

"I – I – have memory lapses sometimes," he said. "But above all, I am an honest man."

He managed to stand up, awkwardly but with stiff resolve. He looked Rhonda straight in the eyes.

"It must be the truth if Paula said so." He crossed his arms firmly, as if daring Rhonda to challenge him. "And what if I did? She bought a new electric blanket. Good for her!"

Rhonda was surprised at his defiance. He was not a docile drunk!

"I've stopped to talk to Mary – and John – many times," he continued. "I often helped her with her shopping if I was nearby. I don't remember this incident. For the last few weeks, my memory comes and goes. It's frustrating and so I've made an appointment to see a doctor about it." His eyes filled with tears again.

"That's a very convenient explanation, Diego. I. Don't. Believe. You." With each punctuated word she poked him in the chest. And with each poke, he moved and weaved back a step until he was hard against the wall.

Just as well he'd reached the wall, Rhonda deduced, because he was unable to hold himself up steady for much longer.

"Leave him alone, Rhonda," Paula pleaded, her gaze anxious as she watched Diego struggle to remain on his feet. "It doesn't matter. It changes nothing. Mary Robbins is still dead."

"You are a sad person, Diego Santo." Rhonda's anger waned. It always did in the end. Paula was right. It wasn't worth it. She had to set free the obsession she had and the suspicions around the fire that killed poor Mary. The pot of sauce simmering on the stove top reminded her of how hungry she was. In her urgency to see Diego, she skipped breakfast. Diego caught her glance at it. Surprised to see him move effortlessly into the kitchen, he stirred the sauce lovingly, almost like a caress.

"What an odd man you are, Diego Santo." Rhonda shook her head in surprise at his sudden agility. And his tears were gone.

"Cooking makes me happy," he replied, softly.

"You need professional help, Diego!" Rhonda bit back. "Get off the vino, eat less pasta and you will be better for it. Make sure the doctor puts you into one of those rehabilitation programs."

"Want some pasta, ladies?" he teased.

Rhonda rolled her eyes, let out an exasperated sigh and turned to leave. Paula smiled her goodbye and followed behind.

Thirty-Two

Early Afternoon

"I wonder what demons drive Diego to drink," Rhonda said. "When I first met him, he was garrulous, fun loving, sometimes even cheeky. Like just then. Yes, he enjoyed a drink or two at happy hour, but who didn't?"

As usual, they were back at Rhonda's house. She turned to a silent Paula, who watched her calmly.

"Diego didn't consume wine as much in the early days," Rhonda continued. "But in recent weeks, it's escalated to a point of being dangerous."

"What did he mean by seeing visions and hearing voices?" Paula asked. "That's a bad sign for a drinker. Terrible."

"He's a grown man who should know better."

Rhonda gazed at Paula. A mousey figure, she thought. Whilst petite in stature, Paula had a Plain Jane look about her. Rhonda couldn't fathom what drew Diego and Paula to each other. Their friendship made little sense. Their personalities were very different. And surely Paula would not put up with the drink either.

"It's strange, Paula," Rhonda gave her friend a thoughtful look. "You never mention Diego or how much time you spend together."

"There's nothing to say. We are friends, that's all."

"Today, you showed care and concern for him. He called you a 'good' friend."

"Of course. That's what friends do for each other."

And yet, since the fire, Paula and Diego spent little time together. Up to that fateful day, they regularly shared walks, sat next to each other at the clubhouse, even went for swims in the heated pool together. Rhonda had seen them often enough.

Not so any longer. Interesting. Very interesting. Mary's death had adversely affected everyone at Possum Walk in different ways. Perhaps Diego and Paula were victims of that fallout too.

"You're better off without Diego. Until he sorts himself out, he is no good to anyone," Rhonda snapped. "Least of all to himself."

"Are your suspicions about the fire now squashed?"

"I suppose so," Rhonda replied reluctantly. "If Diego carried a new electric blanket out of Mary's car, then it changes everything. Even though he doesn't remember it right now."

"The fire must have been an accident, a terrible tragedy."

"Yes, an unfortunate case of faulty equipment. It happens." Rhonda didn't really sound convincing, even to her own ears.

The likely explanation of faulty equipment offered Rhonda a window of hope. She prayed the nightmares that haunted her every night would stop. She'd controlled and manipulated much of her life up to now. Sheer survival instincts. But her dreams? They tortured her in their own unique ways.

She glanced at her watch. Time for Yoga soon. Perfect timing. She looked forward to these classes, which always relaxed her body and soul.

Rick Lewis would have to wait.

Thirty-Three

Day 22 – Afternoon

Kate was physically and mentally exhausted and still reeling from the crippling effects of the police interviews and house search. What made it worse was she'd heard nothing from Detective Abbott or any police officer in four days. Four long and agonising days.

Her day started badly. She had emails to follow up on. The distraction would be welcome and so pushed herself to spend some time on the computers available at the clubhouse for residents. However, she could clearly see that her day was doomed. Other residents occupied all four computers. It seemed they'd settled in for a long time.

As she attempted to exit the clubhouse, Rhonda called her over to where she was sitting with several other residents, Paula, Julie French, who was Kate's next-door neighbour, and Cathy Eldridge amongst them. A motley crew indeed, she thought. She saw Diego at a safe distance in the billiards room to the side of the main community space, playing pool with a few other people.

She caught Paula's eye, who grimaced at her with a shrug. She must know why Rhonda called her over. Kate's exhaustion made her a little grumpy, so she would not be so forgiving of Rhonda's typical directness today.

"Kate, we were just discussing poor John and wondering how he is. Julie suggested we send him a care pack. Cathy suggested flowers. I think I should do the right thing and visit him again. He missed his wife's funeral, which was for the best, really. Has his health improved enough for him to have visitors now?"

That was the last thing she expected from Rhonda, given her one and only visit to John, had distressed her. She hesitated. The police had released no information to date, so it wasn't her call to reveal the attempt on John's life. It was too risky given the murderer was yet to be exposed and living in Possum Walk.

"That's not a good idea, Rhonda," Kate replied with a hint of irritation. "As far as I'm aware, he can't have visitors just yet."

"How is he?" Paula asked with a little shiver. Kate recalled Paula's sensitive reaction to John's episode when he went to 'the other place'. She'd left abruptly.

"I've heard nothing recently, to be honest." Which was true. Neither the detective nor Adrian had given her any update on John's health.

"I thought you would be more informed about John's well-being after the police visit the other day." Rhonda stared at Kate meaningfully.

What a witch! Suddenly, all eyes were on Kate and watched her with increasing interest. Rhonda would have absorbed everything from her window with glee, watching the police leave with bags full of evidence. Rhonda knew exactly what had taken place and she made sure Kate realised it. There was no need for a response.

"Maybe I'll call the hospital and ask if he can have visitors," Rhonda persisted.

From the corner of her eye, she caught Diego silently edge towards the group. No one noticed because their backs were to him. He was avidly listening to the conversation.

"That's up to you, Rhonda," Kate replied sharply. "But I wouldn't be surprised if he's not well enough to accept visitors."

Rhonda seemed determined and Kate was not in the mood to argue with her about the pros and cons of visiting John. She quickly said her goodbyes and left before anyone else interrupted her.

Five minutes later, she was in her car, eager to get to the library. Adrian tapped on her side window as she reversed out of her driveway.

"We need to talk." He looked grim, angry. She hesitated. "It's urgent!"

Kate groaned. What now! Her stomach churned in response. Her head suddenly pounded. Once inside, he didn't speak straight away. Instead, he paced the floor. His agitation was plain to see.

"What's happened?" Kate couldn't stand the suspense.

"The police are on their way."

She didn't expect that.

"Within the hour," he added.

Her heart sank and experienced a sudden dizziness and

nausea. With the last dregs of energy, she mentally and physically pulled herself together, as much as she could. She was determined not to collapse. She just couldn't!

"Am I going to be arrested?" she asked quietly.

"No. But you have some serious explaining to do."

"About what? I've told them, and you, everything I know. There's nothing else to tell."

"You've been concealing the truth about what you know. Repeatedly, you professed your ignorance about the Robbins' history, their background. And lied all along. You nearly had me fooled. I should have known better. And then using the ruse of a missing research folder and how it mirrored the crimes."

"I don't understand. I know nothing more than what I've told you all. And my research folder *is* missing."

"Good try," he sneered.

"It's true! The solution to everything that's happened to Mary, to John, is in their past. In England. And my research is being applied by the murderer."

Adrian's smirk didn't soften. He shook his head at her. He clearly didn't believe her.

"Why am I telling you what you already know?" His stance exasperated Kate. "For goodness' sake! It's all your fault! If you weren't so stubborn about it, and trusted me enough to share what you know, I wouldn't be trying to do my own detective work. Why would I possibly want to hurt Mary and John?"

"Trust. Now there's a word." His tone dripped with mockery. "You don't have to pretend any longer, Kate. It's all there. The police found the evidence on your hard drive."

"What evidence?" Her mind quickly went over what she had stored on her laptop. She had no idea what it could be.

"You've been playing me since we met." Adrian was relentless. "What I can't understand is why? Either someone got to you or... Who are you working for? Who's behind all this?"

The doorbell rang. Neither moved, eyes locked, charged emotion flowing between them. It rang a second time. Followed by a sharp knocking.

Kate was the first to turn away. She waved both detectives Abbott and Penrose inside. A quick glance outside told Kate there were no other police cars present. Perhaps they too were on their way.

"I thought I told you to wait for me to get here, Adrian." Detective Abbott looked annoyed.

"I need answers," Adrian responded tightly.

"We'll discuss that later." The detective would not let him off lightly, it seemed.

Kate stood quietly, bracing herself for what was surely going to be another gruelling session.

"I assume Adrian told you why we are here today?" Detective Abbott turned his full attention to her, his eyes piercing.

"Frankly, he's made no sense since he arrived. Just get it over with, detective. I don't have a clue what incriminating evidence you found as part of your search. But I sound like a broken down record repeating myself over and over. I'm confused, I'm exhausted and I'm discouraged."

"Well, let's start with the following," he said as he took out some notes. Detective Penrose did the same. "For the moment, I remind you that you remain a person of interest in this case."

Kate let out a sigh of relief, knowing she wouldn't face arrest today. Her headache continued to thump hard against her temple regardless.

"You won't be surprised to hear we uncovered information from your computer about a range of murder scenarios, poisons, case studies, and the manuscript you're currently working on," the detective said. "Interesting read, by the way. You're good."

"Er – thankyou detective," she murmured. His unexpected compliment took her aback. Hysterical laughter bubbled up inside her, but she quickly squashed it. His timing was bizarre.

"Let's continue." His tone was brusque once again. One sweet moment of reprieve and then it was gone. "Here's the other interesting thing. It was easy to link most of the data to your novel. Even the poison chalices on the shelves."

Was the detective having fun at her expense? Kate's bewilderment grew. Adrian remained silent and sullen. Never once did he take his eyes off her. She felt herself squirm under his compelling gaze.

"What about my research that's missing? Did Adrian tell you about that?"

"Yes. Unless we have details or evidence, we can't really consider a folder that doesn't seem to exist or has disappeared. I think you understand what I mean."

Kate was gobsmacked. Of course, her research was part of the evidence. "Can't you link it to the websites in my search history?"

"We are onto it. Admittedly, we found a few references to specific scenes which are similar. A strange and chilling theory."

"Theory, detective? I think it's a genuine possibility," Kate persisted.

"Let's discuss another interesting find on your computer. A curious section that didn't fit in with the others." Detective Abbott paused as he frowned at her.

"I don't know what that might be, but you're going to tell me, aren't you, detective?" Kate's agitation grew.

"Lidia Ciambella."

Those two words hung in the air. Kate felt an electrifying jolt through her body, leaving her speechless. The room fell into a vortex of silence and dragged for long, agonising moments.

"The Mafia Queen?" Kate finally croaked and mentally kicked herself. Too late, she remembered the day she'd searched the internet for information on Adrian's background.

"What is your interest in her?"

"Nothing specific," Kate replied cautiously.

Painfully aware of Adrian watching her carefully, she couldn't tell them the real reason was her curiosity about Adrian. It would mortify her. More importantly, Kate couldn't predict how he'd react. Not well, she guessed.

"I came across her by chance," Kate said, which was the truth. "Her story fascinated me." Which was also true. "The rise and fall of the first woman to lead one of the most powerful Mafia clans in Italy - now there's a story! It gave me lots of ideas for a future book."

Adrian finally spoke up. "Ideas? Of all the thousands of crime stories in the world, how did you land on her?" His voice was softly deceiving. She sensed an undercurrent of tension in his words.

"I really don't know," she shrugged. "It was just a lucky find. I scroll through the internet all the time. You can see for yourself in my search history."

She saw the disbelief in his eyes and flushed under his continuing scrutiny.

"Are you sure that's all it was?" Adrian sneered. "There might not possibly be any other explanation?"

"What more do you want me to say?"

Adrian and Detective Abbott exchanged a peculiar look. They seemed to communicate because she saw Adrian nod slightly at him.

"Did you know," the detective said slowly, "that Adrian was heavily involved in Lidia Ciambella's case when he was in the Australian Federal Police?"

So Kate's instinct about Adrian's big break in an international case was correct after all. "No, I didn't know," she replied. "Wait!" She turned to Adrian, puzzled. "You were with the Australian Federal Police, not the State police force?" No wonder she found nothing about his career in state government data. He was a federal agent.

"Yes," he nodded. "I was part of an international taskforce for several years. But that's a story for another day."

"It's curious, don't you think?" Detective Abbott resumed. "The one case that impacted Adrian's life forever is found on your hard drive. What are the odds?"

"I see how this might look, detective. But I assure you, it is a mere coincidence. It must be a rather famous case under the circumstances, but I'd never heard of Lidia Ciambella before. When I stumbled across it, the story captured my imagination.

A young woman who rose to be the Mafia Queen, dominating and surviving in a man's world. That alone is remarkable. Then to be charged with the murder of one of her own."

"It was one of the longest trials in Italy lasting nearly three years," detective Abbott said. "She received a life sentence."

"Only to be murdered in her cell just before her fiftieth birthday," Kate continued, turning to Adrian. "Were the rumours true it was a hit by the mob? Even from prison, she must have been a threat – or liability. It would make a great movie!"

Adrian didn't answer her, instead turning to the two detectives. "I'm not convinced!" he snapped. "She's holding back information. I know it!"

Kate didn't bother to hide her confusion. They were wasting time and effort quizzing her about the case of a Mafia Queen who lived and died on the other side of the world nearly thirty years ago.

"Why the interest of a local detective in a long-ago international case?" she said to no one in particular. "It makes little sense. Other than it was a case Adrian worked on many years ago."

Even before Kate finished speaking, the world tilted on its axis, leaving her breathless and disoriented. Her mind went blank, unable to comprehend the sudden turn of events. There was a connection between the individual cases of the Robbins and the Mafia Queen. She'd accidentally stumbled onto something big.

"Both cases are linked!" she said, turning to Adrian for confirmation. They stared at each other and for a heart-stopping moment, time stood still. She saw a flicker of something deep in his eyes, but his expression gave nothing away.

"Who are you working for?" Adrian resumed his attack.

Kate shook her head slowly at him. He'd never believe her denials or explanations, she realised. She didn't know how to convince him otherwise. Feeling mixed emotions and frustration, she needed time to consider what she had just learned. They were all connected to this case. Adrian, Mary and John Robbins. That had to be it. If not, why the hostility and suspicion?

"I think it's time for a break." Detective Abbott's voice pushed into her thoughts. "Adrian, come with me."

Both men went outside. Detective Penrose, who up to now had not spoken, finally turned towards Kate.

"It's been a rough time, hasn't it?" She sounded sincere. "How are you holding up?"

Kate refused to let her guard down. The other woman was a police officer, after all. "I'm okay," she replied, distracted by the unexpected developments of the past half hour. Her mind was buzzing in overload.

She tried to recall all the information she'd read about Lidia Ciambella, her profile in the international criminal underworld. She'd been tough, a force to be reckoned with in a man's world. Until she got caught in a murder.

Mary Robbins warned her against asking Adrian questions that last day. Perhaps it was less about Adrian and more about her and John's own history. Was this the case that brought them all together? Where deep friendships formed?

Once again, that sense of betrayal by her friend reared up inside her. Mary had lived a lie. Was their friendship part of that lie? On a fundamental level, she really didn't believe it was. Adrian accused Kate of playing games. Deplorably, she was the one who'd been played. By all of them. If the subject was classified, Mary should never have spoken about it.

Detective Abbott returned. Alone. His poker face was in place once again. A quick nod to his offsider, who moved beside him.

"Is there anything else you'd like to add to your statement today, Kate?"

"Where's Adrian?"

"He received an urgent call from the hospital."

"About John?" Kate's heart sank. "Is he alright?"

"He didn't say," the detective replied evasively.

"I hope John hasn't relapsed. He's had so many challenges."

"Adrian will keep us informed if anything develops. But now, back to the matter at hand. Is there anything you'd like to add to what we've discussed today?"

Kate felt guilty about the one detail she'd deliberately omitted. She'd not been exactly truthful about why or how she'd stumbled across the Mafia Queen. Not being totally transparent scratched at the edge of her conscience. Her conscience won out.

"I found the Mafia Queen online because I was searching for information on Adrian Kaufman." A wave of relief washed over her.

"We assumed as much when his name appeared several times in your search history." Detective Abbott seemed pleased with himself. "Yes," he continued, "we uncover these things pretty quickly, Kate." Kate flushed at his dry tone. "The question is why?"

"It's simple. I was curious. He knew why the Robbins' lives were in danger and, of course, refused to reveal anything to me. Mary once told me Adrian was involved in a high-profile international drug bust several years ago. John claimed Adrian knew their secrets. I believed him." She hesitated before adding defiantly, "despite his dementia."

Detective Abbott nodded. "Go on."

"I felt compelled to understand why Mary died. It seemed so..." She struggled to find the right word. "Futile," she added. "I owed it to her."

She felt her emotions close to the surface. It had been a tough day, one of the worst she'd ever experienced. So much to absorb, to consider. She exhaled slowly before continuing.

"In order to do that, I had to try to unravel the mystery of why the Robbins were targeted and who might wish them dead. I had no choice."

"I see," Detective Abbott replied, glancing at his colleague. Another silent exchange between them. "And what have you concluded?"

"That's just it! Nothing yet!" Her frustration was unmistakable. "It's so much easier plotting and weaving murder scenes and mystery in my novel!" She took a deep breath. "I wasn't certain that the Lidia Ciambella case applied to Adrian. Until today. I don't know how or why the Robbins are involved. For surely they must have been. And now there's a risk of whatever secrets are in place being exposed. Otherwise why your interest – or Adrian's fixation - on my so-called involvement? If someone stole my research folder, they are the murderer. No shadow of a doubt in my mind. I have no motive. It makes little sense. You have the wrong girl, detective."

Detective Abbott finally relaxed his expression. Turning to his colleague once again, he said, "It appears to be as you surmised, Joyce." Giving Kate his full attention, he continued. "It seems you have been one unlucky woman. With thanks to my colleague here. She's the one who called it from the beginning. A comedy of errors."

"Comedy of errors?" Kate looked from one to the other, puzzled.

"Your meddling in this case nearly landed you in prison," Detective Penrose said. "You were caught up in a sequence of events so complicated, so unusual, as to be unbelievable. Only it's all true."

She grinned at Kate, shaking her head at the same time. "It was plain to see from the outset but we had no choice but to throw the book at you, to grill you relentlessly. Due diligence being what it is, we had to eliminate every possibility about your innocence or guilt."

"You mean I was never seriously a suspect?" Kate wasn't sure whether to be relieved or angry.

"Let's not sugarcoat this," detective Penrose said. "You definitely were a person of interest. High on the list. Particularly after the attempt on John Robbins' life by poisoned chocolates. Chocolates you brought him to the hospital. We had to examine all the evidence. We are now satisfied you had nothing to do with either Mary's murder or John's poisoning."

Kate felt tears of relief well up. The nightmare was finally over. They believed her. Her body trembled, an involuntary reaction after the intense scrutiny she'd endured. Whether Adrian believed her now that the police exonerated her was another matter.

"Thank you detective, both of you," Kate's voice quivered with emotion.

"We need to get on with finding the real offender, Joyce." Detective Abbott made his way towards the front door. "Kate, I'll arrange for your things to be returned to you today."

"Wait. There's something else you need to know."

Both detectives turned to her.

"I think you should interview Rhonda Kavich. She thinks she saw a person jump the fence the night of the fire. Between the Robbins and Diego Santo's houses. She's been reluctant to come forward because she's not sure of what she actually saw. Could have been an animal."

"We'll follow up on this information as soon as possible," detective Abbott replied. "Thank you for alerting us to it."

"One more moment of your time please, Detective." Kate still had so many questions. "Mary and John Robbins' connection to the Mafia Queen. Did it have anything to do with drugs?" She thought of Diego's story about his family and the ruthlessness of the Mafia. She shuddered at the thought of something similar occurring to Mary and John.

"Their lives were in danger because of something that happened in the past." Kate continued. "Adrian's role as a federal agent must have been pivotal. What I don't understand is what happened?"

"Unfortunately, I can't tell you," detective Abbott replied. "It's still highly classified at a national and, in fact, international level. Not for the Victoria Police to disclose. We will continue to work with federal and international colleagues to find out who's behind Mary's death and John's attempted murder."

Kate's disappointment showed.

"Don't worry, Kate," detective Abbott reassured her. "You have good instincts. You just might figure it out first."

As both officers took their leave, Detective Penrose turned back to her and chuckled.

"Kate. Try to stay out of trouble from now on."

Thirty-Four

Early Evening

They told him his name was John. John Robbins. He didn't believe them. It was not a name he recognised. And now a stranger, a doctor, gazed down at him with a grave expression on his face. A nurse stood silently beside him.

"You gave us quite a scare this time, John," the doctor said. "How are you feeling?"

"Like a truck ran over me – twice," he winced. His voice sounded shaky. The pain was everywhere. Not pain exactly. More of a deep ache which radiated through his body. He felt bruised and battered. Tubes, which were secured to his arm and the back of his hand, connected to an IV bottle hanging beside his bed. The monitor blinked a lot of numbers and graphs, quietly doing its job.

"What happened to me?" he asked.

"You had another heart attack, but you're going to be just fine. You need a good rest and time to recover your strength."

"Another heart attack? How many have I had?" He was alarmed to hear it. He didn't remember having any heart attack.

"Now don't fuss over it. What matters is you getting better. Quickly."

Another man entered the room.

"Adrian!" He recognised his friend instantly as he grasped his hand and held it to his chest. Adrian had a worried expression on his face as well.

"How are you feeling, old friend?" Adrian's voice was gentle. "You've given us quite a scare, John."

"Aching all over. Is my name really John? I didn't want to believe it when they told me. I don't think it is." He glanced at the doctor and nurse behind Adrian.

"I've known you for many years and indeed, your name is John Robbins."

He mulled over that information. He knew he implicitly trusted Adrian with his life. But didn't know why. He couldn't remember anything other than this man was important to him. His name must be John Robbins if Adrian said so.

He must be truly ill if he couldn't recall details about himself. Every now and then, he saw fleeting images swirling in his mind, but nothing specific. Accompanied by a sense of loss and uncertainty that he didn't understand. He closed his eyes. The tiredness was taking a hold of him. He heard Adrian speak quietly to the doctor.

"Does he have any lingering symptoms after the coma?"

He was in a coma? He kept his eyes closed, hoping to hear more.

"We're not sure yet. His dementia has been steadily progressing over the past few weeks and since the coma, it's unclear if it will escalate. Three days is a long time."

"And the insulin overdose?"

"Frankly, Adrian, he should be dead after such a high dose. Fortunately, the chocolates he consumed increased his sugar levels and his body didn't take the full impact straight away. The night nurse came early to check on him and basically saved his life."

"And should we be concerned that he's had another heart attack so soon?" Adrian's voice was heavy with worry.

"His body has gone through a lot. His heart is weak. We'll continue to monitor him closely for the next twenty-four hours. We should know more by then."

His heart rate jumped in response when the doctor's words finally sunk into his brain. His eyes snapped open and panic set in. Alarm bells rang on the monitor. Both the doctor and the nurse rushed to his side. It took less than thirty seconds for the drug to take hold once the doctor administered it through the line in his hand. His panic subsided and he felt relaxed and sleepy. But he had to know. Before he succumbed to sleep. He grasped Adrian's hand to pull him closer towards him.

"Adrian, please tell me it's finally over." His voice was an urgent whisper.

Adrian nodded reassuringly. "Yes, it's finished. You're going to be alright now. You're a tough guy."

"I hope so," he sighed. "Because I won't allow the evil to force me to my knees ever again."

As he drifted off to sleep, a familiar name came to him,

floated into his mind like a soft cloud finding its resting place. The name wasn't John Robbins.

Thirty-Five

Day 23 – Morning

Kate wasted no time in seeking Adrian out the next morning. She'd slept fitfully worrying about John and what had caused Adrian to rush off to the hospital the day before. She stood on his porch for a few moments to calm her nerves and subdue the feeling of dread from taking a hold of her.

Adrian didn't believe her. In her. Despite the police clearance. She was innocent. Instead, he accused her of working with someone to kill the Robbins. Which was absurd. For a federal agent, he was single-minded and stubborn. At least where she was concerned it seemed.

The door opened. "Come in. I saw you standing out there. Stalling." He flinched, giving her a semblance of a smile.

"I'm worried about John. Detective Abbott told me you received an urgent phone call from the hospital."

"Come in, Kate." She hesitated. "I promise not to bite." He sounded remorseful. "I'm sorry about yesterday. My behaviour was unforgivable. I guess I owe you an explanation."

Once inside, she watched Adrian pace the floor before her, agitated. He seemed to do that a lot. His face was pale, the dark shadows under his eyes a giveaway that he probably wasn't sleeping well. Perhaps not eating properly either. The burden of responsibility for his friends, first Mary's demise, then the attack on John, was taking its toll.

"When's the last time you had a decent meal?" she asked.

"Er – I..." He stopped pacing. "I can't remember, to be honest."

"Right! I'm going to make you some breakfast and then – then we talk. Just tell me one important thing. Is John okay?"

He nodded. Finally, he sat down and relaxed into the sofa.

"Good. Breakfast it is."

Fifteen minutes later, he tucked into a plate piled high with toast, eggs, grilled tomato and sliced ham. She joined him at the table with a cup of tea whilst she nibbled on a piece of fruit.

"I needed this," he said, between bites. "Thank you."

He sipped from the steaming cup of coffee she'd placed in front of him. When they cleared the table and refilled their cups, she was ready for answers.

"Is John going to be alright?"

"He suffered another heart attack."

"Another? You mean he's had one before now?"

"Yes, the night someone tried to kill him."

"I suspect as a result of the poison he ingested in the chocolates."

"I think so, combined with the insulin shot. Staff recalled seeing a person in the shadows of the corridor. It must have been the killer dressed as a nurse. Couldn't tell if it was a male or female. The killer plied John with chocolates injected with Valium, followed by a lethal dose of insulin."

Kate felt nauseated, lightheaded. "Go on," she whispered.

"He would have died except the night nurse, the real one, checked on him earlier than scheduled and found him in the middle of a heart attack he wasn't even aware of."

Kate listened with growing horror. Her hands grew clammy and cold shivers radiated throughout her body. It couldn't be true. Not again!

"I wrote that same scene a few days ago." Her voice trembled. "I double checked the details of the murder to make sure they were medically authentic. It's all there in the missing research folder. I curse the day I printed the information. I should have kept everything electronically."

"Whoever stole your research is our murderer. And it validates the theory he or she lives right here in Possum Walk." Adrian's words were sobering. "John consumed so much chocolate that he had high levels of sugar in his system. Enough that the insulin overdose didn't affect him immediately. The killer made a mistake this time."

Kate tried to digest everything Adrian revealed. Someone at Possum Walk went to the trouble of stealing her folder and then deliberately applying the research to plot the Robbins' murders. But who could that possibly be?

"When I found out that Lidia Ciambella appeared in your search history, I didn't want to believe that you might be responsible. And, in my thinking, there was no way it was a coincidence. I couldn't move past it. Finding who did this to Mary and John is all I care about. To see justice done."

Kate wanted to be honest with him too. "I stumbled on Lidia Ciambella's name by accident. I saw a small article from a British newspaper dated over twenty-five years ago that caught my eye. As I explored further, I became obsessed with finding out more about this Mafia Queen. On the one hand, her life story fascinated me. It also repulsed me.."

"I felt the same when it all went down." He gazed intensely at Kate. "That's a story for another day. I promise I'll share it soon. Please trust me for a little while longer."

"Of course. I understand."

"Which brings me to my outburst yesterday." Adrian took a deep breath. "I'm sorry for behaving so badly." She heard the sincerity in his voice. "You seem to bring out the worst in me. My actions where you are concerned have been inexcusable."

"No more accusations?" she asked, with a hint of mischief and a faint blush on her face.

Adrian laughed. "Agree. Truce?" He offered her his outstretched hand.

His grip was firm, warm, causing her heart to miss a beat. Kate's breath caught in her throat. She suddenly became aware of his nearness, the smell of his essence. Her heart fluttered. She didn't know where to look.

Embarrassed, she stepped away from the table to put some distance between them. Her reaction to him took her by surprise. What was wrong with her? She felt like a giddy teenager on her first date.

Thankfully, Adrian seemed oblivious and remained seated. "Joyce, Detective Penrose, told me from the beginning that you weren't anything other than what you presented, that I was looking under rocks where there was nothing to find. But they had to be certain and prove it."

"A 'comedy of errors' is what they called it," Kate replied softly. She'd manage to pull herself together.

"It sure was. And now there's no time to waste. We have a murderer to catch."

"Agree. Mary and John got involved in the Mafia Queen case. Which led to their being in danger all these years later. Just what, why or how I haven't figured out yet." She looked at Adrian expectantly.

"I can't tell you," he replied. "I'm desperately trying to find out who's behind this after all these years. Working with the police at all levels. It's complicated."

"So you were an Australian Federal Police officer throughout your career?"

Adrian nodded. "My commanding officer recommended me to the international taskforce. It was the chance of a lifetime."

"And that's how you met the Robbins?"

"Yes. But that's all I can say for now."

"How can I help?" That was the least she could do.

"It's too dangerous. We are dealing with a ruthless murderer who has flown under the radar all this time at Possum Walk. Someone who carefully planned two murders and succeeded in one. I don't want you in unnecessary danger."

She knew that's what he would say. And understood why. Eventually, the police would uncover the culprit and solve the mystery. But whilst there was a killer amongst them living in Possum Walk she couldn't afford to let her guard down, couldn't trust anyone.

Who could the killer be?

Thirty-Six

Day 24 – Morning

Kate woke with a start. Something had disturbed her sleep. Frowning, she listened for what it might be. The chime of the doorbell reverberated in the house. Twice in quick succession. Someone was impatient. By the time she reached the front door, her head was clearer.

"Adrian!"

His appearance shocked her. He looked as bad as she felt right now. His blond hair was sticking out from all angles. No wonder. He kept combing his hands through it in a nervous gesture. What startled her more was that he was unshaved and looked like he'd just jumped out of bed. Her mind automatically turned to John Robbins.

"What's wrong? Is it John?"

"No, nothing like that."

She was alarmed. She glanced at the kitchen clock. It was seven thirty. Too early for anything except bad news.

"The police have called an urgent meeting for residents at Possum Walk, scheduled for eleven o'clock this morning."

"What are they planning?"

"I don't know. Detective Abbott has been unusually tight-lipped about it. He sent me a text early this morning to alert me."

"Perhaps they're giving an update, maybe even about the attack on John's life?"

"It's likely that's what it's about. Perhaps to make a statement about the fire. The Fire Services should have completed their investigation by now. We'll know more in about three hours," Adrian replied, his expression grim.

"It's going to be a long wait," Kate sighed.

Both their mobile phones pinged at the same time. A text message. From the Possum Walk community managers.

"The Victoria Police has called an urgent community meeting for residents of Possum Walk at eleven o'clock this morning in the club-house. The police are urging everyone to prioritize their attendance, if possible."

Kate looked up from her phone. "It seems the wheels are in motion for an announcement. Why do I feel apprehensive?"

"It's normal to feel like that, especially when we don't know what we're walking into. In the meantime, I'll contact Detective Abbott and try to get more information out of him."

"We need to watch the crowd today," Kate said. "Gauge individuals' reactions as the session proceeds. The murderer won't pass up the chance to hear what the police have to say. Maybe they'll drop their guard."

"That's true. But you must stay out of the way. The police will already have plans in place."

"There's nothing dangerous about making observations and comparing notes afterwards, is there?" she asked innocently. She knew he was uneasy every time she offered her help.

Adrian looked at her in frustration. Once again, he combed his fingers through his hair with jerky movements, making it even messier, if that were possible.

***

The residents' reactions across the board to the text message were pretty much as Kate predicted. A few who had work commitments dismissed it as they prepared for their day. Most were curious, even anxious, about what was going to be said and promptly scheduled it into their calendar. A handful were ambivalent and didn't care one way or the other if they attended the meeting. But they might as well go along. They had nothing else to do.

One person experienced immense glee. Did a little dance in their kitchen.

"John Robbins must be dead!"

The toast burnt, the kettle boiled and the cup with a spoonful of coffee grains left unfilled. It didn't matter. Nothing mattered anymore.

It was going to be a wonderful day!

***

Late Morning

Over one hundred residents gathered in the clubhouse for the meeting. By the time Kate arrived, it was standing room only. She stood at the back of the room to give herself a vantage point from which to observe the crowd. Too late, she realised Rick

Lewis, the reporter, was also standing nearby. They nodded to each other, but neither spoke. There was a steady hum of voices as everyone waited for proceedings to start.

Adrian stood with Detectives Abbott and Penrose at the front of the room with three other uniformed officers, two of them from Fire Services. He was angry, although most people would not notice the subtlety. Whilst he appeared at ease, she saw the tightness around his mouth and his stiff and unyielding stance. He and Kate had no chance to speak to each other prior to the meeting. She mentally braced herself for what the detective was about to say. Her stomach twisted in knots and the nervousness simmering under the surface heightened.

"Ladies and gentlemen, may I have your attention, please?"

Detective Abbott's voice rang out across the room. He used the microphone on the podium.

"Thank you for making yourselves available at such short notice. This session has been called to give you an update on the investigation of the fire at the house of Mary and John Robbins and the subsequent death of Mary Robbins. After we present the information today, we will be available for a short time to answer questions. I must remind you it is an ongoing investigation and we may not have the authority to address all of your concerns."

Detective Abbott referred to a wad of notes in front of him. "We have two major updates to share with you today. It's especially important that you receive the information prior to a press conference that Victoria Police is holding later today."

A collective murmur echoed across the room. Residents

shuffled in their chairs as though trying to get more comfortable. The tension among those present was electric.

"First, a quick recap on what we have so far. Investigations into the cause of the fire have been completed. The police have interviewed all residents. Relevant staff and contractors too. Forensic medical officers have completed a post mortem on the deceased."

Detective Abbott stopped, peering into the crowd of residents. Anticipation filled the air. If she didn't know better, Kate suspected he'd paused for dramatic effect, his poker face well and truly in place. He looked down at his notes for several moments. It seemed like forever in Kate's mind.

The tension in the room, the restlessness amongst the residents, heightened. People turned towards each other, as if seeking comfort. The crowd seemed to hold their collective breath. Kate's own tension escalated. She felt a coil of anxiety rise inside her, trying to escape, and she struggled to push it down.

"It has been a time of upheaval and uncertainty for all of you over the past few weeks. We can now reveal the investigation found evidence that is conclusive regarding the fire at the Robbins' house and Mrs Mary Robbins' death. Evidence gathered confirmed the fire was a deliberate act of arson. Toxic levels of sleeping pills were found in Mrs Robbins' system, which we believe caused her to become unconscious. As a result, the fumes overwhelmed her, which ultimately caused her death. This case is now a homicide."

For several seconds, the room fell into a stunned silence as the shocking revelation hung in the air. But then, everything erupted. Several residents stood abruptly, causing their chairs to fall over with the force. Their shocked expressions reflected the reaction of most of the people present. Kate let out a long breath she didn't realise she was holding, her heart racing at a rapid rate. Hearing the detective's stark words was unsettling, the admission of arson frightening.

"Please remain seated." The detective's voice grew louder and the microphone boomed eerily. It took several minutes for the room to quieten. Detective Abbott appeared under a lot of pressure but Kate thought he managed the situation fairly well under the circumstances.

"Please stay calm," the detective continued. "We have more information to get through. We know from the forensic evidence that the fire was deliberately lit. The wiring of an electric blanket on the bed had been slashed in places. As a result, it sparked and ignited as the blanket heated, severely compromising its integrity."

The detective's sobering words caused a chill down Kate's spine. She glanced at Adrian. He had not moved, nor had his expression changed. But she instinctively knew he was hurting and haunted by the image of his friend's last moments.

"Regrettably, as the case has become a homicide, it also means that Possum Walk is a crime scene. Police will set up a temporary base at Possum Walk from today. If you have any information that you believe may be helpful to the case, even if it's only a minor detail, it may be the one of most significance. Be assured we will overlook nothing to solve this case."

Several residents asked questions from the floor but Detective Abbott motioned them to stop.

"There is a second and final announcement. Many of you

are aware John Robbins has been in the hospital for some time. A little over a week ago, whilst in the hospital, there was an attempt on his life, the details which are unnecessary for now. Thankfully, he survived and is going to make a full recovery. Investigators believe this attack is linked to the death of his wife."

There was no stopping the frenzied reaction from residents following that statement. For several minutes, the detective let the crowd take it in, absorbing all they had heard. People hugged each other, others cried, some remained stoic. Shock greeted Kate as she looked around, which reflected the powerful impact of the police announcements.

How would Rhonda be feeling right now? Kate searched the crowd for her. There, seated next to Paula. But instead of a look of triumph she expected to see on her face, she looked stunned, rooted to her seat. Frowning, Kate wondered at her reaction. Surely after the other woman's persistent suspicions, she would be jubilant. But no, she showed no reaction. Perhaps she felt overwhelmed at the truth of what she suspected.

"We are seeking specific information from anyone at Possum Walk of any suspicious behaviour leading up to the fire. During the next few days, we will conduct further interviews with residents. And we will continue to pursue this case. I promise you we will do everything in our power to solve it quickly."

For the next half hour, a barrage of questions from residents followed. Detective Abbott contained the frenzy quickly as he directed residents to speak into a roving microphone. People directed several questions at the Fire Service officers while others were directed at the police. Overall, the questions were predictable.

As Kate made her way towards Adrian, Rick Lewis stepped in front of her.

"That was intense," he said wryly.

"It had to be done, Mr Lewis."

"It seems most residents were oblivious to the possibility of arson or murder. I found that interesting for arson was a hot topic around here during the past few weeks as I've interviewed a number of residents. At least now, people will be more aware of their surroundings. And friends." He gazed at her speculatively. "I don't suppose you have suspicions about who the killer might be?"

"Do I look like I do?" she said in exasperation. He asked the most ridiculous questions for a reporter.

"Somehow, I think you do, Kate. And maybe you believe as I do that the suspect lives right here at Possum Walk. Are you fearful for your life?"

"You're the last person I'd share any thoughts with, Mr Lewis. So you might as well give up on your questions. Because I'm not giving you any answers."

"And do you have any comment about John Robbins and the attempt on his life?"

Kate didn't reply.

"I'd even go further and suggest the suspect may live in your street. What would you say to that?"

Kate was startled. Did the reporter mean Diego? Who else would he be referring to? And why? She didn't trust herself to speak and walked away.

"What was that about?" Adrian asked as she reached him. He nodded towards Rick Lewis, chatting to a group of residents.

"He wanted to know if I suspected anyone of the crimes. He added that the suspect lives at Possum Walk, maybe in our street."

"He's fishing," Adrian replied. "People are going to look at each other as potential suspects, or worse, as murderers, from now on. Which is why I pleaded with the police not to release all the information in one hit. But they insisted because the press conference later today will announce it anyway. They believe the residents have the right to know before the media does."

"I agree. It would be worse to see or hear about it through the media. This meeting was a good compromise."

"The murderer may be harder to uncover and remain undetected among all the surrounding hysteria this meeting has surely created."

"You're right," Kate said. "Which is why we need to act quickly by identifying some suspects of our own. We have access to more evidence about the Robbins than is public knowledge."

Adrian gave her a quizzical look. "We? Kate, I've told you before to keep out of it. It's dangerous."

"We could make a good team," she said lightly. "If you let me help."

Adrian gave her an exasperated look. "You never let up, do you?" But he smiled.

She grinned back at him. The mood between them eased. She knew what had to be done. They parted, agreeing to meet again later that day after the press conference.

Kate was grateful for the time to follow up on her own suspicions, a couple of residents who required a closer inspection. Diego for one. She'd noticed him earlier, sitting quietly at the edge of the crowd, not interacting with anyone. His claims and counterclaims about what he saw and didn't see the night of the fire were contradictory.

What about his family's connections to drug wars and the Mafia? Given the Robbins' connection to the Mafia Queen, was there also a Mafia link to Diego's background? That was the most promising lead.

Rhonda was the other person who fascinated Kate. She had insisted the whole time the fire was no accident, nor Mary's death. Why so adamant? What else did she know she wasn't sharing? Was there a crossover in her own Polish background that connected to the case?

Both Diego and Rhonda needed to explain themselves. Kate felt she was in a never ending vortex. For without full knowledge of the Robbins' background and the danger they faced, she couldn't understand what drove the killer. Without understanding the killer's motive, she couldn't consider any relevant suspects. And not having those missing pieces of the puzzle made it extremely tricky and complicated.

Adrian and the police, who collectively held comprehensive information and knowledge about both the Robbins and the Mafia Queen cases, couldn't figure out the murderer's motive or identity. With all their resources at hand, they were still stumped. Perhaps Kate, with a fresh set of eyes, could find the critical missing pieces.

Regardless, time was of the essence and Kate was determined to seek the answers. For her friends. She had no choice but to pursue wherever the journey took her.

***

"...he survived and is going to make a full recovery."

Detective Abbott's words echoed over and over. They bounced off the walls. They screamed like banshees. They were horrifying.

John Robbins was alive! John Robbins was not dead! What went wrong? The instructions were followed to the letter.

The hatred raged inside, the anger threatened to spill out for everyone to see. The shock rendered the body immobile. Frozen to the chair.

What to do. Must get out of here before being exposed. Yet the body was fixed down, refused to move. The emotional and physical paralysis was overwhelming. The eyes, the devil eyes as the enemy named them in fear, desperately searched the room for a miracle. But there was none.

Breathe.

In. *Your eyes are special, not a curse.*

Out. *Your eyes must be shielded from the ugliness of the world.*

Breathe. *Your eyes are a weapon. Against the enemy.*

Slowly the tension released. The body calmed a little more with each breath. Everything would be better now. All around, people's reactions to the detective's news were the same. Distress. Disbelief. Fear. No one expected murder to be the topic of the day.

Fools! Fools! Fools! All of them!

The eyes followed Kate Trellow as she made her way to stand next to Adrian Kaufman. They spoke in low tones, bodies leaning towards each other. Well, well. What a cosy scene. That might be a bonus piece of information to store away for future use.

Kate Trellow was the biggest fool. It was *her* fault that

John Robbins was still alive. What was purportedly a foolproof method of killing a person had proven to be flawed. Her material was false.

She would be punished.

She *must* be punished.

And John Robbins was already a dead man. This time there would be no mistake.

Thirty-Seven

"...The fire was a deliberate act of arson...case is now a homicide..."
Rhonda's face turned pale with shock at the detective's words. She was furious, her body stiff and her chest squeezed tight. Her eyes burned and watered. It was some time before she could compose herself enough to move and go straight home. No one noticed her leave amidst the chaos.

She should have trusted her instincts. Just for a little longer. Paula and Diego's claims of Mary Robbins replacing her old electric blanket days earlier hijacked her conviction, created doubt in her mind. Mary was murdered as a result of arson. And sleeping pills. The police had validated her today. Which left two burning questions in Rhonda's mind. Who would want to hurt the Robbins? And why?

The police raid of Kate Trellow's house a few days earlier must be related to the case. Perhaps she was under suspicion. Rhonda couldn't imagine Kate as a killer, despite that awful tattoo. It was surely someone with easy access to the Robbins. Hmm, she wondered...

Adrian Kaufman. What a guarded character he was. He never

talked about himself and rarely engaged in conversation. And he was a friend of the Robbins. Being an ex-police officer he would be familiar with lots of different crimes including homicides. Maybe they'd had a falling out and he was seeking revenge.

Even as she thought it, Rhonda dismissed it. It didn't feel right. Adrian was no killer either. There was something deeper going on and no one had worked it out. Otherwise the killer would already be under arrest and in jail.

Who else? Diego was too drunk all the time to be useful in plotting and delivering a murder. And not capable. Yet, he did have Mafia connections. Had he reached out to them?

Cathy Eldridge? Her acid tongue was strong enough to burn through anything and anyone, she thought callously. But whilst she irked her no end at the Social Committee meetings, she was no killer either. Nor were any of the other women who were in that group.

Rick Lewis told her something big was going down and that the police were responsible for a huge coverup. Today's meeting proved it. He'd asked for her help. Maybe she would accept his offer. They seemed to be the only two people not to be fooled from the beginning. She realised Rick Lewis was very much a person like her. Passionate and fearless about what he believed in. And unpopular, ostracized as a result. Just like she was.

She reflected on it a little more. She'd give Rick Lewis a call later. In the meantime, she'd discuss it further with Paula. What they'd do after that, she had no idea.

Distracted once again by her burning eyes, she realised her contact lenses were irritating her. Why were they playing up so much lately? She felt another infection coming on and was annoyed. Carefully, she removed them from her eyes and placed them in the solution on her vanity basin. She stared into the mirror. Her eyes looked awful. Puffy and red. Like she'd been crying for hours. Which wasn't too far from the truth. She'd in fact been crying for many years. But enough indulgence now. She had to stay focused.

Thirty-Eight

*BREAKING NEWS * BREAKING NEWS * BREAKING NEWS*
This is Rick Lewis reporting from Possum Walk Over 50s Community in Robinwood where police made an astonishing announcement at a residents' meeting earlier today confirming that arson was involved in the death of resident Mrs Mary Robbins in a fire at her home three weeks ago. Her death is now being treated as a homicide. The electric blanket, at first thought to be faulty, was deliberately tampered with. In addition, police revealed a large quantity of sleeping medication was found in her system.

In a further twist in this homicide case, police also revealed that John Robbins, the husband of the deceased, is under protective care since an attempt was made on his life in hospital whilst recovering from pneumonia. Little information about that investigation is available to date.

Residents who choose to live at Possum Walk do so for the security a gated community offers and the tranquillity of the semi-rural surroundings. Many residents have told me they fear for their lives since the death of their friend, worried that a murderer might be living amongst them in plain sight, ready to strike again.

***

Late Afternoon

The press conference was streamed live on all the network television stations. This time it was an Inspector Linda Crawford who represented the Victoria Police and responded to all the questions from attending journalists. Kate noted that both Detectives Abbott and Penrose stood behind her along with several other officers.

Kate watched and listened carefully to make sure she didn't miss anything besides what the residents were told earlier that day. However, it was the same information. It just looked so much more dramatic and seriously formal.

She wasn't surprised when Adrian showed up at her doorstep soon after. He had a folder under his arm. Once they settled at the dining table, he retrieved the documents inside the folder.

"We know that someone at Possum Walk must be the killer. Here is a full list of all the residents. It suddenly occurred to me this afternoon after watching the press conference that we have considered none of the staff and contractors who were here at the time of the fire."

"That's a good point," Kate said. Her eyes widened as she scanned the extensive list of potential suspects in front of her. "There are nearly three hundred names on this list. How are we going to shortlist those who might have the motive and or opportunity?"

"One by one," Adrian said grimly. "We have to start somewhere."

"Why have you changed your mind about sharing information

with me? You've been so determined to keep me at a distance for my protection."

"This is research. And you're exceptionally good at it. I regard this exercise as keeping you at a safe distance. We can pull together data on each of the people listed and rate them according to a scale of 'persons of interest'. How does that sound?"

"Sounds like a plan," Kate said excitedly. "I'll use my laptop to create a spreadsheet. That way, we can record each person's details." She quickly retrieved her laptop from the study and within a couple of minutes, the spreadsheet was ready for entries.

Adrian watched her work, a look of admiration on his face. "I'm impressed," he said at one point. "You're fast and efficient."

Kate blushed at his compliment. She did it again. Acting like a teenager. Where Adrian Kaufman was concerned, he affected her equilibrium like no other person had in many years. And she didn't like it. Not one bit.

"Before we go through each name," Adrian said, "who would you consider a person of interest right now?"

"Diego Santo and Rhonda Kavich," Kate replied without hesitation.

"Let's list what we know about each of them and why they have your attention."

"I have more questions than answers about each of them, but enough to make me think their behaviour strange."

"Let's start with Diego. What puts him on the list?"

"I preface this by stating Diego is not a reliable *witness*." She quoted with her fingers mid air. She quickly told him about her conversations with Diego.

"It appears the alcohol has taken a grip on him," Adrian said after Kate finished.

"He has flashes of being in the Robbins' house the night of the fire. How is that possible unless he really was there?"

"It will be difficult to sift through what is real or imagined."

"I have to get to the bottom of it. Talk to him again." Kate noticed Adrian's frown as she spoke.

"That's a firm 'no'. Not negotiable. We don't know if he's the murderer. You can't be on your own with him."

"That's ridiculous, Adrian! There's no reason for the murderer to come after me or anyone else except the Robbins. Besides, I'll be in a public place when we speak."

"I don't like it!"

"That's not your decision. I'm not about to close myself off from the world until the perceived danger is over. That's not who I am!"

Adrian must have realised not to argue further against her resolve and said, "What else do we know about Diego?"

"He has family connections to the Mafia. But a tragedy in his teens changed the course of his life. Could be a coincidence. Or is there a crossover with the Mafia Queen case?"

"The Feds regularly monitor the Australian mafia families. I'll follow it up with my contacts and see if they know anything about his background."

"Regarding Rhonda," Kate continued, "She's not as high on the list as Diego is. She acts like the champion of truth, crusading to save Possum Walk from itself. In this case, Rhonda has insisted right from the beginning that the fire and Mary's death were suspicious. What gave her that conviction? It was out-of-the-box thinking in those first few days. She voiced strong concerns from the night of the fire. Yes, she hooked onto the premise of *'did she or didn't she have an electric blanket'* pretty quickly. But on reflection, it's almost like..." she hesitated, trying to find the right words, "she knows more the rest of us don't. I think she might be hiding something. I just can't put my finger on it."

Adrian mulled over what Kate said. "I've had little to do with her. To be honest, I try to avoid her where possible. She tried to engage me in conversation one day about my police background. Not so subtle either. That was enough."

"On the surface, she's opinionated to the point of being offensive, and single mindedly focused when she's onto something she believes in. Underneath, she has a good heart," Kate replied. "She's befriended Paula Vincent initially because she was so shy, but there seems to be a genuine friendship now."

"What do we know about Rhonda's background?" Adrian watched Kate add notes on the spreadsheet.

"She's Polish. Was married but her husband passed away some years ago. And she has three children who rarely visit. Not sure where they live."

They discussed several more residents on the list but no one else was a standout except for Rhonda Kavich and Diego Santo. Before he left, Adrian again warned Kate.

"Don't be careless, Kate. Remember, there's a killer on the loose."

"I'll be careful and apply my energy into armchair research only." She gave him a reassuring smile but his expression remained serious.

"If the killer attacked you whilst they were snooping around in the Robbins' house, that's even more reason to watch out."

"Adrian, I have received your message loud and clear."

"This isn't a joke, Kate. You're already on the killer's radar. He or she is close enough in your life to have had the opportunity and the gall to steal your folder from under your nose. You didn't even notice. And now it's being used as some kind of twisted inspiration for murder."

He was right, of course. Kate knew it. But a tiny voice inside her couldn't let it go. She needed answers from both Rhonda and Diego. As soon as possible.

As he left, Adrian glanced across the road to the Robbins' house. The police tape and the canvas hiding the front bedroom wall were still in place.

"Fire Services have cleared the house and I have permission to access it," he said. "Forensics have finished their onsite examination. What's left undamaged by the fire has to be sorted and..." His voice trailed away. She heard his voice catch on the last word.

"I'd like to help."

Kate realised what she was getting herself into. It would be a daunting undertaking. Adrian obviously needed support.

"Would you, Kate?" He sounded a little relieved. She nodded. "Thankyou."

As she closed the door behind him, Kate thought of the shift in Adrian's attitude towards her. His suspicions about her were finally gone. Once again, she gained insight into a softer Adrian. It was subtle, but welcome.

Instinctively, she knew Adrian had the potential to become

an important person in her life. She felt something special between them she couldn't explain. The Robbins' case flung them together reluctantly into a harsh world of mistrust, anger and sorrow. And strangely, those same things drew them together. At first, there was conflict. Now a common purpose united them.

This could grow into a special friendship.

Anything more was not for her. Ever.

Thirty-Nine

Day 25 —Morning

Rhonda rang Paula's doorbell several times. What was the matter with that woman? She was never home!

She was eager to discuss potential suspects with her. Surprisingly, the door was unlocked and she quickly made her way inside the house. She braced herself against the clutter but all the blinds were closed and the house was coated in gloomy shadows. Even so, she saw nothing much had moved off the furniture.

"Paula?" Silence. "Paula, are you home? It's Rhonda."

Maybe she was asleep. At this hour of the morning? It was nearly ten. She moved silently towards the back of the house where the two bedrooms were located. Both doors were firmly closed but she saw a sliver of soft light from the gap under one of them.

She approached that door and slowly turned the knob. She didn't know why she was being so cautious but the house spooked her for some reason she didn't understand.

"Paula!"

Rhonda's voice held a note of relief as she saw her friend in the room. Paula's back was to her and she whirled around at Rhonda's voice. She held a book open in her hands and snapped it shut, clasping it against her chest.

"Rhonda! What are you doing here?"

With her hair dishevelled, hanging limply in front of her eyes, Paula's face was deathly pale. Her nightgown peeped out from beneath her woollen dressing gown. The light from the bedside table gave off an eerie glow in the room. Despite being mid morning, the window blinds were closed tight.

"Are you alright?"

"Ah– yes." Paula sounded distracted, agitated, a look of confusion on her face. She dropped the book on the bed.

"What's wrong?" Rhonda was becoming increasingly bewildered by her friend's bizarre behaviour. Was she on some kind of medication or, worse, illegal drug which was affecting her?

"I'm fine, fine." Paula murmured. "I had – er – a..." her voice faded. Suddenly, she crouched down, covering her face with her hands, rocking back and forwards. A wail escaped from between her lips.

Rhonda knelt down beside her friend, trying to pry her hands away from her face, but they were stiff and unyielding.

"My eyes, my eyes," she wailed. She kept rubbing at them.

"What's wrong with your eyes?" Rhonda didn't know what to do. "Perhaps a splash of cold water on your face will help, Paula."

As suddenly as it had started, the wailing stopped. Gently, Rhonda put her arms around the other woman and helped her to her feet. Paula no longer seemed tense. But her eyes were tightly closed. With soft words of encouragement, Rhonda led her to the bed and helped get her under the covers. Paula fell asleep instantly.

Rhonda stared down at the other woman for a long moment, still shaken by what had just occurred. What had just happened? Paula seemed to be in some kind of trance at one point. The more she thought about it, the more Rhonda was convinced Paula might be taking illegal drugs.

Her gaze moved around the untidy room. Just like the rest of the house. How someone could live like this was beyond comprehension. Toiletries and other small items crowded together, cluttering the dressing table, making it impossible to see the top of it.

On the bedside table was a set of contact lenses resting in solution. Strange she'd never noticed Paula wore contact lenses. Infected or sore eyes had likely caused her wailing. She didn't really know. Maybe that was the simple answer to her odd behaviour. Her eyes were infected from the contact lenses. After all, Rhonda's eyes were infected from her own contact lenses at the moment too. These things happened.

Still...

One thing she realised as she stood there, immersed within the chaos that was Paula Vincent's house. Paula was not what she presented to the world. Not at all. Well-groomed and friendly, yes. Yet this house...the undeniable sensation of an oppressive heaviness within its walls. the house cried out to be rescued.

Rhonda couldn't stay another minute.

She glanced down at the book Paula had discarded earlier. It was on the bed, its title glaringly visible.

"Ancient Potions and Spells."

Forty

Late Morning

Kate wasted no time pursuing Diego to get answers about his alleged visions. She didn't know how she was going to achieve it but determined to help him unlock the memories he struggled with.

She'd just about given up after ringing his doorbell three times when she heard muffled sounds from within the house. Finally, the door opened. Diego's appearance startled her. He looked terrible. Blood-shot eyes, ashen unshaved face, dressing gown hanging off one shoulder. And ready to collapse at any moment.

"Kate! Come in." His grin belied his drunken condition.

It would be a waste of time trying to reason with him in his current inebriated condition. He didn't seem fully cognisant. She went inside anyway. A quick glance around the living room into his kitchen was a surprise. It was reasonably tidy except for the empty glass of wine.

"I can come back later if it's more convenient," Kate said.

"No, I need the company," he replied. "I don't enjoy being alone these days," he added.

"Can I make you some breakfast, Diego? A cup of coffee, perhaps?"

"Maybe a strong coffee. I need to wake up. I'll get it." He made to get up but stumbled back on the sofa, cradling his head with both his hands. Squeezing his eyes shut for a moment, he groaned and then gave her a sheepish look.

It didn't take long for the coffee to be made and set before Diego, who took a big gulp. "There's some cake in the fridge I made the other day. Please have some, Kate."

"I'm ok. I wanted to follow up about the night of the fire." Kate didn't want to waste any time.

"I panicked, regretted telling you. I must have sounded like a crazy person. Sorry for lashing out at you at the funeral. I didn't mean it when I told you it never happened." He frowned down at his coffee. "In the first few days, I saw only flashes. Like a snapshot. Mary sleeping on the bed. Flames. It was all jumbled and made no sense. Recently, I'm seeing bits of a moving scene. A shadowy outline of a person standing beside me, whispering in my ear. We are both in Mary's bedroom. I see her asleep on the bed. It's as though I'm not in my body but watching from a distance. It's disturbing and yet it feels so real. I'm convinced more and more that I was there the night of the fire."

"Is there anything else? Think! It could be important."

"I've tried. Time and time again. The only thing is..." He jolted upright. "Eyes. I remember the eyes."

"What eyes? Someone else was with you?"

He shuddered and gave her an agonised look. "Devil eyes," he whispered. "Burning right through my soul."

The reference startled Kate. John had also mentioned devil eyes. 'Evil', he'd called them. Warned her against the danger. Lidia Ciambella had strangely coloured eyes, sometimes referred to as 'evil'.

"Devil eyes, Diego? Why do you say that? Who has devil eyes?"

"That's just it. I don't know. I just see a fragment of a blurred face. And eyes. I see them clearly. Red and raw, piercing and glowing, staring at me, mesmerising."

"Do you recall any facial features? Hair? Male or female?"

Diego closed his eyes tightly. "I just can't grab the image."

Kate sat patiently. Silently watching. Waiting for Diego to sift through his mind for any more pieces of the puzzle. The more they spoke, the more she believed he had in fact been in the Robbins' house the night of the fire. Why and how had yet to be determined. He was holding up very well for someone who looked decidedly seedy and probably suffering a massive hangover.

"There's something else," he murmured. "I went back to the house a few days after the fire. The place was a total mess. The police had it all sealed off. I shouldn't have gone there but just had to know. It was the middle of the night and sleep escaped me. I was doing no harm if I went there. I thought it might trigger my memory about that night, help fill in the blanks."

Kate felt a tingling sensation up and down her spine. A soul deep shiver of disbelief coursed through her.

"I slipped in," Diego continued. "It was the middle of the night. I looked around for a few minutes but then I heard a noise.

Someone else was there. I panicked when I saw a person's outline in front of me, thinking it was the killer come back to the scene of the crime or something like that. Acting purely on instinct, I knocked them out of the way and ran out the back door."

He stopped, a look of awe on his face. "That's the first clear memory I've had in weeks. I even remember jumping the fence back into my place next door."

"That was you?" A paralysing realisation washed over Kate, making her limbs feel heavy, as if anchored to the ground. She couldn't process the enormity of what she'd just heard. In shock, she barely got the words out.

Diego must have noticed her reaction and then had his own light bulb moment. His eyes widened as he looked at her in horror.

"That was you?"

She nodded. She didn't trust herself to speak. Adrian's words about putting herself in danger popped into her head and a ripple of dread twisted inside her. She thought the killer had attacked her that night. She was alone inside Diego's house. He'd just admitted to attacking her and she stood there, unable to move. He appeared to have recovered conveniently from when he'd first opened the door. She had to get out of there. Fast!

"I have to go, Diego."

She couldn't look at him. Stay calm. Don't panic. She felt her anxiety levels rise. Oh no, not now.

"I am so sorry, Kate. I had no idea it was you. Please forgive me. I would never hurt a woman." Diego sounded very sincere and concerned.

Kate felt her throat closing up, the tightness begin inside her chest. Reaching the front door, she became alarmed as Diego's arm shot out to hold it shut.

"Please let me pass, Diego," she said as calmly as she could.

He shook his head at her. "Not before you accept my apology, Kate. Why were you there, anyway?" He watched her intently.

"I saw a light inside the house and checked it out. That's all."

"The torch," he nodded. "That was foolish of you to put yourself into a potentially risky situation. Alone." He emphasised the last word with an odd smile.

"I accept your apology, Diego. I really must go."

Kate never looked back. She felt Diego's eyes bore into her with every step until she locked her door behind her. She managed to get herself back under control once she fled Diego's house. The panic attack she'd felt coming on didn't eventuate but she felt drained emotionally. And foolish.

She half expected Diego to follow her once she escaped. For that's exactly what she did. She freaked herself out so badly, her mind filled with thoughts of danger and murder. The extent of her crazy behaviour took her by surprise. She'd fled like the very devil was chasing her.

She'd ignored all of Adrian's warnings. Be careful. The killer is out there. Don't find yourself alone in a sticky situation. Once in the safety of her home, she realised Diego's shock was just as genuine as hers once they both grasped the significance of what actually took place that night.

Unless Diego faked his reaction, there was no other conclusion. Diego was not the killer.

Forty-One

✺

Afternoon

Kate agreed to meet Adrian at the Robbins' home later that afternoon to sort through their belongings. They navigated their way past the police tape, ducking and weaving across the debris strewn over the garden, which looked tragic.

Kate's heart felt heavy when she saw Mary's once beautiful orchids trampled beyond recognition. Mud and slush covered the lawn and once beautiful garden beds were indistinguishable.

For some reason, Kate felt apprehensive about returning to the Robbins' house. The discovery that Diego was the one who assaulted her that awful night didn't help settle her nerves. But she needed to get over it and only by taking the first steps inward would she do so.

Once she and Adrian stepped inside, they both stopped in their tracks, absorbing the magnitude of damage the fire caused. The carpet was waterlogged, the walls and furniture stained and damp. The potent smell of smoke still lingered weeks later. She felt the deep sorrow of Mary's death radiating off the walls. Where to start?

"I suppose there's no easy way to do this." Adrian winced as he looked around and picked up one of the packing boxes he'd brought with him.

"Before we start, I have to tell you something important." Kate didn't mean to sound so sharp. Her nerves were stretched.

"What is it?" A frown knit his brow.

"I went to see Diego earlier today." She braced herself for Adrian's reaction. But all he did was stare at her in astonishment, his expression grim. She saw the muscles in his jaw tighten.

"He told me inadvertently that he was the one who attacked me," she continued.

"What! And you were alone with him? In his house?"

"He hoped by coming here it might trigger the fragments of his memory from the night of the fire. He heard a noise and panicked when he saw someone else was here. Unfortunately, that was me. You know the rest. Oh, by the way, he jumped over the adjoining fence into his house in no time."

Adrian paced. As much as it was possible to pace in the surrounding mess. His agitation was evident, a classic giveaway. Kate waited patiently for the lecture she was certain would follow. Instead, he halted before her and searched her face carefully.

"Are you alright? That must have been quite a shock to you."

His voice held a tenderness she'd not heard before and her heart raced. At the same time, her stomach did a backflip. She nodded because she didn't trust herself to speak. What was it about this man that caused such intense feelings inside her?

With a muffled curse, he pulled her into his arms, holding her close. Kate, at first startled, quickly settled into their warmth and safety. It felt so right being there. They remained together like that for long, wonderful moments. The emotions and stress of the morning slowly melted away as she leaned against his hard chest. Warm sensations like butterflies danced in her stomach. Adrian pulled back a little, gazing down at her face. She felt a tingle of anticipation.

"The truth is," Adrian said, grazing his fingertip along her jawline in a slow motion, "I can't pinpoint the moment you started becoming important in my life, Kate. But you are."

Lowering his mouth to hers, they kissed, a soft kiss, delicate, a promise. Her senses filled with all of him, his mouth, his touch. She felt consumed as she leaned into the kiss. Everything around her ceased to exist.

Adrian was the first to break the kiss and take a step back. "Sorry, I shouldn't have done that."

"What are you talking about?" she breathed, holding his gaze. "That was...it was...good." Kate knew that something special had just happened between them, something amazing. Unexpected. It was a moment that would stay with her forever.

"Good?" His voice was hoarse. Clearing his throat, Adrian laughed a little before kissing her again. This time it was longer and ever so sweet. She hardly breathed.

When they finally pulled back from each other, Kate laughed back at him.

"That was better," she said with a smile. It felt easy between them. He hugged her tightly for a moment more before putting some distance between them.

"I can't think straight when I'm around you, Kate," he admitted. "There is so much between us we need to discuss but the timing is..." he looked at her helplessly.

"I know," Kate sighed, "not quite right. Too much at stake for us to be distracted right now," she finished, accepting the situation they were in.

"Only for a while," he whispered. "We will find the person responsible for all of this, I promise. And then, we'll work through what is happening between us."

"I'm okay with that."

"About Diego." Adrian's expression turned serious. The man's name sobered them both instantly. "Does he know it was you he attacked that night?"

"Yes. And he looked horrified when he realised it. I couldn't leave his house fast enough. Your warnings kept ringing in my ears. I admit I was terrified and panicked."

"The police should arrest him right now!"

"No, please don't. He was genuinely remorseful. Shocked as much as I was. I want to believe what he's saying. It's too bizarre to be made up."

"I see that stubborn gleam in your eyes, Kate." Adrian watched her keenly. "And it bothers me." She didn't deny it.

"Alright!" he sighed heavily. "Together, we'll visit Diego. And Rhonda."

"Great."

"I hope you appreciate now that you must be extra careful." Adrian's concern for her was evident. "Possum Walk is a ticking time bomb and a killer is on the loose. Your actions, however well intended, could cause him or her to react dangerously. We don't know what we're dealing with yet."

"I know it." Kate felt just as concerned. "I'll be careful from now on, I promise. Oh! One other thing. Diego told me his memory about the night of the fire is filling out. Someone else was in the Robbins' house with him."

"The plot thickens," Adrian murmured. "What can we believe?"

"My one regret is that I never had the chance to ask him about his Mafia connection."

"A couple of colleagues are onto it. They should have some news soon. In the meantime, police need to take a closer look at Diego Santo."

"For now, let's get to work!"

Kate and Adrian systematically walked through the Robbins' house to ascertain the extent of the damage and determine what to salvage or dump. The crime scene investigators had added their mark to the chaos. Fine fingerprint powder covered everything and they couldn't avoid disturbing it wherever they moved.

"The back of the house is the best place to start," Adrian said. "The kitchen and dining areas are the least damaged."

It took over two hours. They piled boxes into three categories – storage, charity and rubbish. Kate felt like an intruder attempting to steal precious possessions. There was no option but to get it done.

"Once John is stronger and settled into his new accommodation, I'll help him go through the things put aside. It's best he doesn't see this place ever again. It would be devastating for him. To be honest, I'm barely coping with this destruction," he added.

Kate felt exactly the same as she looked around what used to be a house full of love, laughter and life. Now it was just a shell of a house, destruction of a home, end of a family.

Forty-Two

❦

Day 26 – Late Morning

Adrian arranged for Kate to visit John the next day.

"John's been moved to a high security ward on another floor," Adrian told her. "Usually reserved for prisoners needing medical treatment. Under the circumstances, it's the safest place for him. We can't take the chance our killer will try again."

When Kate exited on the third floor of the hospital, a security guard immediately approached her. She gave her name and who she was visiting. The guard passed a security device over her body. He inspected the contents of her handbag and finally allowed her to enter the ward.

Once inside, she noticed several uniformed police officers at various stations and standing guard outside some rooms. Hospital staff moved freely in and out of the doors. She was directed to one of the guarded rooms down the hall.

"Hello, John." Happy to see him sitting up watching a television installed on the opposite wall, she greeted him with a warm hug. No response. No welcoming smile or greeting, just a glance and nod her way. He returned to watch the screen, a vacant look in his eyes.

Kate's heart sank. Adrian warned her that John's condition had worsened following the attempt on his life. The overdose of drugs had certainly taken a toll on him, physically and mentally. She studied his familiar face. It broke her heart to see how grey and haggard it had become since her last visit. He'd been through so much. His hair was even whiter than she remembered.

"I have some chocolates for you today." Kate offered the brightly coloured bag of goodies to him. John's gaze fixated on the screen, not a flicker that he heard her.

She sat next to him in silence. Gazing around her, she felt sad. Hospital rooms were notoriously uninviting, but this one was particularly sterile and harsh. There was no window for a start. Just that awful fluorescent white lighting that hurt your eyes if you stared at it long enough. Which she shouldn't have done.

She played with the light switches and found a dimmer switch. That was much better, she sighed. The only furniture in the room, apart from the bed, was a medical stand on wheels. It had a jug of water with a glass on it. No bedside table or wardrobe. The barest 'decoration' was an IV pump with a bag of fluid attached into one of John's veins.

"Kate! When did you get here?" His voice sounded frail. But his smile was ever present.

John was back! Grateful for whatever quality time they had together, Kate gave him a warm smile and handed him the chocolates. Predictably, he took them with pleasure and started eating them. But just as he was about to consume the second one, he stopped and frowned down at it.

"I think these are bad for me, Kate." He continued to stare down at the chocolate.

How thoughtless of her! She could have kicked herself. Of course, somewhere in the deep recesses of his mind, the chocolates were giving off warning signals. She placed her hand over his.

"It's okay, John," she reassured him. "These are safe. They won't hurt you."

He stared at her, appeared satisfied with her comment and ate the chocolate.

"How are you feeling?"

"Never better. Adrian told me it's all over. Finally, we can go on with our lives in peace. Will you tell Rosie it's safe now?"

"I will," Kate replied gently. "When I see her, I'll let her know."

"But no!" John tried to sit upright, but his weakened condition wouldn't allow it. In defeat, he slumped back down onto the pillow. "She's gone, isn't she?" The physical effort left him breathless.

Kate nodded. "I think so. Who is Rosie?"

John's face lit up. "She was the sunshine of my life. We laughed all the time. I fell in love with her from the first moment I saw her." Tears formed in his eyes. "Do you believe in love at first sight, Kate?"

"Yes," she said. "I believe it happens to some people. I've never experienced it."

"We were so young and married quickly. Her parents disapproved. But we didn't care. We had the rest of our lives to grow old together."

"Rosie was your first wife?" Kate started to piece the 'Rosie' puzzle together. She realised now why he talked about her so often. Young love and, she suspected, first love was a powerful force.

John nodded. He had a faraway look in his eyes. "But it wasn't meant to be. She was taken from me. In the cruellest of ways."

"What happened to Rosie?"

"We never speak of it. It upsets Mary too much."

"Why would Mary get upset over Rosie?" She was reminded again there was more about the Robbins that she may never uncover.

"She blamed Rosie for everything that happened. Our troubles started because Rosie insisted on a certain path. Despite all the warnings against it."

John grasped Kate's hands in his. "Kingfish was toxic," he whispered, giving her his full attention. "Those responsible should have made sure it was safe."

"Are you saying that kingfish killed Rosie?" Kate asked, alarmed and confused.

"Yes! We were in danger the whole time and didn't know it. Adrian saved us. It could have been far worse. We could have died."

Kate didn't know what to make of it. If true, what a tragedy. To lose your wife to fish poisoning would have destroyed him. So young too. But she wasn't absolutely sure that's what he meant either. Rosie must have died around the time the Robbins became involved with Lidia Ciambella. John said Adrian had been a part of their lives for a very, very long time. He implied he'd known Rosie. More pieces of the puzzle coming together.

"I'm so very sorry, John. It must have been a difficult time for you."

He nodded. He looked exhausted. His face was beaded with perspiration. He'd over exerted himself and a pang of guilt hit her chest. Recalling his first wife must have been too much. And Kate had stayed too long.

"You rest now, John," she whispered. "I'll visit again soon."

She closed the door softly behind her.

***

"Kate!"

Kate was about to exit the ward when she heard her name called behind her.

"Libby!" It was the nurse she'd met on a previous visit to John and subsequently saw at the Orchid Show with her daughter Grace.

"Are you working in this security ward?" Kate was happy to see a familiar face.

"Yes, I do. You just visited John Robbins? I've looked after him quite a few times. He's such a sweet man."

"I didn't see you leave the Orchid Show that day. I looked for you, but you must have gone."

"Grace felt unwell and we had to leave." Kate thought she looked a little uncomfortable.

"Sorry to hear it. I'm worried about John to be honest. Since his last health scare..."

"You mean the attempted murder?"

Kate was startled by Libby's directness. "Yes," she replied slowly. "He's deteriorated quite a bit."

"Agree, he's weakened. Heart attacks on the elderly are challenging. But, with bed rest and no further incidents, he will gain his strength in time."

"I hope so. We've all been so worried about him."

"Are your friends from the Orchid Show also worried about him?"

Kate wasn't sure whether she imagined the coolness in Libby's voice and wondered why she was acting strangely. She'd been full of warmth and friendliness in the past. Today she was different. Perhaps she was having a difficult shift.

"You mean Rhonda and Paula? Yes, of course. We are all friends. They both visited him when he was in the other ward a few weeks ago."

Libby glanced around them, suddenly appearing nervous. "Look Kate," she lowered her voice. "I'm probably breaking heaps of rules here, but I need to speak to someone about John. I've listened to him tell me – on repeat sometimes – about things in his life, his past. I think I know him reasonably well by now. Since the attack, I've had a crazy theory buzzing inside my head and I don't know what to do about it."

"What do you know about John's situation?" Kate's response was sharper than intended yet she was instantly on guard. Who was this woman?

"I'm sorry. I didn't mean to offend anyone," Libby replied.

"Why don't you tell me what's bothering you and we'll try to figure it out together?"

Libby vigorously shook her head. "No, Kate. I don't want to bring you into this. It's so outrageous an idea that I'm not even sure I want to open up the possibility. I might cause unnecessary pain on others."

"Libby, you're talking in riddles. I can't help or advise you if you don't give me more."

"Maybe it's a matter for the police," she murmured, almost to herself. "If you can tell me who to contact, I'll arrange to speak with them soon."

"The police?" Kate frowned. She was becoming more alarmed with every passing second. Libby was making little sense but she obviously had something important she wanted to share.

"Detective Michael Abbott is the lead officer in the Robbins' investigation. He might be a good start for you. I'll give you his number." She did so on a notepad Libby handed her.

"Thanks." Libby sounded relieved. And gave Kate her first genuine smile since seeing her. "I've got to attend to another patient. Bye for now."

Kate watched her walk away, grab a file at the nurses' station and disappear into a room further down the hallway.

Kate's head was spinning. She felt deeply unsettled. Confusion seemed to be her nemesis because it followed her at every turn.

She exited the ward, making her way to the lifts. Deep in thought, she tried to unpack what Libby had said. A theory relating to John?

She stopped.

What the hell just happened?

Forty-Three

Mid Afternoon

Kate met Adrian outside Diego's house. They quickly discussed their approach.

"The chief aim is to get his account of the night of the fire and if he recalls any more. And we need him to open up about his family background." Adrian's focus was clear.

Diego was surprised to see them both standing on his porch and hesitated before waving them inside. He appeared sober and steady on his feet. Kate thought he looked better than the day before.

"I'm sincerely very sorry about attacking you," Diego said to Kate, tears pooling in his eyes. "I just didn't know what to think! It happened so fast and I was in a state." He shrugged in a helpless gesture. "It was unforgiveable. And I haven't touched a drop since then. It frightened me to think I did something like that to a woman."

"Apology accepted," Kate replied. In her heart, she didn't really want to believe Diego was guilty of murder. Or anything else criminal. "Let's not dwell on it any longer. We have a favour to ask you."

Diego looked from one to the other warily.

"Adrian knows about your visions."

Diego looked visibly startled but stayed silent.

"Could you please recap your experience for my benefit?" Adrian asked. "Kate said that your memory of that night is coming back gradually each day. Maybe it will help to tell me."

Kate noted Adrian's body language as he sat forward towards Diego in a non-threatening manner. Diego searched Adrian's face, possibly wondering whether to trust him, Kate suspected. Finally, he nodded. Taking a deep breath, he eased back onto the sofa. He'd made his decision, it seemed.

"It's very simple. I'm a drunk. Have been for many years. But lately, the drink affects me in ways that I've never experienced. I have lapses in memory and time. Hours go by that I don't remember. Sometimes days. I suffer from headaches that pierce my brain." He touched his fingers to his temple. "And then I see random images of me in situations or places that frighten me. I can't tell if they are real or imagined by the drink."

"You're doing well, Diego. Go on." Adrian's tone was calm and reassuring.

"On the night of the fire, I see myself in the Robbins' house with flames around me, a searing heat on my skin. I see Mary Robbins sleeping on the bed with a blanket covering her. But she's not moving."

Diego became agitated and took a deep breath. With a strained voice, he continued. "The fire is licking at the blanket but she's not moving. And I'm in the corner of the room watching it happen. After that, it becomes a blur. Just fragments. Like looking through shards of glass. You know what I mean?"

Kate and Adrian both nodded, their attention fully on Diego.

"Can you describe any of those bits of fragments?" Kate asked.

"There's a flash of someone standing over Mary, looking down at her. I can't make out who it is. Another image of me looking down at a bottle of pills in my hand. Pouring thick liquid, maybe soup, down the sink."

Again he paused, his breathing laboured, like it had been a tremendous effort. He dragged his shaking fingers through his hair. Tears dampened his cheeks but he wiped them away.

"And then the eyes. They haunt me," he continued. "You asked me if I remembered what colour they were, Kate. Well, I concentrated hard. They were a brilliant green, like cat's eyes, that glowed. They weren't human. They were the devil's eyes, burning through me." He shuddered. "They enticed me, in my mind. I felt mesmerised, pulled into their power. I've never been so afraid in my life."

Kate caught the fleeting look of alarm cross Adrian's face before he quickly replaced it with a deep frown. Both of them hung on every word Diego uttered. These eyes were becoming a common theme difficult to ignore. What did it all mean? No one she knew had the eyes as described by both John and Diego. At least not at Possum Walk.

"The last thing I remember is jumping over a fence and falling into a bush into my backyard. I found a bruise here the next day." He indicated the right side of his torso. Diego stopped talking but not before he hung his head down and whispered, "Please make it stop."

Kate put her hand on Diego's shoulder, trying to offer some comfort. Talking about it had been a gruelling effort for him.

"Thank you for sharing this with me, Diego," Adrian said evenly. "I understand how hard it must have been."

"I think this is a good time for a coffee break."

Both men welcomed Kate's offer. Diego didn't stop her as she went into the kitchen. He looked utterly defeated. And there were so many more questions she and Adrian wanted to ask him.

The break was exactly what they needed. Kate felt energised and Diego looked less tense. Adrian said little and appeared distracted. He roamed around the room aimlessly, stopping here and there. Kate noticed he stopped and spent a bit more time near the side cabinet. Mostly, Kate chatted to Diego about the upcoming billiards tournament that he was involved in. He became quite animated on that topic, which he obviously had a passion for.

It was Adrian who changed the subject dramatically.

"Diego, do you or your parents have any involvement with the Mafia families in Australia?"

Diego didn't seem overly bothered by the abrupt change. "I have nothing to hide. It's a terrible and senseless tragedy. During the fifties, my uncles were targeted by the local Mafia in Italy. Both of them had modest businesses in the small town where we come from. In the mountains of Calabria in southern Italy. One of my uncles was the local tailor. The other had a small general store. In those towns, the Mafia ruled the economy. It could make you very rich or destroy you. If you paid a weekly 'contribution', they left you alone. If you didn't pay it, they would run your business to the ground.

"The 'Ndrangheta," Adrian murmured.

"Yes," Diego replied. "My uncles didn't want to bow to their blackmail, so they walked away from their businesses, packed up their families and migrated to Australia. They left everything behind. I missed my three cousins when they left. We were close in age and did everything together. My family followed them to Australia a few years later. I was excited to be here because now I would be reunited with my cousins and life would be good."

Diego's tears flowed freely. His body heaved and trembled. "Unfortunately, my cousins had changed. The 'Ndrangheta found them through their contacts in Australia and threatened to kill them all if they didn't hand over my cousins as recruits, mainly in dealing drugs."

"And that happened over how many years?"

"About seven years. When I saw my cousins, it was four years after they'd been recruited. They made a lot of money, too much they didn't know what to spend it on. But it was not worth it. They were dead inside. They did what they had to do to save their families."

"What happened after that?" Adrian prompted.

"One by one, rival clans killed all three of my cousins, mostly in cross fire wars and paybacks. My uncles and aunts, all four of them, were involved in a fatal car accident not long after. But that was no accident."

"Were you and your family ever drawn into any of it here or in Italy?" Kate asked.

Diego shook his head. "My father owned nothing they wanted.

He was a poor man compared to his brothers. He worked a small patch of insignificant land an hour's walk from our town. Strangely, even in Australia, they left us alone."

Diego was not their killer, Kate was sure of it now. Only a shattered man who carried much sorrow from his youth throughout his life. What he was experiencing now, his memory lapses, his confused state, was because of his drinking.

"I'm so sorry," Kate said. Such inadequate words but she didn't know what else to say.

Adrian glanced at Kate, a warning in his eyes. What was he trying to convey? That Diego was guilty? His frown deepened as he turned back to Diego.

"Just one more question, Diego. Kate and I will then take our leave. Have you ever heard of a woman called Lidia Ciambella?"

Kate watched Diego focus on the name. "No, I don't think so," he replied. "The name isn't familiar. Should I have?"

"It was a chance question. I met her when I was in the police force and she was part of the Italian Mafia."

"I kept far away from anyone or anything to do with the Mafia clans here and in Italy. I never made it my business to find out. I hate them for what they did to my cousins and their families." He spat the last few words.

"I understand your sentiments," Adrian responded.

"Why did you ask me questions about the Mafia?" Diego asked as they stood to leave.

"I was curious. Kate told me a little about your background and I was curious if you knew of Lidia Ciambella." Adrian's response was smooth and convincing. However, Kate sensed he was hiding something. He gave Kate a quick, reassuring smile before turning his attention back to Diego.

"Lidia Ciambella was not only a member of the Mafia. She was their 'capo', their leader, for many years. People knew her as the Mafia Queen."

He paused, possibly hoping for some reaction from Diego. But there was none. "Here's an interesting fact about the Mafia Queen, Lidia Ciambella," Adrian pushed ahead. "She was renowned for her unusual eyes. Shaped like cat's eyes. Some people called them 'devil eyes'. People described them as a brilliant green colour. Apparently, it was quite unnerving to look into their depths."

Diego was stunned the instant he realised the inference of what Adrian said.

"You mean she's here? At Possum Walk? I don't understand."

"No, that's not possible," Adrian replied. "She's been dead for many years. But it's curious that you described eyes that appear much the same way. Why is that?"

"I – I don't know. I can't think!"

"It's a simple question, Diego." Kate was baffled by Adrian's tone, which had decidedly chilled.

"The same unusual eyes? How can that be?" Diego said, his expression anxious.

"Maybe you're playing games with us, Diego," Adrian shot back.

"No, I would never do that! I don't know how to explain it." Diego shook his head vehemently. He started to cry.

"Then perhaps you can explain this!" Adrian quickly moved to the side cabinet behind Kate and removed an item peeping out from under a stack of newspapers. It was a thick, purple coloured folder. He threw it down between Diego and Kate on the sofa.

"Diego!" Kate leapt out of her seat. Her heart pounded in her chest so fast she felt as if she would collapse. "That's my research folder!" She turned in horror to Diego. "It was you! You're the killer!"

Diego's expression mirrored the horror on Kate's face. He stared down at the folder.

"I'm no killer!" he shouted at Kate and Adrian. "I've never seen this before in my life!"

"You have some fast explaining to do before I call the police." Adrian pushed the other man back down as he attempted to rise from where he sat.

Kate's initial shock was wearing off to be replaced by a rage so intense it pulsed through every pore of her body. Her blood pressure must be sky high because her face felt on fire and her head pounded. The evidence was overwhelmingly against Diego.

"You played us all. On our emotions. And manipulated us at every turn." Kate's voice shook, her own emotions overtaking her.

"What are you talking about? Who am I supposed to have killed?" Diego cried out.

"Mary Robbins," Adrian replied coldly. "You used the information in that folder to plot her murder and then try to kill John."

All the time Adrian spoke, Diego vehemently shook his head.

"And then attacked Kate and pretended it was an accident."

"No! I would never hurt Kate or any woman."

"Stop pretending, Diego." Adrian said. "It's over." He handed his mobile phone to Kate. "Can you please call detective Abbott? Tell him to get over here urgently." All the while, his gaze remained fastened on Diego. The other man didn't stand a chance of escape with Adrian in the room.

"Why are you calling the police? I've done nothing wrong." Diego's own anger had shifted to heavy weeping.

"Why did you do it, Diego?" Adrian was unmoved, relentless. "What's your connection to the Robbins?"

"I'm innocent. I have done nothing."

"Did the Mafia put out a hit?"

Diego continued to weep, not responding.

"Was it a hit? Tell me Diego!"

Kate laid her hand on Adrian's arm to calm him. He was hurting and she felt his pain and frustration radiating out from him.

"It's no use, Adrian," she murmured. "You know he won't crack that easily. He's fooled us all for too long."

"You're right. The police can have him." He kept his attention on Diego.

For the next few minutes, the only sound in the room was that of Diego sobbing and occasionally moaning. Eventually, he stopped and stared down at the floor, hands clasped tightly in front of him. He remained silent.

When Kate went to pick up her research folder, Adrian stopped her. "Don't touch the folder, Kate. I should've known better. It's evidence that needs to be handled as little as possible before being dusted for fingerprints."

What a day this turned out to be. Her visit with John earlier felt far away. So much had happened since. Diego was the murderer. She shuddered, thinking of the times she'd unwittingly been alone with him and potentially placed herself in danger. That he was the one who attacked her made her skin crawl.

It didn't take long for detectives Abbott and Penrose to arrive. It seemed they'd brought the entire police force with them. Diego didn't resist as officers handcuffed him and led him away. He was docile and didn't make eye contact with anyone.

"You have one interesting story to tell me," detective Abbott said to Kate and Adrian. They quickly told both detectives what happened over the past two hours.

"I want to be present when you interview him," Adrian said firmly.

"Not this time, my friend," detective Abbott replied, just as firmly. "I'll keep in touch. You've had a big day. Get some rest, both of you. I think you've earned it."

Kate offered Adrian to come back to her place after the detectives left. Several police officers remained, undertaking a search for more evidence. The police officers had already bagged the research folder, ready for forensics. She watched the all too familiar process unfold. She didn't stay to see anymore.

***

Rhonda couldn't believe her eyes. Police cars were again lined up in the street. This time outside Diego's house. She watched in shock as he came out of the house, his head hung low, his wrists handcuffed. Several police officers accompanied him into a car that quickly whisked him away.

Just over a week ago, the police had been at Kate Trellow's house removing bags of evidence. A few days later, she saw them return with the bags. So whatever trouble Kate found herself in at the time seemed to have vanished.

Instead, Diego's situation appeared more serious. Officers left with bags of evidence. She saw Kate and Adrian exit and go to Kate's house. Perfect!

She didn't waste any time. She had to find out what was going on. Now was as good a time as any, she decided. Kate looked tired when she opened the door.

"I saw the commotion at Diego's house." Rhonda didn't do preambles very well. "The police took him away."

"He's being questioned about Mary's murder and John's attempted murder."

Adrian stood behind Kate and Rhonda eyed him with contempt. "This your idea?" she scoffed at him. "Diego isn't capable of murder!"

"Rhonda, there's been some pretty damning evidence uncovered, which suggests otherwise," Kate replied drily.

"Diego may be a drunk, but he's no murderer. He doesn't have the stomach for it."

"Well, time will tell," Kate replied. "I'm really not up to talking about it right now, so if you will excuse me?"

"Wait!" Rhonda said as Kate was about to shut the door. "If there's anything I can do to help, I'm here."

"Thank you, Rhonda." The door closed firmly in her face.

Well! The manners of that woman! It was that tattoo. Dead giveaway. She hoped Paula was home. She couldn't wait to share the latest with her. Besides, she should check up on her after yesterday's strange episode.

But luck was not on her side. Her friend wasn't home. At

least she didn't respond to the several doorbell chimes nor the loud prolonged knocking. Nor was the door unlocked. Perhaps she was at the clubhouse. It wasn't one of her work days.

As she entered the clubhouse, she found everyone gathered round immersed in animated discussion. Several people spoke at once, others raised their voices to be heard. Whatever they were talking about must be serious. She spotted Paula amongst the group and went to stand beside her.

"I need to speak with you," she whispered to her friend.

"Have you heard the news?" Paula replied.

"What news?"

"The police have arrested Diego and taken him into custody. There are rumours he might be the killer!"

"I know! I saw police take him away in handcuffs. That's what I came to tell you. I can't believe it. He doesn't have the stomach for murder."

"How do you know that?" Paula looked at her sceptically.

"You know, a robust constitution. Nor the heart. Besides, he cries at the drop of a hat!"

"Maybe he's deliberately acting out a part, convincing everyone that he's not a cold, calculating murderer."

"No, I can't believe that. No one is that good. Besides, his alcoholism is real. You can't pretend to be drunk the way he seems to be, especially lately. I can smell it on him!"

Paula said nothing in response. They both listened as the other residents continued to talk about the arrest. Most couldn't believe it, but others said maybe it could be true. Altogether, it was a very polarising discussion.

Rhonda thought about Paula's episode the day before. Today

she looked her normal self. But she wondered what caused her behaviour yesterday.

"How are you feeling today?" she asked.

"Good, thank you. Why do you ask?"

Rhonda urged the other woman away from the group for some privacy. She noted a couple of nosey residents nearby and didn't want to chance them overhearing the conversation.

"Do you remember me entering your bedroom yesterday morning? You were crying and confused, kept saying something about your eyes."

Paula looked shocked. "I don't remember any of it."

"I helped you back into bed. You fell asleep straight away."

Paula gazed at Rhonda in disbelief. "I had a migraine yesterday. I slept it off most of the day."

"That explains it." Rhonda was relieved. "I was worried about you."

Paula's stance stiffened visibly. "No need," she replied, but her words were sharper than expected.

She fumbled with her hair, stroking it in jerky movements. Her other hand was tightly clasped. She appeared distracted. Rhonda felt the tension emanating from Paula and wondered why.

"Are you sure you're alright?" she persisted.

"Yes, fine." Clipped reply.

Rhonda remembered the contact lenses on the bedside table and gazed intently into Paula's eyes. There it was. A faint outline around the pupils. She again was surprised she'd never noticed before.

"You wear contact lenses."

Paula looked startled. "Er – yes." She hastily looked away. "Is that a problem?"

"No, not at all. I wear them as well. I hate wearing them. I hate the constant infections. Sometimes they just irritate me. I'm thinking of going back to glasses."

"Might suit you," Paula snapped.

There was suddenly a strange awkwardness between them. Rhonda wasn't sure why. She shook it off.

"I'd better be heading home now," Paula said, abruptly.

Rhonda watched her walk away, stumped. She suspected she had just missed something significant. And had no idea what it was.

Forty-Four

Day 27 – Early Morning

*BREAKING NEWS * BREAKING NEWS * BREAKING NEWS*
This is Rick Lewis reporting live with an update from Possum Walk Over 50s Community in Robinwood, an outer suburb north of Melbourne. A male suspect has been taken into custody where he is currently being interrogated by police for the murder of Mrs Mary Robbins and the attempted murder of her husband Mr John Robbins.

The 74 year old resident of Possum Walk was murdered nearly a month ago in a fire caused by a faulty electric blanket, which was later found to have been deliberately tampered with.

More to follow as information comes to hand.

***

Mid Morning

"Has there been any update on Diego from the police?" Kate asked. She and Adrian were continuing the daunting task of packing up the Robbins' house.

"None. I've been trying to reach detective Abbott since they arrested Diego yesterday."

"Would they have charged him by now?"

"The police can hold him for questioning for up to forty-eight hours."

"There's nothing to be done except wait," Kate admitted. "My mind can't reconcile the killer to be Diego. Even though the evidence points to him. Why he did it is not obvious."

"The common denominator between Diego and the Robbins is the Mafia," Adrian replied. "His motive is complex. It doesn't add up right now and there are still plenty of missing pieces."

"Have your federal colleagues found anything yet?"

"No, it might be too soon. They have to liaise with their overseas contacts. It will take several days."

"Maybe Diego's family has ties to Lidia Ciambella. Diego mentioned his cousins were dealing drugs. That's a link. Diego was open about his background, but he strongly emphasized that neither he nor his family had anything to do with the local Mafia."

It was useless going round and round the facts and second guessing Diego's motives. Kate decided it was time for something more tangible.

"In the meantime," she said, observing the living area, "we have some work to do."

As they waded their way through the mess, it was clear much of the furniture in the living room suffered extensive water damage, with some pieces being scorched by the fire. This was the room which adjoined the bedroom where the fire started and the smell of smoke was the strongest here.

"What a tragedy that this beautiful oak bookshelf got ruined," Kate said softly, running her eyes over the solid piece which filled one entire wall. It had caught the brunt of the fire that reached this room. The beautiful wood suffered from severe scorching.

"Most of the books appear to be waterlogged," said Kate, as she picked one up. It lay limp in her hand. Many were the same where they rested on the shelf. Others had fallen from the shelves and were scattered on the wet carpet, which amplified their sorry state. Remarkably, a few ornaments remained standing, untouched and unbroken, on the shelving.

"Where to start?" Adrian murmured, gazing across the room.

"I'll start with the bookshelf." Kate drew a deep breath, mentally bracing herself against the daunting physical task. "Maybe there are a few books we can save."

"There are quite a few books not too badly damaged," Kate said in surprise, after nearly an hour on the task.

As she moved along each shelf, the 'save' pile in the box beside her grew steadily that she had to start a second one. Many others were so severely soaked through that the pages disintegrated in her hands.

She paused at a book covered in brown leather. Although the leather was water stained, it was soft. The pages inside showed minor water damage and were well preserved. It looked quite old because the title on the spine had faded. It was unreadable, yet strangely she was reluctant to dispose of it in the rubbish pile.

She set it aside for later. She turned to place it on the coffee table behind her when it accidentally slipped from her fingers. Kate watched in dismay as it landed on the floor, open, face down.

"No!" She couldn't believe her clumsiness. She stared down at the book for a moment. It didn't look pretty. Why she was so taken with this particular book she didn't know. It definitely belonged on the scrap heap now.

Carefully, she picked it up. A photo peeked out from within its pages. It must have dislodged when the book fell. Extracting it, she noted the photo was discoloured and its details dull and unclear. Two young people, a man and a woman, stood close together, smiling at the camera. Their fingers made the 'V' sign of peace. The words "With love, Peter and Rosemary Winslett. 1974" were written on the back.

She studied the blurred faces staring back at her. The man was tall, much taller than the woman beside him. His broad features appeared similar to those of John Robbins. Perhaps a relation? The woman was slim with straight long hair reaching past her waist. She looked ethereal, like a forest nymph. But Kate couldn't make out her face at all.

"Adrian, look what I found in one of the books!"

She held out the photo. Adrian stared down at it for the longest time. He turned it over and read the words. Kate saw his lips purse and the muscles in his jaw tighten.

"Do you know them?" Kate asked. Adrian gave her a startled glance, then looked back down at the photo and studied it. "He has similar features to John. They might be related," Kate added.

"I know little about their younger days," Adrian said. "They look like the typical seventies couple at Woodstock, don't they? Without a care in the world."

"John told me yesterday that you knew Rosie, his first wife."

Adrian gaped at Kate, a startled expression on his face. She smiled back innocently at him.

"He did?" Adrian said slowly. "What else did he tell you?"

"Only that he and Rosie were very much in love and were married young. Apparently she died tragically from kingfish poisoning. It sounded awful. He said you saved his life."

Adrian said nothing for the longest time. She really must have taken him by surprise. He watched Kate closely and appeared to reflect on what she'd told him. He looked down at the photo once again, then back at Kate. His brow puckered and he started to say something, then stopped.

"He said Mary was his second wife," she continued. "I was surprised. Mary never mentioned that in all the time we chatted. I guess there were lots of things she never told me. Did you know John's first wife, Rosie?" she repeated.

"Yes," he said, after a pause. "She was a very special woman. And yes, she died at the hands of kingfish."

Suddenly, he picked her up off her feet and twirled her about, laughing. Once he put her back down, he landed a long kiss on her lips. She automatically kissed him right back.

"You're endearing," he said. "I don't know why I ever thought you capable of evil deeds."

"Thank you. I think?" she replied a little bemused.

She became serious while she recounted everything John told her. Adrian listened intently, nodding here and there.

"That's why John was always so sad every time he mentioned Rosie." Kate said.

"Yes," Adrian nodded. He studied the photo closely.

"What's wrong? You look worried."

"Do I?" he said, giving her a reassuring smile. "I'm just thinking about the photo and what special meaning it must have had for them. They kept it all these years."

"We found no other photos in the house from their earlier years. Don't you think that's strange?"

Adrian shrugged. "We might never know. They may have kept them in the bedroom closet. Unfortunately, the fire destroyed everything in that room."

"Should we try to trace Peter and Rosemary Winslett? It's a long shot because it was many years ago but at least we have names. You said they had no next of kin or friends that you knew of. This might be the break we need."

"What would that achieve after all these years?" Adrian looked uneasy.

"You don't think it's worth a try?"

"No," he said firmly. "They've not been part of their lives for many years. I know it."

Kate was a little perplexed by his reluctance. Adrian held all the cards of knowledge, so she believed him if he said so. Still...

"Can I take this photo for a while?" she asked.

Adrian gave her a quizzical smile. "I know what you're up to, Kate. It won't work. You won't find anything."

"What makes you so sure about that?"

"I asked you to trust me. Just for a little while longer. It's nearly over."

"What's nearly over? I'm working blind here, Adrian. It's time you give me something." She'd reached a point of deep frustration. "You ask me to trust you, Adrian," she persisted. "When will you trust *me* with your secrets?"

She watched a mix of emotions flit across his face as he considered the challenge she'd flung at him.

"I think I've earned it, Adrian," Kate murmured softly.

"Yes," he said slowly, "I think you just might have, after all."

At last. Kate felt apprehensive yet excited that she would hear the entire story of the Robbins. But Adrian's next words quickly quashed her excitement.

"Kate, you deserve to hear the truth. And I look forward to finally sharing everything with you. But I have one last favour to ask of you." His eyes pleaded with her. "You'll understand why I've been unable to say anything when you know the full facts. Once the police formally charge Diego, I will tell you. Deal?"

He held out his hand to Kate. She didn't know where this new relationship would lead but she didn't care for now. For the first time in ten years, she trusted a man. This man. Felt safe with him.

"Deal."

***

Late afternoon

"Diego is being released." Adrian said, with no preamble.

"What!" Those four words sent shockwaves through Kate's body. She'd just joined him at a local café after receiving his text message ten minutes earlier to meet him urgently.

"Not enough evidence to hold him but still considered a person of interest."

"Not enough evidence? My research folder found in his house, his Mafia contacts?" Kate couldn't believe it. "Is he considered innocent now?"

"They are still examining the items taken from his house. Detective Abbott said they are waiting for an urgent toxicology test to be reported. They couldn't legally hold him any longer."

"So he's home?"

"Will be by the end of the day," Adrian checked his watch. "It's just on three thirty."

"So what now?"

"We stay vigilant and continue to investigate all possibilities. I heard from my federal police contacts late last night. Diego's family has no connections with the Ciambella family or their Mafia clans. The 'Ndrangheta cells loosely connect family groups based on blood relationships and marriages. Diego's links are to another southern Italian organisation." He offered a smile and added, "They don't tend to – er – associate."

"Could they be rivals and out for revenge on them? Perhaps because of Diego's cousins and their involvement, the net is wider than we think."

"That's a possibility. They have a couple more leads to follow up."

"That line of investigation might be redundant," Kate said. "It all comes back to the motive. There must be some association between Diego and the Robbins. Otherwise, nothing makes sense. Their lives must have intercepted somewhere."

Adrian's mobile phone rang.

"Detective Abbott." Adrian's tone was sharp. He listened to the other man for some time, then moved away where it was more private. Kate saw a surprised expression on his face, followed by a frown which deepened by the passing minutes.

"This is getting stranger by the day," Adrian pocketed his

phone and sat back down. "You wouldn't believe it. Police tested an open bottle of wine found at Diego's house. It was spiked with an illegal substance. They're waiting for the toxicology report for more details."

"That makes little sense. Diego is an alcoholic. Mixed substances would be a certain death sentence if you didn't know what you were doing."

"They've returned to his house with the forensics team on site this time. Maybe they'll find something that was missed."

"I read up on this," Kate said. "There are several legal and illegal drugs that cause death, accelerated if combined with alcohol and…" She stopped. "Surely not!" Her heart raced at the sudden thought that popped into her head.

"You did research on this topic?" Adrian gazed at her intently. "It's in your research, right?" She nodded slowly, feeling a coldness deep in her bones.

"Diego might have read it." She bit her lower lip, a worried expression marring her face. "Why would he do such a thing to himself, knowing the risk?"

"Detective Abbott referred to him as a 'double dipper', someone who likes to indulge in multiple drugs for extra thrills."

"I can't get my head around it."

"Diego denied it, of course. Emphatically. Said he didn't use illegal drugs nor ever did. Especially after seeing the destruction they caused his cousins."

"What will happen to him now?" Kate felt nervous about Diego's return to Possum Walk.

"They will keep him for a further twenty-four hours pending evidence from this second search."

"Thank goodness!" Kate breathed a sigh of relief. "I'm not sure what the reaction from the other residents will be if he's released. But I don't feel comfortable at all. Everyone's talking about it. And he's already guilty in the court of public opinion at Possum Walk."

"Yes, that's what happens. I'm not sure if they will release him soon. The odds are stacked against him."

"We're still no closer to uncovering his motive."

"No, but Mary and John deserve justice. And if Diego is guilty, I'm determined he never sees the light of freedom ever again."

Kate couldn't agree more.

Adrian's phone rang again. "Detective Abbott again." He listened without replying for a lengthy period. "Kate's with me. I'll get back to you shortly."

"They found an earring wedged between the sofa cushions at Diego's house. He's sending a picture now."

"An earring?" Kate frowned. A coincidence? Surely not!

Adrian's phone pinged. They both looked at the downloaded photo. An earring in the shape of a crescent moon, dark blue, studded with gems.

Very pretty...

Very confusing...

The identical match to that found by Kate and Rhonda in Mary's garden.

"How can that be?" Kate whispered, overwhelmed by the thoughts racing through her mind. "Rhonda and I found its other half in Mary's garden a few days ago. What does it all mean?"

They continued to stare down at the picture.

***

Kate and Adrian arrived at the police station in record time. They'd stopped briefly at Kate's house to collect the earring she'd found in Mary's garden. It needed to be checked against the one the police had retrieved from Diego's house.

"It's a match," Detective Abbott said, a grim expression on his face. The individual pieces lay side by side. It was unmistakable.

"Perhaps Diego's visions are factual events, after all," Kate said. "He must have been present in the house when the fire started and somehow the earrings got entangled in his jumper."

"Yes," Adrian responded. "That could also explain why and where you found one in the garden. He must have brushed against the pair, hooking them in his jumper. One fell to the ground when he jumped over the fence."

"And yet," detective Abbott said, "someone, Diego perhaps, went to the trouble of wiping all fingerprints clean from the second earring found at his house. Why is that?"

All three continued to stare down at the earrings.

"A deliberate plant?" Adrian said. "Someone trying to implicate Diego."

"And take the scent off the actual killer," added Kate.

Detective Abbott nodded. "It's the most plausible explanation. Diego denies all knowledge of it, which is what I expected. He appears consistent in his ignorance of the details associated with this case. Either he's brilliantly wily or actually innocent. If he's guilty, we'll break him down."

"It's time to push Diego hard. Either break him completely into confessing or send him home." Adrian's determination was visible in his tone. "And I'm not leaving till we get one or the other."

"You know the drill. That's not possible, Adrian," detective Abbott told him firmly. "Take Kate home and wait to hear from me. That's your only option for now."

Forty-Five

Day 28 – Early Hours

Kate couldn't relax. Sleep had eluded her for the last hour. The past couple of days were like being on a really fast train, one that never reached the station. Since Diego's arrest, she'd been on edge. It didn't seem real that the Robbins' attacker was finally behind bars. She became nervous at the thought of his release. And it bothered her.

Then there'd been her conversation with Libby. Still perplexed by it, she mulled over what information the other woman felt compelled to share but was hesitant about. Frustrated, she realised she would not sleep anytime soon. She was wide awake and decided to do something productive. So she made herself a cup of tea and sat at her computer.

She'd neglected her novel, leaving her characters frozen and waiting for her to revive them back into action. She spent the next half hour reviewing and updating the last few chapters she'd written. Although engrossed, she yawned and her eyes drooped. Perhaps now she was ready to try the bed once again.

She was about to shut down the computer when an email notification popped up. Ordinarily, she would ignore it. At this time of night, it was likely promotional material. But it caught her eye when she saw the title 'Your query re Lidia Ciambella trial.'

It was from the Daily Chronicle newspaper whose article she had stumbled upon nearly two weeks ago. That minor news item triggered her fascination with the Mafia Queen's life. She'd emailed the editor that same night requesting any related information the paper may have in their archives. It was a long shot. Perhaps it had paid off after all.

The email was lengthy and had several attachments. She was fully alert as she read the contents. The editor who'd sent her the email, Joanne Cronston, was a rookie reporter in 1997, the year of Lidia Ciambella's trial. She'd written the original article.

The attachments covered the court case. The presiding judge ordered the names of witnesses be suppressed, the file sealed for twenty years and media reporting on the case banned. What Joanne sent her was her own research and articles never released.

What were the odds of the same journalist being with the newspaper after all these years? Now editor-in-chief, Joanne explained.

"My father was the owner and editor of the newspaper at the time of the trial. I was a rookie reporter fresh out of university and did a summer stint with him. I took over the business after my father's death nearly ten years ago."

Her notes and articles were thorough. Lidia Ciambella murdered her second in charge in a small village on the outskirts of Rome after uncovering his plot to overthrow her and take control. According to internal sources, he had the numbers and would have succeeded.

"The execution-style murder was witnessed by a British couple on holidays in Italy. It was their critical evidence that doomed the Mafia Queen to a life sentence in prison. They were placed under Protective Services for the three years of the trial following at least two attempts on their lives."

In another attachment, Kate read that in handing down its sentence to Lidia Ciambella, the Court acknowledged the bravery and sacrifice of the star witnesses throughout the long process.

"The couple, whose names were suppressed for their own protection, were involved in a fatal car accident a few months after the trial ended. There was never any proof the Mafia was responsible for their deaths but speculation ran rife."

The irony of the tragedy was not lost on Kate. She read on.

"Now that the suppression has expired, the couple's identity can be revealed. Their names were Peter and Rosemary Winslett, a married couple from Lyme Regis in Dorset."

Kate's hand flew to her mouth, muffling an involuntary gasp. She felt a shiver run down her spine, a tingling sensation that spread like wildfire. Stunned, Kate sat back in her chair for a long while. The unexpected revelation sent shockwaves through her entire body.

Why did the Robbins keep a photo of Peter and Rosemary Winslett in their home? Were they related? Friends? Had they supported their friends during that terrifying period of their lives? Kate's brain was in free fall, too many questions firing at her.

She wondered...

With hands trembling uncontrollably, fingers twitching with nervous energy, Kate wrote back to Joanne Cranston, hoping the other woman would deliver a miracle.

***

Later

When Kate woke, it was late morning. Not surprising given that she'd finally fallen asleep after dawn. She lay in bed, going over what she read a few hours ago.

She tried to reach Adrian for several hours. His phone went to voicemail each time and she left two messages. His car was not in its usual parking spot in his driveway either.

Adrian told her repeatedly the Robbins' story was not his to tell. So she would make it easy for him and tell him what she knew. That way, it addressed his moral dilemma.

Adrian. Whenever she thought of him, she couldn't help but remember his kisses and how he made her feel. She hadn't felt like this for many years and it was nice to have a connection with a man again. Her former husband, Charlie, had left his mark on her emotionally. They had said hurtful things to each other during that last argument before he stormed out of the house to his death.

"Just tell me the truth, Charlie!" She'd been in tears. "Are you having an affair?"

"Are you crazy!" he yelled back. "I have never cheated on you, Kate!"

"I don't believe you!"

So many little things had changed gradually between them. She knew there was someone else. She'd suspected one of his female co-workers. Too many late nights. Working on deadlines, he said.

"You're an emotional cripple," he continued. "I need someone who's a little warmer than the ice queen!"

His words continued to haunt her over the years and created barriers every time she got close to someone. She was always the first to back off any potential relationship. She wanted to give this budding romance with Adrian a chance to survive. She liked him. Very much.

Adrian rang her later in the afternoon.

"Diego is being released within the hour," he said.

Her stomach churned. "The police must know what they're doing," she replied.

"I don't have any details but will try to find out more. I've been with my federal colleagues most of the day," he continued. "There's been some big developments and I have news to share with you. It's blown this case wide open."

"I look forward to hearing it. I've been busy too and must tell you something important too."

"I always want to be honest with you, Kate," his voice was serious. "It's time to tell you about the Robbins, Lidia Ciambella, all of it."

Kate felt her heart swell with emotion. "No more secrets," she murmured.

"No more secrets," he replied. "See you soon."

***

Late Afternoon

Diego was home! How could that be? The police should have locked him up by now. And thrown away the key! Things were not going to plan. Deep frustration welled up inside. It was time to visit Diego to see what was going on. He needed an extra shove if he was going to be of any use to the endgame.

Of course it was obvious as soon as he opened the door that he was drunk.

"It's you!" he said dismissively. He clung to the door frame, his speech slurred. He looked like he was about to collapse. His skin looked ashen and there were beads of perspiration on his brow.

Inside, on the dining table, there were three empty bottles of wine with a glass beside them. Three more bottles were unopened.

"Don't mind me," Diego said as he swayed precariously on his feet. "I started the party early."

"I'm sorry about what happened. I thought you could do with a friend."

Diego's response was to slump to the floor, unable to stand on his feet any longer.

"Since when have you been anyone's friend? I don't need you. Leave me alone."

"What happened? I heard the police think you're responsible for Mary's death and John's attempted murder. Please tell me that isn't true."

Diego nodded, his head slumping down near his chest. "Yep, I did it alright. They just can't pin it on me yet." He giggled, his whole body shaking. "Apparently, they don't have enough evidence."

"That's good news for you, right?"

"No. I'm still under suspicion. They're waiting for blood results."

"What blood results?"

"Apparently I'm a drug user. Did you know that about me? I certainly didn't. They found drugs in the wine taken from the house."

His giggles turned to hysterical laughter. It was alarming to watch as he slid down even further along the ground. From there, he curled his body into a foetal position. He continued to lie there, laughing to himself. Now and then, he'd stop but then he'd start again.

The wine! An unfortunate and careless slip up. Should have emptied the bottle down the sink and thrown it away! That was sloppy work, leaving incriminating evidence out in the open like that.

Diego struggled to raise himself off the floor, but he was too unsteady. He refused any help. Finally, he stopped trying and remained where he was, mumbling incoherently under his breath.

"What did you say, Diego?"

"How did the drug get into the wine?" he asked a little louder.

"I don't know. Where did you buy it?"

"I don't know," he answered, his voice rising, agitated. "I don't know. I don't know!" He shouted the last sentence.

He seemed to gasp for air and clutched his hand to his chest. He fell silent, not moving. Had the wine finally knocked him out? No. His eyes opened and they locked gazes for the longest time. A scowl formed on his face as he appeared to mull over something.

Was he finally working it out?

Too late did he realise who he was dealing with?

What a pathetic human being. He'd served his purpose. Too bad it was over for him. For he had to be disposed of. One drink should do it.

Diego's gaze locked with the other person, as though seeing for the first time. He looked comical as the emotions flitted across his face from confusion, uncertainty and finally shock.

"It was you!" he said, fear in his voice. His words came out garbled but were unmistakable. He massaged his temple, shaking his head as though trying to clear it. "You gave me that last case of wine." He stumbled over the words in his haste to get them out. "It was you I saw in the house the night Mary died. You killed her!"

A sneering grin was his answer.

"Why are you smirking like that? You put those drugs into the wine?"

A nod.

"Why would you do that?" Anger laced his words.

"Because I needed your help and couldn't risk you remembering afterwards."

An expression of horror from Diego. "The dreams. Blackouts. I thought I was going out of my mind." He finally sat upright.

Diego looked comical in his attempts to regain a level of control over his body, but the alcohol he'd consumed hampered him. He wouldn't be sober any time soon. No matter. He was harmless. Toying with him was fun.

"I admit it took a bit of experimenting on my part." A maniacal laugh escaped. "Had to get the dose just right. Enough to make sure it was effective for what had to be done."

"And that's why I've been so confused and out of it for the past few weeks? You treated me like a lab rat!"

Diego's look of disgust was comical.

"Get over it, Diego. It wasn't personal. I had no choice. Mary and John Robbins had to die."

Diego's look of horror changed to that of disbelief. "You're crazy!" he said. "What did the Robbins ever do to you?"

"You'll never know what they did to me and my family!"

"Who are you?" Diego whispered.

"Who am I? That is a fascinating question." The voice crooned with a chilly eeriness.

The time was near to finally unleash the power. Deep inside, it ripped through every cell, demanding release. With trembling fingers, the veil was lifted away from the eyes. To reveal secrets hidden from the world since a young child.

The unusually brilliant green eyes penetrated Diego's very soul as they turned their full force on him.

"Noooooo!" Diego screamed his terror. "Devil eyes!"

He frantically tried to scramble to his feet but his movements were sluggish. Suddenly, his breathing laboured, he clutched at his chest and slumped back to the floor. He lay there, unmoving.

Good! The wine had finally knocked him out.

What a waste of time and effort Diego turned out to be. Useless to the endgame now. Had to hurry before he woke up. And stopped, frowning down at Diego, watching him carefully.

Was he even breathing?

His chest was still.
No pulse at his wrist.
Stark realisation hit...
The pathetic fool! Diego was dead!

Forty-Six

Evening

Kate jumped in her chair as a blood-curdling scream ripped through the silence of the early evening. It came from nearby. She rushed out into the street, trying to locate the sound. The scream had also drawn the attention of Rhonda and several other neighbours. Just at that moment, Adrian pulled up in his car outside his house.

He looked around at everyone outside. "Everything alright here, Kate?"

Another scream. This time, they all heard it. Coming from within Diego's house. Everyone rushed towards it. Just then, Diego's front door flung open and Paula ran out, hysterically crying.

"He's dead! He's dead!" She collapsed against Kate, sobbing uncontrollably. Rhonda put a protective arm around her. Adrian charged inside shouting "Call ooo" to Rhonda.

"What happened, Paula?" Kate asked.

"I went to see if he needed anything. I saw him get home in

a taxi earlier. But when I got there, he was…he was…" She shut her eyes tight for a moment. "I saw him collapsed on the floor. His skin was cold and clammy when I touched him." She gave a shudder. "I knew he was gone."

Kate moved towards the house when Paula grabbed her arm. "Don't, Kate. You don't want to see it."

"Adrian might need help."

When she entered Diego's house, Adrian was standing in the living room, looking down to where Diego lay. So many overwhelming emotions coursed through her as her eyes gazed at Diego's slumped body. She felt tears slip down her cheek. What a tragic end to a tragic life. She wanted to believe he was finally at peace.

"He's dead," Adrian whispered. "Touch nothing, Kate. We should probably wait outside till the paramedics arrive." She heard sirens in the distance, getting closer.

Once again, emergency services filled the street. Kate had a sense of déjà vu'. It was becoming all too real and too often.

"What do you think happened to him?" Kate asked when they went outside. She'd managed to pull herself together after the shock of seeing Diego but her heart was still thumping loudly in her chest.

"Not sure. There doesn't seem to be any visible trauma that I can see."

The paramedics had a brief word to Adrian before entering the house. Detective Abbott arrived minutes later, accompanied by several uniformed police officers.

"What's the story, Adrian?" Detective Abbott surveyed the

group of residents and then turned his attention to Adrian and Kate.

"Diego Santo is dead. Can't see any obvious trauma. Could be from natural causes."

"We released him only a few hours ago." The detective said and followed the officers inside the house.

"What now?" Kate asked, feeling cold. She'd rushed outside without a cardigan and her light top was no match for the evening chill. She wasn't sure if the chill was from the weather or from her reaction to Diego's death.

"This is not a good sign." Neither saw Rhonda behind them until she spoke. "A second suspicious death in Possum Walk in a month."

"We don't know that yet, Rhonda," Kate replied. "Where's Paula?"

"She went home to lie down," Rhonda said. "She got a terrible shock. I offered to help her but she refused. Said she wanted to be alone."

"I'm not sure leaving her alone in her state is a good idea," Kate said. "Maybe we should stay with her for a while, make sure she's alright."

"The police will want to talk to her shortly," Adrian said. "Maybe you should leave her alone for now. She needs time to process what she saw, to deal with the shock."

Rhonda snorted. "She's tougher than she looks, that one!"

"Why do you say that?" Kate asked. Paula tough? Not a word she would associate with the other woman. Shy. Timid. In fact, Kate worried Paula was not tough enough to cope with what she'd seen. Maybe the paramedics should check on her once they were free.

"Sometimes she lets her guard down." She didn't elaborate. "And her house is a pigsty. There is no other word for it. A pigsty!"

The vehemence of Rhonda's words alarmed Kate.

Thankfully, detective Abbott exiting Diego's house distracted them.

"It looks like he suffered a fatal heart attack," he said when he reached them. "He must have been drunk out of his brain. There were three empty bottles of wine and one opened, ready to pour. He must have purchased the wine on his way home from the police station. We removed all there was after we finished searching the place the second time."

"Yes, that would be correct, detective," Rhonda nodded. "He was carrying a rather large and heavy box when he got out of the taxi. So there are no suspicious circumstances, detective?" Rhonda asked.

"Not that is apparent, Mrs Kavich. But it is only a preliminary finding. We will need to wait for the autopsy result to confirm it." He gave her a speculative look. "Can you see Mr Santo's house from your front windows?"

"Yes. I'm on the corner and have a clear view down the entire street on both sides."

"Did you see anyone go in or out of Mr Santo's house after he returned to his house?"

"Only Paula. She was in there for a bit the first time."

"The first time?" the detective pressed her.

"Yes, Paula visited Diego twice today. The second time she ran out screaming within a minute or two of entering the house."

"I see. No one else?"

Rhonda shook her head.

"Thank you, Mrs Kavich. I might get back to you with more questions soon."

Rhonda nodded and walked away towards another group of residents.

"Diego's death changes things," detective Abbott said as soon as they were out of earshot.

"Yes, we may never know for certain if he was our killer," Adrian replied.

"You mean he might be innocent?" Kate was taken aback.

"We only have circumstantial evidence against him," detective Abbott replied. Not enough to charge him formally. The advice we received from the prosecutor's office suggested it would never stick in court."

"What about the illegal drugs he was taking?"

"He was charged with possession of an illegal substance. However, there's no evidence that links him to the Robbins."

"Except Kate's research found in his home," Adrian said drily.

"He vehemently denied any knowledge of it. There is a real possibility that he might be innocent and the actual killer planted it there." The detective sounded just as frustrated as Kate felt.

"Just like someone could have planted the earring," Kate added.

"Why would anyone go to all that trouble? Adrian asked.

"To distract the investigation away from the real killer," Kate replied.

"There's still the lack of motive," the detective prevailed, "which is the main sticking point. Nothing makes sense without it."

"Have you received any further update from the Federal Police?" Adrian asked.

"Yes, we are in regular communication, particularly regarding the potential link to Lidia Ciambella's case. There are unlikely to be any family relations between the Australian Mafia families and the 'Ndrangheta, the Mafia Queen's domain. Which surprises me, to be honest. The 'Ndrangheta has far-reaching influence and power internationally."

"That's what my contacts tell me," Adrian nodded. "Just this afternoon, they advised of a fresh development. I should have more details soon. They had to follow up with their leads to confirm. It's big apparently."

"I wonder if it's connected to the rumours I've heard lately." Detective Abbott didn't elaborate.

"So that leaves us with two options," Adrian continued. "Either Diego was our man and his motive is yet to be uncovered…" He stopped.

"Or?" Kate prompted him.

He glanced at Kate. "I'm sorry Kate, for what I'm about to say won't make much sense. I'll explain everything soon, I promise. *Or* the Robbins' location has been compromised. It's all about honour for the 'Ndrangheta. Lidia Ciambella's Mafia family may want to settle the score. To finish what was started all those years ago. Their drug business was in shreds as a result."

"You may be right," the detective said. "That certainly makes more sense. Regardless, we need hard evidence. Guesswork won't solve this case."

"Weren't Peter and Rosemary Winslett key witnesses to Lidia Ciambella's murder case?" Kate turned to Adrian with a frown.

Both men gave her a startled look, then a half smile from Adrian.

"You know about Peter and Rosemary Winslett?"

"It's a bit of a story about how I found out, but yes. Their evidence was crucial to Lidia Ciambella's life sentence. They both perished in a fatal car accident not long afterwards. Do you think the Mafia intentionally killed them for their testimony?"

Both men glanced at each other. Detective Abbott coughed, looking a little uncomfortable. Adrian grinned at Kate, shaking his head.

The detective turned to Adrian. "Can I take up a little more of your time please Adrian? Could you come back to the station with me? There are matters to follow up that you should look at."

They left with another apology from Adrian and "I'll see you tomorrow" as a farewell. Secret men's business, she thought, a little peeved to be excluded. There was no reason for Kate to remain outside in the chilly air, which was turning colder by the minute. After speaking briefly to some residents who lingered, she returned home.

She felt on edge and couldn't explain why. The impact of Diego's death hit her hard. It was unexpected, yet not surprising. The heavy drinking killed him in the end, after all. Such an unhappy situation. Whether they would ever have enough evidence against him to confirm if he was innocent or not was anyone's guess. An unsolved case was not ideal. The Robbins deserved better.

Taking John's safety for granted was never possible again unless there was certainty. Someone might still be out there who wanted to finish the job. It was probably what Adrian and Detective Abbott were discussing right now.

She made herself a cup of tea and sat down at her computer once again. She glanced at her new emails and saw another one from Joanne Cranston. Feeling excited and hopeful, she wasted no time in opening it.

"Hi Kate. You asked for any photos of Peter and Rosemary Winslett taken during the trial. This one was taken in August of 1997. Hope it is useful. I'll keep looking for more."

Eagerly, she opened the attachment. The photo was of a middle aged man and woman holding hands, leaving a court-house. She gasped and the colour drained from her face. She blinked rapidly, trying to process the unbelievable sight before her, her mind struggling to reconcile reality with the shock.

The faces were younger yet distinctive.

Mary and John Robbins.

Forty-Seven

Day 29 - Morning

Kate had a second sleepless night in a row. How could she have missed the clues? The Winsletts and the Robbins were one and the same couple. John's ramblings and cryptic comments all made sense now with her newfound information. His constant references to Rosie. And Mary. She'd accepted them as two separate women. In his mind, they probably were.

She was anxious to speak to Adrian as soon as possible. Fortunately he rang her earlier asking her to meet him at the local café in half an hour. He was on his way there from a meeting with Detective Abbott.

He greeted her with a warm hug and kiss before they settled in for their chat.

Kate quickly told him about the emails from the UK newspaper, the unpublished articles about the Winsletts and their role in the Mafia Queen's trial.

"It must have been some trial for the judge to ban all media for twenty years," she added. "I realise now why it was impossible to find any information."

"It was the biggest story of that time. The drug cartel she ran was destroyed, her accomplices scattered but we managed to find some of them who quickly made deals and gave up their colleagues."

"The last email I received from Joanne Cranston was a photo."

Adrian's gaze was intense and he looked uncertain, a little worried.

"No more secrets," he murmured. "A photo of whom?"

"Peter and Rosemary Winslett."

Kate let that statement sink in. Of course, Adrian knew its significance instantly. This must surely be a tough moment for Adrian. All the secrets he and the Robbins had safeguarded for many years finally exposed.

"So now you know," he said with relief in his voice. "Peter and Rosemary Winslett were indeed key witnesses at the Ciambella court hearing," he said. "They were kept under protective care for three years to make sure no one got to them. Although there were two failed attempts."

"It must have been a terrible time for them."

"Peter and Rosemary Winslett were remarkable throughout the years leading up to the trial. Their lives changed forever from the moment they saw Lidia Ciambella pull that trigger. They were in constant danger but displayed exceptional courage and determination far beyond what was expected of them. They believed that justice should be served and were prepared to take the risks."

"Is that when you met them?"

"Yes. I was assigned to Operation Kingfish together with two of my colleagues."

"Kingfish?" Kate frowned at the reference. "John mentioned kingfish several times."

"Operation Kingfish was an international taskforce set up specifically to bring down Lidia Ciambella's drug empire," Adrian continued. "They had newly established cells in Australia."

"John told me kingfish killed Rosie, his first wife. He was referring to the taskforce, wasn't he?" Adrian nodded. "And you didn't correct me. You let me make a fool of myself by prattling on about her being poisoned by fish!" She flushed, mortified at how naïve she'd been. In that moment, she wished the floor would open up and she'd disappear into it. What must Adrian think of her?

"I'm sorry but I had no choice," he said. She heard the sincerity in his voice. "It was not my story to tell and I had no authorisation to do so. So many times, I came close to revealing everything to you, especially in the past few days when things escalated. The Robbins' secrets never weighed as heavily on me as they have since Mary's death. And not because I take responsibility for John now. The pressure to find the killer was overwhelming at times."

Kate saw the rising tension in his stance and clasped her hand in his, trying to give him some comfort as he continued.

"My fears from the beginning were that their cover was breached. And validated when John's life was threatened. My protective instincts kicked in. Everyone and every action were suspicious in my mind. It's no excuse but that's why you copped the brunt of it initially. Of course, I was singularly focussed on catching a killer. Unfortunately, it was at your expense in those early days. I'm sorry again, Kate. Can you ever forgive me for being such a jerk?"

"There's nothing to forgive," she said gently. "We're at a totally different point in time now."

Adrian leaned over towards her and gave her a swift kiss. Kate happily took it.

"You're one in a million, Kate Trellow. Thank you."

Just being near Adrian made Kate's heart skip a beat, her face warm up. But she wanted to know more about the Robbins. "What about the trial? And how did Mary and John, er – Peter and Rosemary – end up in Australia."

"Operation Kingfish was infiltrated by the Mafia. They blackmailed one of the taskforce members who passed on the Winslett's every move. Lidia Ciambella's buddies were so desperate to get rid of the damning evidence that twice they nearly succeeded in having them killed.

Kate felt physically ill at the thought of the constant fear and terror John and Mary must have gone through during those years.

"After the trial and Lidia's life sentence, Peter and Rosemary Winslett entered the Witness Protection Program and were relocated to Australia with new identities and new lives."

"And then John was diagnosed with dementia. No wonder Mary showed such sorrow at times."

"They were both worried about what it would mean as his illness progressed. John started to manifest his old life as Peter Winslett and said things from their past that didn't make any sense to others, thankfully."

Adrian's phone rang. It was Detective Abbott. "I just left the station," Adrian said with a frown. The call was brief.

"He wants us to meet him at Diego's house as soon as possible. He said Diego was set up."

Forty-Eight

Afternoon

Kate and Adrian arrived at Diego's house to find Detective Abbott together with another man waiting for them.

"This is Inspector Frank Royston from the Australian Federal Police," Michael said. "He and his team are working closely with Victoria Police on this case." They quickly exchanged pleasantries.

"Good to see you again, Inspector," Adrian nodded in acknowledgement. "I've been consulting with some of my former colleagues who are in your team."

"The Robbins' case was brought to the attention of my team, the International Liaison Unit," the inspector said. "They've been following the developments locally with much interest."

"We received the forensics report back for the wine bottles taken from this house," detective Abbott said. "results which I thought you should know about."

"You said something on the phone about Diego being set up?" Adrian sounded unusually anxious. Kate's heart raced and her anxiety levels suddenly jumped. She had a bad feeling about what the detective was about to say.

"Yes. The unopened bottles were tampered with. Forensics found a small pin prick in the cork and the foil around the mouth carefully resealed. There were traces of the drug in the cork too."

"Number four," Kate murmured. She suddenly felt faint, unable to breathe. Adrian grabbed her as she swayed.

"Kate!" He easily caught her, but her face was pale and her eyes wide with shock. "Kate, talk to me." He sounded worried. She felt the world spin.

"I'm okay."

She struggled out of his arms, but he seemed reluctant to let go just yet. She glanced at the other two men who wore equally concerned expressions on their faces. She managed to stand on solid ground. Detective Abbott offered her a glass of water which she sipped gratefully.

"I'm sorry," she said, embarrassed. "It's just that – er – it's yet again another murder scene I detailed in my research. Number four to be precise."

All three men stared at her, startled. Adrian quickly told the inspector about Kate's research being used in the case to copycat the actions taken by the killer.

"It appears that Diego was indeed set up, detective," she added, regaining her composure in the meantime. "The folder was planted here by the murderer to lead us to Diego and away from the actual killer. Diego referred to his fear of the 'devil eyes'. It looks like his wine supply was deliberately drugged. Maybe his erratic behaviour, his memory lapses, were drug induced."

"It certainly looks that way," the inspector said. Adrian and the detective nodded in agreement.

"We have a cunning and very clever criminal on our hands, always one step ahead," Adrian surmised. "We are missing something crucial."

"There's been a late and surprising development in the Lidia Ciambella case," the inspector said. "Which might be the missing piece we need." The Mafia Queen case was classified as a priority at the highest level in Australia, in fact internationally, back in the 'nineties. When the judge quashed all reporting on the trial the case was buried instantly. But we never stopped monitoring the main players and the overall activities of the cartel.

"When the Winsletts were attacked here in Australia over twenty five years later, we quickly got in touch with our overseas sources to check on any recent activity within the 'Ndrangheta that we should be made aware of."

"Our agents confirmed that there was none," Adrian added. "But we had strong suspicions from the beginning that this case was somehow connected to the Winslett's role which ultimately imprisoned and killed Lidia Ciambella. Nothing else made sense."

"Overnight we received intel from an undercover agent in Italy," Inspector Royston continued. "He'd been unable to communicate for some time and the intel was a few weeks old. We are still checking it out, but it appears legitimate."

Kate was totally engrossed and hanging on every word the inspector said.

"It appears that Lidia Ciambella had a deeply buried secret

of her own," the inspector continued. "She gave birth to an illegitimate daughter in 1965 when she was fifteen years old."

A prickling sensation shot up Kate's spine and the small hairs on the back of her neck stood on end. She clutched her chest, feeling her heart beat, a thunderous echo of the shock gripping her. From the expressions on both detective Abbott and Adrian's faces, and their eyes wide in disbelief, they were just as stunned as she was.

"The daughter has the same unusual green coloured eyes as her mother did?" Kate whispered, her voice shaky.

Inspector Royston nodded his answer.

Adrian recovered first. "So where is she now?"

"We're trying to track her down. According to our source, the baby was adopted out to a European family living in England. We know she grew up in the northern country. But she seems to have disappeared from her mid teens. If she's still alive, we have no idea where she is nor what her name is."

"She would be about fifty seven or eight today," Kate said. "Both John and Diego talked about 'devil eyes'. Isn't that the expression people used to describe Lidia Ciambella's unusual eyes?"

"Yes," Adrian replied. "Some also described them as 'cat eyes' and 'evil eyes'. I saw her a few times up close and I admit her eyes were startling and unnerving every time."

"I think we know exactly where the daughter is, inspector," Kate said. "What are the odds that two people living at Possum Walk described similar eyes they saw here? That person must be Lidia Ciambella's daughter. And the killer. She's a resident here."

"You're onto something there, Kate," Adrian replied. "So all we have to do is narrow down the suspects to those in the same age bracket living at Possum Walk and check them out."

"Don't you think that someone with such unusual eyes would already be a stand out?" Kate started to have doubts about her theory.

"Maybe," Adrian said slowly, "unless she hides behind coloured contact lenses."

"It's very possible that a woman, in her late fifties, a resident of Possum Walk, wears contact lenses to hide the true colour of her eyes," Kate summarised. "She's the one."

"Our first priority is to review the list of everyone who was onsite the day of the fire," said detective Abbott. "Who is in her late fifties. Our killer is on that list."

Forty-Nine

Day 30 – Morning

EVERYTHING. WAS. FALLING. APART!!!!!

With Diego Santo gone, another way must be found. John Robbins was still alive. It was virtually impossible to get into the security ward at the hospital. Useless to try.

Rage flowed through her like lava. He had to die. Now!

It was risky, dangerous, even crazy. Kate Trellow's research showed great imagination. Another inspiring murder option ready to go. Simple. A saline bag injected with poison and put through his body intravenously. Take your choice of potions, ladies and gentlemen! A cackle of laughter escaped.

In hindsight, she should have applied that method in the first place. It would surely have been more straightforward and successful. But no. She had to be clever and make it more interesting and complex. Look at what that accomplished. Nothing! He was still not dead!

It seemed from that point onwards, everything became more difficult, more challenging, more complicated. Plans did not go to script. She had to carefully craft the last battle. This time, failure was not an option.

It had taken twenty-five years of waiting. A desperate need to avenge the wrongdoing cast upon Lidia Ciambella, her incarceration, her murder. What they had done, leaving her daughter motherless, was unforgiveable.

Peter and Rosemary Winslett died in a tragic car accident soon after the trial. Or so it was reported. She didn't believe it for a moment! They were somewhere out there. The search to find them over the next fifteen years was in vain. During those long painful years, her resentment and anger festered and grew like a tumour inside her. During that whole time, she went through a constant revolving door of mental institutions.

In. Out.

Inpatient. Outpatient.

New drug trials. Change of medications.

Voices. Inside her head. At her. In her. With her.

The doctors were fools! All of them! There was nothing wrong that revenge couldn't fix! No more being their guinea pig!

Alas, eventually the painful decision to move on with life had to be made. The relocation to Australia was impulsive and made no sense. All the time spent in hospitals made her think and ponder about a new future. One nurse, who was Australian, was always kind to her. She spoke about Australia with affection and longing. It sounded like the place to be. Why not?

Ten years of burying the past in Australia passed quickly. Only to find by a bizarre twist of destiny an article in the local news about a couple who recently purchased a home in the new development of Possum Walk Over 50's Community.

There was no shadow of a doubt it was them. The photo showed a much older version of Peter and Rosemary Winslett, now known as John and Mary Robbins. Ironically, they lived less than forty kilometres away. How close she had been to them all these years.

That day was truly life changing. All the old feelings, the anger, resentment, intense hatred, flooded back. Everything changed in a split second. One singular purpose was uppermost.

To kill John and Mary Robbins.

For killing them both would exorcise the ghosts of Peter and Rosemary Winslett forever.

And Kate Trellow was next.

Fifty

Late Evening

It was a spur-of-the-moment decision for Kate to go for a swim so late at night. She'd had trouble sleeping lately. The events of the past weeks were overwhelming, as was the information overload. So much had been revealed and so much was yet to be resolved. It was an unsettling time. A swim in the heated pool would relax and help her get a good night's rest.

She didn't expect anyone else at the pool at this hour. To her surprise, Paula was there, swimming laps. She didn't notice Kate straight away. On the side of the pool was a towel and bag.

"Hello, Paula. You had the same idea for a late night swim, I see."

Paula twisted around from the other end of the pool. The lighting was dim and her face in shadow.

Slipping off her robe, Kate placed it, along with her bag, on the nearby chair. She slipped into the pool with a long sigh. Paula remained at the other end. Kate spent the next few minutes soaking up the heat of the blissfully warm water against her skin. She felt all her tension melt away as she alternately floated and swam a few gentle laps.

Each time she swam close to Paula, the other woman slipped under the water and swam her own lap away from her to the opposite end. The other woman's fortitude to stay underwater for the length of the pool was impressive. Kate knew she herself didn't have the stamina or fitness.

Both continued their laps, neither engaging in conversation. For a moment, Kate felt guilty for not chatting to Paula, but then it was gone. She suspected Paula was happy enough to relax with her own thoughts, just as she was.

The pool was working its magic already. Kate enjoyed the quiet, the feeling of calmness washing over her literally and emotionally. With each stroke, she felt her mind empty, piece by piece, until the all-consuming clutter lifted. Eventually, her mind was still. She felt mentally liberated and energised at the same time.

Her thoughts turned to Paula. She felt for the other woman. Finding Diego's body must have been such a shock to her system. Paula didn't strike her as being very strong or tough. Rhonda, on the other hand, was tough enough for the both of them. Their friendship, whilst odd, seemed to work. And her calm and gentle demeanour seemed to quiet Rhonda's brashness and insufferable ways a little.

Libby. A slight frown marred her features. She must ask detective Abbott if she'd contacted him yet. With all the turmoil of the past few days, she'd forgotten to tell Adrian about her conversation with the nurse.

She floated aimlessly for a while, enjoying the feeling of

weightlessness. She wasn't' sure exactly how much time passed before she realised Paula was nowhere to be seen and she'd not noticed her step out of the pool. She listened for the shower but heard nothing. Paula's bag and towel were still on the side of the pool. There was total stillness and silence around her.

Suddenly, a disturbing thought came to mind. She prayed she was wrong. Taking a deep breath, Kate dived underwater, searching. She saw Paula immediately. She lay unconscious at the bottom of the pool. Grabbing the other woman's arms, she pushed her up above the water. Her face was turning blue.

Kate didn't have time to lose. With all the strength she could muster, she pulled Paula's upper body safely out of the water onto the tiled floor. She put her ear near the unresponsive woman's mouth and nose whilst watching her chest for any signs of breathing. No pulse. She quickly began chest compressions, praying desperately that she remembered her training from a few years ago. Her heart raced. And her body trembled all over. She felt breathless as she pushed down on Paula's chest.

1 – 2 – 3 – 4 –5 and onwards…

1 – 2 – 3 – 4 –5…

Paula didn't respond.

Again! 1 – 2 – 3 – 4 –5. Breath in.

Panic set in. Please breathe. She didn't know how long she worked on the lifeless woman but suddenly Paula's body convulsed as she spluttered and coughed up water and spluttered some more, gasping for air. Kate twisted her to her side as more water released from her mouth.

Relieved in every pore of her being, Kate saw the colour return to Paula's cheeks. Slowly, she opened her eyes. They looked dazed and confused. They were also an unusual vivid green colour, like cat eyes. Some said they were like the devil's eyes.

Kate instinctively and suddenly pulled away, horrified. She felt a scream rise in her throat. But nothing came. She felt paralysed with shock and stared down at Paula Vincent, the secret daughter of Lidia Ciambella.

Kate saw the moment Paula twigged onto her. Her true identity was finally exposed and she was fuming. Her previously dazed confusion had cleared to a chilling and deadly rage.

Kate had to get away from the other woman. Her life depended on it. Paula would not let her escape now that she knew her truth.

Fifty-One

Rhonda felt unsettled, on edge. She didn't know why. She watched her favourite show but didn't seem to have the appetite for it tonight. So much had happened over the past few weeks and her little community of Possum Walk was falling apart.

To add to her mood, she'd developed an infection in the right eye, which became red and swollen. Probably due to her contact lenses. Which were useless now. She was definitely going back to glasses. She looked ugly, she decided, as she studied herself in the mirror that morning. She'd stayed indoors the last couple of days. And she missed her weekly water aerobics class. It wouldn't do to be amongst people with a swollen eye.

Movement outside caught her attention. Her window shutters were usually open until she went to bed. She liked to look out whilst she was up. She saw Adrian come out of his house and glance towards Paula's house, which was in darkness. Then he ran to Kate's house, banging on her door. Whatever was the matter with him? Curious, she went outside and watched from her veranda.

"She's not home," she called out to Adrian.

"Where is she, Rhonda?" He sounded desperate.

"I saw her leave earlier. Looks like she went to the clubhouse for a swim. It's a bit late. But she'll have company. Paula's over there too."

"Paula!" He was visibly shaken. He started running towards the clubhouse, then turned and shouted out. "When the police get here, tell them to come straight to the pool."

***

Kate tried to lift herself up off the ground when Paula grabbed her arm painfully. Her grip was like an iron vice. No matter what she did, Kate couldn't shake her off.

"You're Lidia Ciambella's daughter!" Paula's eyes were truly remarkable, as Adrian said. A little unnerving. "Those eyes are unmistakable."

"Well done, Kate." Her voice sounded unfamiliar, deeper, cold. "By the way, thank you for the timely research you prepared for me. It was inspiring. And very useful." She laughed. The sound was creepy. "But John should be dead. You didn't get that one right."

Kate felt mesmerised by Paula's eyes, as though she was being drawn into their depths. They were truly extraordinary in colour.

"You wear contacts. I never noticed."

"Nobody ever noticed me. Quiet and shy Paula. Friendly enough and caring. But invisible. How I hated her! I had no choice, ever since I was a child. My mother was in constant danger as she became more powerful. She warned me no one must know about my existence. Otherwise, they might harm me to get to her. She loved me, Kate."

Kate saw a crazy light in Paula's eyes and wondered how long her sanity would hold out before she killed her. For she was certain that was what she would do. She had to distract her long enough to get away.

"Why did you do it? Even poor Diego."

"Diego!" she scoffed. "The stupid man went and got himself dead." She kept her eyes fixed on Kate like an animal stalking its prey, her grip remained tight. Kate's arm was tingling with pins and needles.

"It's simple, actually," Paula continued. "Revenge. The Winsletts, I mean the Robbins, had to die. They didn't keep their mouths shut. All they had to do was walk away and forget what they saw. But no! They had to testify. *It was the right thing to do*," Paula mimicked. "They alone were responsible for my mother's death. If she'd been free, she would still be alive, not murdered in a prison cell like a dog."

"You don't know that. Your mother lived a dangerous life. Anything could happen to her at any time. The person she killed was leading a coup. He had the numbers. Your mother was on her way out." Kate deliberately tried to provoke her, waiting for her to make a move. It worked.

"Liar! All lies! My mother was all powerful. And I was finally going to live with her, by her side, supporting her just as soon as she got rid of the troublemakers. They ruined everything!"

Without warning, she pulled Kate into the pool, pushing her down underwater. Caught by surprise, Kate didn't have time to draw in breath. She struggled against the force of the other woman's strength. She'd underestimated her physicality, small in stature but like a powerhouse. She kicked at her, pushed against her, tried to scratch her face, get to her eyes. Anything to make her release her grip. But Paula held steadfast.

Kate couldn't hold her breath much longer. Waves of panic consumed her and she felt her body shutting down. With every grain of strength left in her, she fought back.

Paula's hands were everywhere, her body surrounding her, unrelenting. It was no use. Kate saw sparks of light before her eyes and realised in those few seconds that she was about to lose consciousness. She felt a strange calmness overcome her, a floating sensation. So this was what it was like to die, she thought dispassionately.

Suddenly, Paula's arms were gone and Kate felt someone pull her out of the water. She gulped in precious air. Her chest heaved from the exertion.

Adrian. For a moment she thought she was dreaming. Somehow, incredibly, he was here, his arms around her, clasping her tightly to him. She collapsed against his warmth.

"I thought I was too late!" he whispered in her ear.

"I thought it was over." Her breathing was laboured. It had been close. She had underestimated Paula, her brute strength.

"Paula!" Kate struggled in Adrian's arms.

"Don't worry. She'd out cold after I hit her away from you." He turned her to look behind her. Paula was on the floor. Unconscious.

"Thank you." She leaned back into his arms.

"It's all over, Kate."

She nodded, tears spilling down her cheeks. Her emotions were raw, screaming in protest at what she'd endured. She was a lucky woman. It could all have gone terribly wrong.

"I'm a blubbering mess," she sniffed against his chest. "I'll be okay. Just need a minute."

"Brave words, Kate. But you're going to need more than a minute. You may not think so, but you're in shock. Be kind to yourself and take it easy for a while."

They heard running footsteps and detective Abbott exploded into the room, followed by several police officers. He took in the scene with one sweep of the room.

"Looks like you have everything under control, Adrian," he smiled at them both. He waved towards Paula and gave orders to the officers to cuff her and take her away. Kate noticed the other woman was starting to stir.

"She's going to have one beautiful bruise. Her jaw will hurt like hell for a while," Kate said with delight. "Well done, Adrian."

Fifty-Two

❦

Very Late

"I'm grateful you didn't wait till the morning to ring me," Adrian said to detective Abbott.

They had all moved to Kate's house. She'd changed into pyjamas and dressing gown. Adrian continued to hold Kate close to him.

"How did you find me?" She looked at Adrian. She was still weak but her breathing was normal and she felt calmer. Earlier, she'd refused to go to the hospital for examination.

"Inspector Royston contacted me late this evening with the breakthrough they'd been searching for," Adrian replied. "Even after the Taskforce wound down officially, our British and Italian colleagues kept tabs on key people. They heard rumours of a daughter very early on but it didn't seem a priority."

"It might all have been different if it had," Kate responded sadly. "Mary might still be alive."

From intel gathered recently," Adrian continued, "Paula was born "Lilliana Rossini", her great grandmother's name. From her teenage years, she kept changing her identity, moved around a lot. In and out of mental institutions throughout her adult life."

"Which reminds me, Kate," detective Abbott interjected. "Your friend Libby contacted me earlier today with an extraordinary story."

Kate was relieved and pleased Libby acted on her concerns.

"She lived and worked overseas in London for a number of years," the detective continued. "At one time, she worked in a mental institution where Paula was an inpatient. Only she didn't know her as Paula Vincent then. She went by another name. The point is that she recognised Paula at the Orchid Show. She'd been an inpatient for a lengthy period and left an indelible mark on Libby. So much so, she started to put the pieces of the puzzle together without realising she held the vital missing clue that would have cracked this case wide open if she'd come to us sooner."

"Who's Libby?" Adrian looked confused.

"Libby is a nurse who has cared for John during his hospital stay," Kate explained. "You may have met her already. I saw her a couple of times when I visited John. I ran into her and her daughter 'at the Orchid Show. Now that I think about it, she kept looking at Paula, then asked her if they knew each other. Paula denied it. The last time I saw her was when I visited John in the security ward. She seemed agitated and made cryptic comments, needing to talk to someone about John's safety. I gave her detective Abbott's contact details."

"When she came to see me today," the detective said, "she told me this wild story about a patient she cared for in London who used to talk about getting her revenge on those who killed her mother. Medical staff regarded it as psychotic episodes and so didn't take her seriously. One day, Paula showed Libby a worn newspaper article about her mother's trial. And she also had an old picture of a middle-aged couple. She used to stare at it for hours, the newspaper article beside her."

"So, are you saying Libby made the connection between Paula and John?" Adrian asked, frowning. "It was a rather long bow to draw to make."

"That's the odd thing!" the detective exclaimed. "When she met John in the hospital, she had a sense she'd seen him somewhere before but couldn't place it. She shrugged it off and thought no more of it. But then she recognised Paula and instantly recalled her revenge story. She realised where she'd seen John before – in the old photo Paula used to stare at for hours. It creeped her out so much she couldn't stop thinking about it. When there was an attempt on John's life, she wondered if what she remembered from the past might play out in the present. She had doubts about it and agonised for days about what to do. She said you convinced her to act on it."

"Wow!" Kate said, shaking her head. "I'm in awe of how the universe transpired to bring all this together. In a world full of billions of people, four people - Libby, Paula, Mary and John - would end up right here in the one place."

"It's truly mind blowing," Adrian agreed.

"Just to wind up what led to uncovering Paula," detective Abbott said, "The Feds were undertaking a background check on all the residents, contractors and staff at Possum Walk as part of their investigation. In Paula Vincent's case, nothing appeared in her background before she moved to Australia over ten years ago."

"That would definitely have raised a red flag," Adrian acknowledged.

"The overseas intel came back with more info this morning, telling us that Lidia's daughter had contacted one of her mother's henchmen. Told him she'd found the Winsletts, that it was past due time for them to pay for what they'd done to her mother. She asked him for help in avenging her mother's death. The one mistake she made was to give him her current name."

"That's when detective Abbott rang me tonight," Adrian said. "He was giving me the heads up they were on their way to arrest Paula. He suggested I monitor her place just in case she got wind of anything. I doubt she knew we were on to her."

"If you'd waited till tomorrow to ring Adrian, I might not be here," Kate whispered. "She was too strong. I couldn't fight her." She felt the tears again. She needed to get a grip on her emotions, but she was physically exhausted and didn't have the mental stamina to fight it.

"I couldn't wait to tell you either," Adrian continued. "I tried to call you, then came over."

"How did you know where I was?"

"Rhonda saw you leave for the pool. She mentioned Paula was also at the pool. I went crazy with worry when she said that. I rushed over here only to find you – well – no point in spelling out the details. But it was my worst nightmare, believe me." Kate heard the quiver in his voice.

"Thank God for Rhonda Kavich!" Kate said. "Who would have guessed her meddling and nosey behaviour would save us?"

They laughed. The case had taken its toll. Detective Abbott looked tired, yet relieved. Adrian had a genuine soft side to him that had started to replace the uncompromising hard edge side he mostly showed the world. It endeared him to Kate even more.

"She certainly fooled us all," detective Abbott said. "She never showed up on our original list of suspects."

Kate shivered at the vision of the real Paula who tried to kill her. She'd seen the ugliness that simmered inside her soul and would never forget it.

"Well, it's been a tough time but we got the bad guy – or in this case, woman - in the end," Adrian said.

The doorbell rang. Detective Abbott returned with Rhonda beside him.

"I'm sorry to barge in like this at such a late hour," she said, nervously clasping her hands together. Uncharacteristically so, noted Kate. "But I just couldn't wait another minute! I have to know what's going on."

Kate, Adrian and detective Abbott exchanged glances, then burst out laughing.

"Sit down and join us, Rhonda," Kate said warmly. "You've earned it."

Rhonda hesitated, initially startled at their laughter. Then visibly relaxing, she gazed at Kate sitting comfortably in Adrian's arms.

"You know," she said, conspiratorially. "I always had a feeling about you two."

Fifty-Three

Two Weeks Later

Kate and Adrian entered John's hospital room. He was due to be transferred to permanent care the next day. Kate was happy, truly happy, for the first time in many years. She and Adrian were taking things slowly and the feelings between them grew stronger day by day. There was still so much they didn't know about each other and she was confident they could work through what mattered.

"Welcome, my friends," John waved them in as soon as he saw them. Kate handed him the bag of chocolates.

"My favourites!" he exclaimed happily. As usual, he popped one into his mouth, pure bliss on his face.

He looked well, Kate thought. His skin had a healthy glow and good colour was back in his face. The ravages of the heart attack had almost disappeared. Freshly shaved, hair trimmed. It made a world of difference.

"How are you feeling today?" Adrian asked.

"Never better," John replied. "And who is this lovely young lady?" He turned to Kate.

"I'm Kate, a friend."

"Lovely to meet you, Kate."

He extended his hand out to her. She smiled back as she took it into her own.

"I'm Peter," he added. "Peter Winslett. Have you met my wife, Rosie?"

THE END

Francesca Pane lives in Melbourne with her husband
and has two grown daughters.
She loved writing since she was a child and has waited decades
before writing her first complete mystery novel.

She hopes you love the adventures of the residents at
Possum Walk Over 50's Community.

www.ingramcontent.com/pod-product-compliance
Lightning Source LLC
Chambersburg PA
CBHW011128190726
48289CB00012B/2957